T0162106

"I knew you'd come," the Mother said. Her voice was smoky and sweet. "You couldn't resist. You're like a child after candy."

She leaned closer. Frank smelled the flowery bodega scent and sweat and the dust of dry places.

"My church is open," she whispered. "Come join us."

The invitation was sensual and erotic, a lover's desire. Frank had an urge to get up and follow the Mother, to dance with her around a blood-red fire in a place where beasts still stirred beyond the pale. She wanted to cry at the moon then bow low to receive the warm sacrament . . .

Frank was surprised to hear herself say, "Never."

The Mother's wolfish eyes almost closed. In a voice like snakes slithering over each other, she warned, "Don't be so sure, child. Never's a very long time."

Visit

Bella Books

at

BellaBooks.com

or call our toll-free number

1-800-729-4992

Cry Havoc

by
Baxter Clare

Bella
BOOKS
2003

Copyright© 2003 by Baxter Clare

Bella Books, Inc.
P.O. Box 10543
Tallahassee, FL 32302

All rights reserved. No part of this book may be reproduced or transmitted in any form or by any means, electronic or mechanical, including photocopying, without permission in writing from the publisher.

Printed in the United States of America on acid-free paper
First Edition

Editor: J. M. Redmann
Cover designer: Bonnie Liss (Phoenix Graphics)

ISBN 1-931513-31-7

For Bunny, for ever,
and that's a *really* long time.

ABOUT THE AUTHOR

Baxter Clare is the author of two previous L.A. Franco mysteries, and a work of nonfiction under the name Baxter Trautman. She lives with her spouse in California and is a biologist working with threatened and endangered species.

A common slave (you know him well by sight,)
Held up his left hand, which did flame, and burn
Like twenty torches join'd; and yet his hand,
Not sensible of fire, remain'd unscorch'd.
Besides, (I have not since put up my sword,)
Against the Capitol I met a lion,
Who glar'd upon me, and went surly by,
Without annoying me: And there were drawn
Upon a heap a hundred ghastly women,
Transformed with their fear; who swore, they saw
Men, all in fire, walk up and down the streets.
And, yesterday, the bird of night did sit,
Even at noon-day, upon the market-place,
Hooting, and shrieking. When these prodigies
Do so conjointly meet, let not men say,
These are their reasons, - They are natural;
For, I believe, they are portentous things
Unto the climate that they point upon.

—Shakespeare, *Julius Caesar*

1

If the devil rode a Harley it would sound like the Santa Ana winds bellowing through the Cahuenga Pass at seventy miles an hour. The dead air gusted into the City of Angels, bent on trailing havoc in its wake. Jails filled, hospitals ran out of beds, doors slammed and dishes were hurled. The desiccating heat was relentless.

Lieutenant L.A. Franco glanced at her Timex. Eight fifteen and it had to be at least ninety already. She watched her rookie detective prowl the scene. The kid's first homicide, and wouldn't it have to be a dead man sitting naked in an '88 Caddy with a headless chicken in his lap.

Dark faces peered from porches and doorways, but the body wasn't drawing the usual onlookers. The lieutenant passed that off to the heat. The last two days had set record highs for October. Still, it was odd that there wasn't a drunk or some cluckhead hanging around the scene hoping to peddle useless information for a pint or a hit off a crack pipe.

Must be the chicken, Frank thought. She studied the gaping smile carved under Danny Duncan's chin. She didn't need the coroner's people to ID him for her. He'd made sure in his short life that everybody knew who he was. Street entrepreneur, hustler extraordinaire for his aunt, Mother Love Jones, the biggest crack dealer in South Central Los Angeles.

Cheryl Lewis paused next to her boss and Frank said, "Congratulations. Looks like your first case is a dump."

Lewis accepted the decision stoically. Frank admired her placid exterior, but the sweat soaking Lewis's blouse wasn't just from the sun. Frank knew the rookie was burning with self-consciousness and second-guessing her every move. Was she missing a waving red flag that everyone else saw? Was she stepping all over critical evidence? Was she making notes that would turn out to be useless? She'd only have one chance to get everything right. Once the body was moved all she'd have to work with were notes, photographs, and whatever was collected as evidence.

Frank watched Lewis eyeball every item on the street, trying to turn each scrap of garbage and litter into valuable evidence. Lewis was walking a thin line between savvy and naiveté. A black woman who had come up through the ranks, Lewis was well aware that her first mistake would bring howls of derision. Lewis's partner, Noah Jantzen, was already calling their victim Colonel Sanders. If Lewis did something stupid enough (or brilliant enough) she'd get a nickname too.

Lewis knelt and inspected a ground out cigarette butt near the car. Noah knelt too.

"Unfiltered Lucky Strike," Lewis noted. "Looks fresh."

"Sure does," Noah agreed.

"Should we have SID bag it?"

"Nah," her partner said. "You can collect little stuff like that yourself. Just mark the date and location on the label."

Lewis frowned, glancing at Frank. She knew that the Scientific Investigation Division collected all the evidence at a crime scene.

Frank nodded and Lewis shrugged. Noah handed her a baggie. Lewis scrupulously collected the crushed cigarette. When she finished, Noah indicated an older cop smoking at the periphery of the scene.

"You see Haystack over there?"

Lewis nodded.

"Okay," he told her. "Give him the bag. Tell him to pick up his own goddamn butts next time."

Her partner laughed as Lewis flushed. Pointing to a house across the street, Noah said to Frank, "The lady in there said she won't come out until he's gone. She said if we keep messin' with the Colonel here, we're gonna get hexed. Her old man was mumblin' somethin' about not truckin' with no hoodoo niggers."

From across the car, Lewis shot her partner "the look."

"What?" he defended. "That's what he said."

"What else?" Frank continued.

"Nobody remembers seeing the car come up this morning and no one remembers it being here last night."

"How late we talking?"

"Midnight. One."

When the Figueroa detectives had arrived on scene Lewis had reached up under the car to see if the engine block was hot. It wasn't. Duncan's eyes were dull and the blood had crusted around his neck. The dump must have been in the wee hours of the morning.

Noah said to Lewis, "You notice something odd about the blood here?"

"There wasn't a lot."

"Right. So where is it?"

"Wherever he got cut."

"Yeah, but you've seen people cut before. A slit jugular's going to gush all over. The Colonel here should be covered in blood. Why isn't he?"

3

"Whoever cut him cleaned him up?"

Noah pulled at his tie and plucked his collar from his neck. He'd already peeled off his jacket and rolled his sleeves up.

"Come on, Lewis, look at this guy. He looks like he spilled tomato soup down his chin, not like he just lost a couple quarts of blood."

He was right. Duncan's hairless chest was daubed with blood, so was his neck, but the rest of his body was unusually clean.

"Where is it all?"

Lewis pouted.

"Maybe he got bled into something so he wouldn't be all bloody and make a mess when they went to dump him," she guessed.

"They?"

Frank constantly rode her crew about supposition and she was pleased to hear Noah do the same.

"He, them, I don't know. All I do know is it'd be awful hard for one man to hold him down and then cut him so clean like. I watched my granddaddy kill a hog one time and he had to have my daddy and two of his brothers help him. They cut its neck over a bucket and got most of the blood but it was still all over. And Duncan here's a helluva lot bigger than that pig."

"Okay," Noah conceded. "Let's say that for the time being. I agree with you. Too neat for one person to have done this."

"Unless he was dead already. Maybe that's why he didn't bleed out."

Noah frowned, shooing a fly away.

"Nah. Even if his heart wasn't pumping he'd have made a lot more mess than this. And look at the way he's clotted. We can assume he was probably cut around the time he died. Coroner might give us a different cause of death, but until then let's say someone bled him like your granddaddy's pig. Hey. Maybe we should call him Arnold. You know, like the pig on Green Acres?"

Lewis scowled, moving off to think on her own.

"Sheeth tho thenthitive," Noah lisped.

4

"You think he was bled somewhere?" Frank asked.

"What do you think?" Noah countered.

"I agree whoever did him did a pretty good job cleaning up after himself. Or themselves. But why?"

"Exactly," Noah said. "Where's the blood? It's like they drained this guy, not just cut him. And what's with the fuckin' chicken? Is that some sorta warning or something? 'Tonight Luca Brazzi sleeps with the chickens?' Jesus," he spat, "only in South Central."

"His aunt does fortune-telling or something like that. Maybe somebody's dissin' her."

In addition to founding a crack empire and running a number of legit side businesses, Mother Love Jones also tended the faithful at Saint Barbara's Church of the something-or-other. Its tenets were vague in Frank's mind, something like a cross between Baptist revival and Catholicism, but Mother Love's psychic abilities were legendary. Her devotees came from as far away as Malibu and Beverly Hills to hear what the Mother could tell them about health, wealth, and love. Some came for prophecy, others for the drugs.

"Maybe," Noah said, scratching under his collar. "But I'd give my left nut for a solid witness."

He and his partner spent the rest of the day knocking on doors, but as it turned out, Noah got to keep both his nuts.

2

Frank circled the array of papers and photographs on her dining room table. She had the guts of an old triple homicide spread out before her, but the Duncan case kept breaking into her thoughts. She walked around the table, absently feinting and jabbing at the Duncan case, but not connecting.

She wished she'd brought that home instead, but the murder of a corner boy hadn't seemed to demand her attention. On the surface, Danny Duncan's death looked like the perfectly normal outcome of the business he was in. The motive was probably drug-related, his assailant an associate, competitor, or client. A garden variety South Central murder.

So why's this bugging me, Frank asked herself. Despite sparring with the facts all night, she still hadn't hit the one dangling right in front of her. She knew her brain at a crime scene was like a sponge dropped in water—when it was pulled out, the conscious thoughts were the ones that ran and dripped. The subconscious impressions remained inside the sponge and had to be squeezed out. Frank was trying to wring the sponge dry. Pulling another Corona from the fridge, she gave up. Sometimes the facts just had to surface at their own speed, a subconscious evaporation that was completely beyond Frank's control.

She flopped on the couch with the remote. Scrolling through the programming menu she realized it was almost Halloween—all the educational shows had a paranormal theme and all the movies were horror flicks. She clicked on a bar that featured *The Exorcist*. The opening credits were still rolling and she settled back with her beer, glad she'd caught the best part of the movie.

It opened with Max von Sydow in the desert, an old man running out of time. She empathized with the priest's urgency, his dread for the battle ahead. The dig was over and Father Merrin still hadn't excavated what he searched for. He returned anxiously to the ruins. It was dusk. His booted footsteps startled the watchman, who jerked a rifle toward the old man. He lowered it in sullen recognition. The priest continued. Dogs snapped and snarled at the ruin edges. Stones rolled under foot. The darkness came closer. The old man stopped. He lifted his head to the leering grin of an ancient stone demon. There it was. Where it had always been. Where he had known it would always be. Time ran between his fingers like sand, yet the priest remained a while longer in the demon's rough shadow. Now he knew what he had to do.

The scene faded to Washington, D.C. Mired in crude shock appeal, the rest of the movie never delivered the opening's promise and Frank clicked the TV off. She wished the movie had focused more on the old priest and his dilemma rather than the vulgarities of demonic possession. Frank sipped her beer, noting the silence stealing into the room. Silence, but not stillness. Frank wasn't moving, but she wasn't still either. She felt a vague disquietude, and thought to blame it on the movie. *Nice try*, she thought, balancing her bottle on her belly. It had been there before the movie. Had been there since she got home.

Unable to explain her unrest, she justified why it was ridiculous. Stats were up, the boss was happy, and her squad was finally recovering from some serious setbacks. Nothing wrong on the work front.

Something with Gail, Frank wondered. She'd been hoping the doc would come over tonight but she had to prep for a big day in court. As the Chief Medical Examiner/Coroner for L.A. County, Gail Lawless had to testify that the mayor's daughter had driven into a jeep at 76 miles per hour, killing herself and three teenaged friends. The then-mayor had threatened to paint Gail's relationship with Frank to the media with a very broad brush, unless the doc reduced his daughter's blood alcohol concentration from a flagrant .36 to a more modest .03. Gail had refused, and the mayor had started outing his ME, but at a politically bad time. Riots during the Democratic convention, accusations of a city council rife with fraud, and a transportation strike that cost the city a quarter million dollars a day, paled next to allegations about who the Chief Coroner was playing footsies with. By the time the case made it to court, the mayor had been voted out, and the new Hizzoner didn't mind rubbing his ex-rival's nose in the dirt a little more.

Frank thought back over the weekend with Gail, trying to pinpoint anything that might be festering under her skin. The doc had dragged Frank to Griffith Park to ride horses. Watching *Mr. Ed* on TV was the closest Frank had ever been to a horse and she'd been reluctant to step up onto one. Surprisingly, she'd had a good time. She shouldn't have been surprised; she always had fun with Gail. Almost always. They had spats, but she was learning she could trust the doc. She could let her guard down and catastrophe wouldn't necessarily strike. It might, she maintained, but if it did, it was beyond her control. There was nothing she could do about that.

She had Clay over at the Behavioral Science Unit to thank for that. Like most cops, Frank lived with the constant certainty that bad things were inevitable. What Frank was trying to learn, and what kept her from going off the paranoiac deep end, was that she couldn't control all of the bad events, or for that matter the good ones. She still had more than a healthy share of cynicism—good cops had to in order to survive—but they also had to learn to put it away at the end of the day or they'd end up eating their guns. Clay had taught Frank how to loosen her emotional grip. It was a hard trick to pull off, but Frank was practicing diligently.

Spinning off the couch, she started pacing. Danny Duncan kept dancing just along the edge of her consciousness and every time she tried to focus on him, he vanished. Frank stopped in the middle of the living room. She folded her arms and listened to the air conditioner. She didn't usually have it on but without it, there was no sleeping through the merciless Santa Anas. The compressor's hum was steady and comforting. Frank stood and waited. She felt like Father Merrin under the rough shadow of the demon.

Her skin prickled, and she caught the merest whiff of it. Subtle, but there it was, a tiny weight hanging against her heart.

Dread.

Duncan felt big. Bigger than it should for the death of a wanna-be baller. Frank was glad no one was around to see the shiver that tickled her. The idea of another big case was repellent. Delamore, then Ike Zabbo—they'd been big enough to last her a career. A lifetime. They were ugly and sad and more than she wanted to face again.

A thud sounded against the front door and Frank's heartbeat trebled. She whirled, half expecting to see the door broken into, but its wood was solid and silent. Her 9mm sat on the kitchen counter amid the debris she unloaded from her pockets each night.

"Who's there?" she called. No answer. Frank grabbed the Beretta and checked the magazine, turning lights off. She simultaneously chided her overreaction and acknowledged the wealth of death threats she'd collected over the years. It was probably just Gail come to surprise her. Frank raced through a plausible scenario. Gail fumbling with her keys on the other side of the door, dropping her briefcase while she clamped a fat folder between her teeth, unable to answer or even curse. She was disorganized like that. Forever losing her keys, her glasses.

Or it was a pissed off parolee with an Uzi in his hands and no thought other than to blow away the bitch that sent him up.

From an angle, Frank peered through the peephole. Nothing. She checked the lateral view from the living room window. She couldn't see the entire alcove, but the front light wasn't throwing any shadows. Frank pressed her back to the wall parallel with the door.

Again she asked, "Who is it?"

No answer. Frank turned the lock, ready for someone to bust in or shoot through the door. Nothing happened. She twisted the handle, pulling it just enough to slip the catch out of the hole. Again she expected someone to ram in. No one did. She shoved the door open with her toe. Only silence. Crouching, she chanced a glance outside.

Shadows danced crookedly on the lawn and the wind sent litter scraps scurrying along the sidewalk. At her feet was a dead pigeon. Taking in the empty cars at the curb, the lighted windows across the street, Frank relaxed and breathed normally.

She shook her head at the bird on her door mat. Its head was bent back at an awkward angle and a drop of blood made a perfect red bead on its beak. Frank picked the bird up by its feet. The scaled legs were warm. She dropped the little body into the garbage can and returned to the insulated silence of her house.

Half a block away, a flock of pigeons settled nervously along an eave. Frank didn't know that birds didn't fly at night because they couldn't see. Nor did she know that they left the safety of their roosts only when badly frightened.

3

The Mother was restless. She'd snapped at the boys during dinner then gone to bed early. She paced, hating how edgy she felt. Now and then she separated the heavy red curtains, looking out into the L.A. night. Headlights streamed up and down Slauson Avenue. A helicopter whomp-whomped not too far off. The sky was the color of old blood, the same as it was every night. Nothing had changed.

But something had. Something no one else could see. The Mother knew it. She knew things before she saw them or heard them sometimes. She was like a bloodhound that could smell a man's scent in the room even though he wasn't there. Something had touched the Mother. She couldn't touch it back, but still she felt it upon her, as thick as warm fog.

She checked her view again, expecting to see lightning but there was only the smudgy maroon sky. She pulled her robe tighter.

Normally the sensuous slide of silk against skin delighted her. Tonight it felt only cold. Everything felt cold—the burgundy chenille spread, the antique velvet chairs, the king-size mahogany bed frame—all the rich textures she loved felt cheap and lifeless.

The Mother paced through her anxiety. It wasn't new. It always happened before a big vision. Sooner or later she would wake up on the floor or in a chair, not knowing how she got there. Concerned faces would be around her, waiting for reassurance. She didn't mind the visions. It was the waiting that vexed her. But the Gods would reveal the vision in time. In Their time. And only if she had prepared properly.

She scrutinized an altar near the window, making sure it was clean and well-tended. Red candles burned amid bowls of rice and honey. Bananas curved around sprays of red hibiscus flowers and black rooster feathers. A plate of fresh crabs and an open bottle of rum stood waiting.

The Mother dipped her hand into a jug of water. Sprinkling the shrine, she murmured an ancient invocation. Wetting her other hand, she washed them together. She crossed the room and pushed a chair the size of a throne from her desk. Opening a satin-lined drawer, she gathered a chain of cowry shells, a wooden mat, and a thick cigar. She pulled a box of matches from her pocket and lit the candles on the desk. One was white, the other red. The Mother opened the mat, sprinkled it with water, and then laid the cigar between the jug and the candles. She turned the lights off. The words of a language as old as the wind melded with the candle shadows dancing against the wall.

Now she was ready. Now They would surely come.

4

Lewis and Bobby Taylor were climbing the steps ahead of her. Frank slowed down to eavesdrop on their conversation. Bobby was explaining, "If you do your job right, you won't be a nigger or a bitch. You'll just be a cop. Period. That's all they'll see you as. But if you don't pull your weight or back your brothers, then you'll be worse than a nigger. You'll be outside forever and nigger will be the *nicest* thing they'll call you. It's all about being the best cop you can be, is all. And that's not to say it's always about justice or law. It's about being treated the way you want to be treated, and you've got to earn that."

"I been earning it eight years," Lewis complained. "How many more times I gotta prove I'm down?"

"Every day," was Bobby's reply. "Every new partner, every new case."

Frank followed quietly behind, pretending to scan one of the memos in her hand.

"Yeah, well they don't give *you* grief. You're not having to prove yourself every day."

"I've been here a long time. These guys know who I am. I've been through hard times with them. And good times too. When you've been around a while and had enough beers with them, and backed them on enough busts, covered for them, then they'll trust you too. But right now, we don't know who you are. You're being tested, Lewis. So just do your best and forget the rest, understand?"

"Yeah, I understand," Lewis blew out. "It's just hard sometimes."

Bobby answered, "If you wants it easy, sistah, best be givin' up this *po*-leece bidness and getting' yo' black *be*-hind down to Sunday school, be teachin' lil' chilrens instet."

It was the first time Frank had heard Lewis laugh. It was a good sound and Frank was grateful Bobby was taking the rookie under his wing. The Ninety-third Homicide Squad had taken some fire lately but it looked like they were going to come out all right.

When Frank had pinned a series of murders on Ike Zabbo, one of her own detectives, her accusations had unraveled the squad. Nook, the last of her good old boys, had quit in solidarity with his indicted colleague and the rest of her detectives furiously questioned Frank's loyalties. Then only a few days after she'd dropped that bomb, Zabbo was gunned down in a parking lot and the nine-three finished unraveling.

Even though it was well outside their jurisdiction, her detectives had clamored to work Zabbo's case alongside the big boys at South Bureau. Frank had forbidden it, adding fuel to their already incendiary acrimony. Even Noah had come down on her. He was the only one with balls enough to voice the squad's increasing frustration about her dispassionate stance regarding Ike's violent, and as yet, unsolved murder.

Frank had warned her crew with deadly sincerity that unless they felt like pursuing new careers they would forget about Ike Zabbo and leave the investigating to South Bureau. After that she'd stormed into her captain's office demanding four new hires. Not one, not two, not three, but four. She'd been under-staffed for years and was crippled without Ike or Nook. More importantly, she'd needed an infusion of new blood to stop the nine-three's hemorrhaging.

Foubarelle had produced, allowing her to bring Lewis on from Robbery and Darcy James in from another division. With Jill back from maternity leave and Foubarelle working on the fourth hire, Frank felt like she was finally heading a decent squad again. There were gaps, but overall the team was solid.

Lewis was raw and sensitive, but she'd proven her street ability as a uniform. Frank had been watching and waiting to bring her aboard. Lewis had the perseverance and curiosity that was vital to homicide. Her skills were still weak but that was to be expected. Frank had paired her with Noah because she'd learn a lot from him, if she was willing. So far they were still testing each other. Noah delighted in pushing her buttons but took equal time in teaching her the intricacies of interviewing the parents of a dead child or how to look at a crime scene before entering it. Lewis paid sharp attention to her partner, constantly alert for tips as well as gags.

Johnnie Briggs and Jill Simmons were working together. It was a problematic combination, but Frank couldn't afford to put Johnnie with someone new nor could she have him operating on his own. Johnnie was a loose cannon and he needed a seasoned partner who could rein him in, which Jill reluctantly did. For a while his drinking seemed to have tapered off; he was actually getting to the 6:00 AM briefings clean and on time. Since the business with Ike though, his sick calls had increased and when he did show up he was often bleary and shaky.

Jill handled her partner with a loose disdain, not really wanting to be back at work, and certainly not partnered with Johnnie Briggs. Her heart was home with her infant daughter but she did what was required. Frank suspected it was only a matter of time before Jill took the chair opposite Frank's desk to tell her she was quitting.

Bobby—quiet, plodding, and dependable as ever—was showing

the new guy the ropes. Darcy James III barely topped five feet eight with his shoes on and Bobby loomed well over six feet. Bobby was slow and deliberate, where Darcy quickly and intuitively interpreted a situation. When pressed, Darcy was equally forthright with his opinions, while Bobby, after considerable deliberation, usually offered a more politic answer.

Then there was Taquito. Frank sighed quietly. Lou Diego had been doubly wounded, first by his partner's alleged treachery, then Frank's refusal to stand by one of her own men. He blamed her for Ike's death. He refused to talk about it and would leave the room whenever Zabbo's name was mentioned. In his own time, with his own logic, Diego was dealing with the reality of Ike's betrayal and the position he'd put the whole squad in. Frank didn't push him. He was a good cop and she didn't want to lose him, but she wondered if she already had. She accommodated his unspoken rage, hoping time and latitude would help him come around.

Even Foubarelle seemed to have calmed down. He was still an asshole, but after four years the captain was learning to stay out of Frank's way and let her do what she did best, which was produce stats for him. Bottom line, that was all Fubar wanted. He wasn't a people man, nor committed to an ideal. He just wanted to see how far his star could climb. Frank enjoyed high clearance rates for a different reason. Her motivation was unconscious, but every murder solved was a vindication of her past. Frank needed homicide as badly as the captain needed numbers.

Tossing some of the memos in the trash, she filed others, and took the rest out to the bulletin board. She was pinning them up when Jill and Johnnie walked in with a suspect. He spit, protesting weakly while Johnnie sat him down, and Jill told Frank, "Now this is the damnedest thing. Darcy came up to me this morning and asked if KD here worked in a restaurant. I said, no, the lazy bastard doesn't work at all. He just mooches off his girlfriend like an over-grown tick. So Darcy asked where the girlfriend worked and I told him she was the night manager at the Jack in the Box on Florence.

He said we might want to check the refrigerators over there. I didn't think much about it, but I had to ask the girlfriend something anyway, so we went over. She didn't want us looking around but she finally consented, and look what we got."

Jill held up a .44 in a plastic bag.

Frank frowned.

"In the fridge?"

"Right where Darcy said. Pretty freaky, huh?"

"How'd he know to look there?"

"Beats the hell out of me." Jill bunched her shoulder. "I just hope the ballistics match."

Twelve hours later Frank had another cleared case for the captain's stat sheet. Darcy James had a note on his desk to see Frank.

5

Jill rushed in ten minutes later than her usual ten minutes late. Bobby finished his meticulous briefing, while her colleagues watched her scramble for notes and a cup of coffee.

"Anything from you?" Frank asked Darcy.

In his basso profundo, he rumbled, "What my partner didn't cover would fit on the end of a gnat's ass."

Bobby and Darcy were both quiet men, but where Bobby's voice was as soft as a spring breeze, Darcy's sounded like a V-8 at a red light. Jill pulled a chair up, waiting expectantly for Frank to continue. Frank was silent for a few uncomfortable beats.

"Nice of you to join us, Detective Simmons. When we're done, get with Bobby and Diego. Find out what you missed. Maybe tomorrow you could try for your usual six-ten. What have you got?"

Jill looked imploringly at Johnnie but he was picking his fingernails. She flipped through pages in her notebook, stalling. "Let's see-ee."

"Want me to get another box of doughnuts?" Noah asked. "Or maybe I should just go ahead and order lunch."

"Okay, okay. Hang on. Let's see. We followed up on the names Cheryl gave us."

Jill was the only one who used Lewis's first name, and Frank thought it was good the two women had a chance to work together.

"Porfiero Hernandez was one of them. By his own admission was friends with the vic. Last time he saw him was around two PM the day vic died. He said"—she paused to decipher her own handwriting—"He said . . . vic was going to go by his aunt's and then after that he'd meet him—Hernandez—at Brenda's Pool Hall. That was supposed to be around eight. Vic never showed. Hernandez played a few games, watched a few, left around ten."

She paused and Johnnie added, "We'll take his picture over and see if anyone can put him there."

"Was he with anybody else?"

Johnnie supplied a name from memory and Frank was pleased to see him on the ball this morning. Today he'd shaved with no cuts, and was fidgeting restlessly like the old Johnnie. He was a couple dozen pounds overweight but his clothes were clean, and amazingly enough, pressed.

"Yeah, and get this," Johnnie said in his gravelly smoker's rasp. "This guy lives right in front of where we found your Colonel. He was parked right in this guy's driveway."

Flipping through a folder, Lewis asked, "What was that name again?"

Johnnie repeated it impatiently, spelling it for Lewis like she was brain-dead.

"Booyah," she said, holding up a rap sheet. "Tito Carrillo. That's one of the names Danny Duncan's sister gave me."

Frank glanced at Noah, who almost imperceptibly shook his head. Pointing to the rap sheet, he asked his partner, "When'd you get all that?"

"Last night," she replied smugly.

"Did you plan on telling me about it sometime?"

"Well, I *tried* tellin' you this morning but you and your *home-boy*"—she sniffed at Johnnie—"were too busy playing which yo' paper dolls."

Johnnie laughed and Noah looked as innocent as a choirboy. Lewis's position on the LAPD women's soccer team had inspired the boys to high artistry. They'd gotten a picture of Brandi Chastain's famous pose and pasted a Polaroid of Lewis's face over Chastain's. Then they'd cut a bullet-proof vest out of a catalogue, clipped it into the shape of a bra and glued it over Chastain's infamous sports bra. They'd even added a tiny shield with Lewis's name printed on it and a full gun belt on her waist.

When Frank had come out of her office for a second cup of coffee, Lewis had been glaring at the masterpiece hanging on the bulletin board. Frank had nonchalantly filled her cup, thinking that the line between sexual harassment and kidding around was easily crossed. This was where knowing her crew as well as she did enabled her to make the distinction between true malevolence and ritual razzings. Before returning to her office, she'd clapped Lewis on the back and deadpanned, "Need to work on that farmer's tan."

Pulling her detectives back on track, Frank commented, "Glad to see somebody actually working around here. What else you got?"

Still unaccustomed to her role as primary detective, Lewis shifted a little nervously, if not proudly.

"Well, this guy Carrillo? He's got a rap sheet from here to Orange County. Mostly all drug charges. Most of them dismissed or settled. His homey, Hernandez, was busted with him twice, in January, and last June. Both on felony possession charges."

Waving another rap sheet, Lewis continued, "I checked on the other homes Duncan's sister told me about. Alejandro Echevarria. Known associates." Lewis paused dramatically, then said, "Carrillo and Hernandez. They've all three of 'em got a bucket of aliases, they've all been busted for felony drug possession or narcotics trafficking, and all three of 'em Nicaraguan."

"Ollie North in there?" Noah cracked.

Lewis ignored him. Her eyes sparkled as she leaned toward Frank.

"I'm thinking maybe little Danny Duncan was trying to get out from under his auntie's skirt and get some action going on his own, know what I mean? Maybe auntie"—Lewis said "aunt" like "haunt"—"didn't like junior straying so far and decided to show her boy what was up."

"If that's true, then we're fucked," Noah said. "There's no way we can touch her."

Frank silently agreed. Maybe this was the big thing she'd felt in her living room last night. If it was, that wasn't so bad. She could handle a crack lord. Narco had gone after Mother Love half a dozen times but the worst they'd done was make her lay low for a couple of weeks. Crackheads had hopped around the streets like fleas jumping off a dead dog, but within a month they'd crawled back under their rocks, back to sucking on pipes and bent antenna rods.

"You talked to her yet?"

Lewis shook her head, asking her partner, "We gonna do that today?"

"I'd hate to see all your hard work go to waste. Let's go talk to the upstanding citizens on your list before we hit the Mother. Maybe they'll drop something we can work her with."

Lewis nodded disappointedly, but seemed to understand Noah's logic. They broke up after another ten minutes and Frank snagged Noah.

"How's paperwork coming for the Colonel?"

"Unless Sister Shaft did it after typing her 40-page suspect list, it isn't."

"That's what I thought. You get it started. I'ma roll with your partner this morning."

"That's not much of a deal," Noah complained.

"You're right," Frank grinned, "but I want to see your girl in action."

21

"How'd she get to be *my* girl?" Noah grumbled. "You're the one that's a god to her."

"How's that?"

"Christ, she thinks you can walk on water." Noah's eye somersaulted when he said, "She says you're an inspiration and that she appreciates how you've kept your eye on her. That you picked her when you could have had any of a dozen vets. You're her angel for sure. She'll be flyin' backwards out there tryin' to please you."

Frank smiled, remembering her mentor. She'd have rather cut off and pickled her toes than disappoint Joe Girardi. Frank started prioritizing her day as Darcy stepped into her office.

"You wanted to see me?"

"Yeah. Sit down."

He settled easily into her old vinyl couch. She thought it curious he hadn't taken the chair on the other side of the desk.

"How'd you know about that .44 in the refrigerator?"

"Just a hunch." He shrugged.

"Helluva hunch."

When he didn't offer anything more, Frank said, "Explain it to me."

"There's nothing to explain. I just kept thinking about a .44 in a refrigerator. A stainless steel one like you'd find in a commercial kitchen. I knew Jill had a vic shot with a .44 and that they couldn't find the weapon. It was just a SWAG," he concluded, some wild-assed guess.

"That's all?" Frank drilled him with her blue beams on high.

"That's it."

Frank studied her cop a beat longer.

"Nice heads up," she finally said. "Leave the door open."

She watched Darcy leave. Her new cop came with a clean record. He hadn't given Frank any cause for suspicion, but then again, neither had Ike Zabbo, and she thought she'd known him a hell of a lot better than Darcy James. Lewis interrupted Frank's rumination.

22

"Noah says I'm riding with you this morning."

Frank grunted, "In an hour or so," and followed Lewis into the squad room. Frank wanted the time to get some background on Mother Love Jones. If Lewis was right, she was riding a pretty fast horse. Frank considered reassigning the case to Noah, but only for a second. She had confidence in Lewis. There were nuances she couldn't be expected to know yet, but under Noah's tutelage and Frank's watchful eye she felt Lewis could handle the case.

Frank pawed through the shelves of cold files. When she was brand new in the nine-three, Girardi had been sweating blood trying to build a case against the Mother. She found the murder book she was looking for and blew the dust off it. The binder was thin but probably had a good bio on Mother Love.

Someone had thoughtfully left a quarter inch of coffee to thicken and burn. Frank dumped it and made a fresh pot. She filled her cup while it still perked through the basket and settled at her desk with the musty binders.

Peter Gough, retired now, had been the primary on the case of an aspiring high-roller torched in his Monte Carlo. Gough had nothing—no prints, no wits, no trace. All he had was street talk. One of Gough's CIs, a confidential informer that was still working with Diego, had passed along what he knew as a minor player. Other CI's reinforced the talk, but it was all hearsay. The vic had burned MLJ—as Gough referred to her in his notes—coming up shy a couple keys in a coke deal. Then the vic compounded his mistake by bragging. A week later he was found chained to his steering wheel, crispy and still smoking. The only thing they knew for sure was what the coroner said, that the vic had been alive when he was immolated and had fought like hell to free himself.

Frank marveled at MLJ's rap sheet; conspiracy, felony possession, intent to distribute, assault with deadly weapon, fraud. Sixteen pages and not one conviction. Frank wondered if she had connections in the system.

Don't even go there, she warned herself.

Gough kept referring to an old case number and Frank delved back into the cold files.

"Whatcha lookin' for?" Noah asked. He was a good detective because he couldn't mind his own business.

"An old case involving the Mother."

"Oh, yeah?"

"Gough caught one when I came on. A baby-baller fried in his hooptie. He keeps referring to this other one. Here it is."

Frank blew dust again.

Behind her Noah asked, "You thinking what I'm thinking?"

"Probably."

Maybe because they'd had the rare LAPD opportunity to have worked with each other most of their careers, or maybe because Noah knew her better than any other human being, they shared an uncanny access to each other's thoughts.

"That if Lewis is right, and I'm thinking she might be, that this case could be a motherfucker?"

"Kinda like that," Frank agreed. "You should see her sheets. Multiples on everything and not one conviction."

"Think she's got an angel?"

"Don't even think that. If she does, she can keep him."

Frank was on thin departmental ice after exposing Ike Zabbo and had no taste for chasing the Mother up a conspiracy tree. She'd jeopardized her career enough with Ike and wasn't about to risk it again over a hustler's slit throat. Narco or the rats in Internal could take on the Mother. Frank wouldn't.

Noah followed into her office. They skimmed through the first case, a Honduran coke dealer who appeared to have fallen off a roof. The autopsy indicated a struggle, as did evidence on the rooftop. The case had been Joe's. Evidently he'd had a wit but she'd refused to talk.

As she considered how the Mother had burned her old boss twice, Noah chimed, "No wonder he wanted her so bad."

"Check on the wit. See if time's mellowed her," Frank said, scanning the Mother's brief bio.

Crystal Love Jones, nee Crystal Green. Married Richard Love in 1963. He died in 1964. Crystal Green inherited two Laundromats and a large property on Slauson Avenue.

"Set up pretty nice for a seventeen-year-old," Noah said, reading over her shoulder.

The young Mother Love, still just Crystal Love then, took over running the laundries and renting the Slauson property. Joe had pulled her income tax records. They were neatly organized by an accountant and showed she paid on time every year. Starting in 1968 the tax bills indicated a large amount of money moving through her newly organized nonprofit Spiritual Church of Saint Jude.

In 1976 she married Eldridge Jones. Four years later he was in Soledad on possession. Around that time the Mother started acquiring serious felony charges. In '80 the Slauson property became her legal residence and she began steadily purchasing a number of businesses—a liquor store, a beauty shop, another liquor store, a corner mart.

"Perfect distribution points," Frank remarked.

During that period she was investigated for the two murders laid out on Frank's desk. In 1991 the tax records showed a church reorganization. Noah whistled at the triple-digit figures funneled through it.

"Hell of a character," Frank mused, reading quickly through the rest of the pages.

"Character, my ass. The woman's a one-man plague. She's probably behind every overdose and crack-related homicide in central L.A."

Frank grinned at her old partner.

"Gotta love her. Job security."

"You know," Noah said, his eyes on Frank now instead of the book, "if I didn't know any better, I'd actually say you were happy."

"You think? Go on. Take these with you if you want," she said to the books.

"It's a nice look on you, Frank. Haven't seen it in a while."

"Yeah, yeah. Go on," she said, shoving the binders into his hands. He grinned, and she checked the clock, making sure Noah left. She'd get enough shit from what she was about to do next and didn't need any extra from him. She eyed the phone a moment, then tapped in a number.

After being put on hold, and transferred twice, she finally said, "Hey, sport. What's up?"

"Well, hey there, LT. Why don't you tell me? Long time no talk."

The drawl that used to shred Frank's nerves was soothingly familiar. Frank smiled only because Allison Kennedy couldn't see her.

"I know. How you been?"

"I been pretty good all right. And yourself?"

"Fair to middlin'."

"That's what I hear. I understand you're keeping mighty fine company these days."

Frank dreaded asking, even as she did, "What mighty fine company might that be?"

"Aw, now don't get all coy on me. You know that doesn't sit purty on you. I mean, you and Doc Law, of course. The way I understand it you two are squeezing together tighter 'an teeth in a tripped bear trap."

"And which credible source might this come from?"

"That's what the grapevine says, and from what I've seen of you two together, I reckon the grapevine's dead on for a change."

"We're friends," Frank allowed.

"And then some," Kennedy choked. "I gotta tell you, I'm a mite jealous."

"You had your chance."

"That's not true, and you know it. I *never* had a chance with you."

Kennedy had a knack for driving a knife straight into the heart of a conversation. Then twisting it.

"Okay. You might be right there. At any rate that's not what I called about. I need a favor."

"That's the only reason you ever call."

Frank ignored the comment, giving Kennedy the Mother's real name and social security number.

"Can't you get this from Figueroa Narco?"

"Yeah, probably. But you've got a wider net there at Parker. Plus I trust you to do a better job. If you're busy though, don't worry about it."

"No, I can do it. Just wondering why you're asking me, is all."

"Because you're a good cop," Frank said stroking her ego. "You'll dig deeper than the suits here would. Besides, this way I get to check in on you. Still having bad dreams?"

Frank hadn't expected the ensuing silence.

"Some," was the tenuous answer. "How about you?"

"Not too often. Hey. You know you can always call. Doesn't matter when."

Regaining a measure of her bravado, Kennedy snorted, "Yeah, I'll bet Doc Law'd love it if I woke you up at two in the morning."

"I'm a cop, she's Chief Coroner. We're used to two AM phone calls. I'm serious. You need me, you call."

"Thanks. It's good to know you're there."

"I am. Always."

Another uncharacteristic pause, then Kennedy said wistfully, "I miss you."

Frank had nothing to offer, could think of nothing more comforting than a softly uttered, "I'm right here."

"You know what I mean."

"Yeah. And you know there's nothing to be done about that."

"I figured as much, but it couldn't hurt to check, huh?"

"Can't hurt," Frank agreed.

For a brief moment, until she remembered how Kennedy hopped from lover to lover, Frank was flattered by the sincerity of her longing. She let the silence hang until Kennedy said, "Well, I'll get on this and get back to you when I know something."

" 'Preciate it."

Adding one of the narc's own parting lines, Frank told her, "Keep your eye on the skyline and your nose to the wind."

As she hung up, Kennedy's laugh came clearly across the line.

"Lewis!" Frank bellowed.

The detective skidded into the doorway.

"Yes, ma'am?"

"You get us a car yet?"

"No, ma'am."

Frank cocked an eyebrow. "What are you waiting for? Come on, Lewis, get with the program."

Lewis made a pissy face but skittered out. Frank smiled. Noah was right. She *was* happy.

6

Having uncovered more of Danny Duncan's history, Lewis was anxious to re-interview his sister. Frank agreed, thinking it would be an easy place for Lewis to start the morning. She surprised the rookie by letting her drive and Lewis took them to a nicely kept bungalow in Rampart's jurisdiction. Danny's mother met the detectives at the door, politely but warily inviting them in.

Her daughter, Kim, was washing the breakfast dishes and both women were dressed and made-up. Lewis seemed to take that in, explaining she wouldn't keep them long. Mrs. Duncan motioned the women to sit on a plastic covered sofa.

Lewis got to the point, asking about the names she'd found through the database. Frank took in the photographs stippling the walls between crosses and plates painted with pictures of saints. The furniture was mostly a matching department store set, but a few older, wooden pieces occupied the clean and tidy room. The house boasted modestly but clearly of a hard-working, middle-class family.

Lewis addressed most of her questions to Kim, who answered readily, though vaguely. Frank felt she was sitting on something and might talk more freely if her mother wasn't in the room. She quietly asked Mrs. Duncan if she could see Danny's room.

"Certainly," Mrs. Duncan agreed, leading Frank out to the garage. She explained almost defiantly that she and Kim each had their own rooms inside and her grandchildren shared the third room. She added, "Daniel was too old to be coming home to his mother whenever he was out of money, so I let him stay out here. But I wasn't going to make it comfortable."

Frank nodded, taking in the austere concrete-floored room. It wasn't uncommon in South Central for garages and storage sheds to be bedrooms or crash pads. They were frequently occupied by men and decorated with cobwebs, pin-ups, and empties, but Mrs. Duncan was having none of that. An armoire and a gently worn chair flanked a single bed, its sheets tucked as tautly as skin on a new facelift. An oval braided rug delineated Danny's half of the space. Tools, paint cans, and the usual garage paraphernalia were neatly stacked and shelved in the other half. A wooden crucified Jesus loomed over the armoire.

Indicating the carving, Frank asked if Danny was religious. Mrs. Duncan's face got hard and she replied through tight lips that he used to be.

"What happened?"

"He started running with that sister of mine, that's what happened."

"How did that change him?"

"Detective, I'm sure you've heard about my sister. She's always been different. Ever since we were babies. She's always had to do things her way, even if it means going against the natural order of things."

Mrs. Duncan quickly checked the sunny, rose-filled yard behind her.

"Truth be told," she continued, "I was glad to have Daniel where

I could keep an eye on him. My sister's an awful influence on young people. She was always filling that boy's head with notions he shouldn't have had in there. I prayed for my son. I prayed that he would follow the Lord's path, but I guess my prayers weren't as strong as hers. I hope she's happy now," Mrs. Duncan spat, "because she's going to spend eternity on a spit in hell."

Frank murmured, "I take it you two don't get along."

"Truth is, Detective, there was a time when I loved my sister, but that time has long since passed. She chose her path and I chose mine. We went our separate ways many a year ago but I still pray for her. I pray for that girl every day."

"Mind if I look in here?" Frank asked at the armoire.

"Help yourself."

She pushed aside a few hangers, some neatly pressed pants and button-downs, a gray suit, a blazer, some winter jackets. A very ordinary closet. Bending to look at some little pellets scattered around a jumble of hightops and a dusty pair of dress shoes, she asked, "What do you pray for your sister?"

"I pray that she returns to the Lord. To the one and true God."

Frank wasn't surprised that the pellets were rice grains. Dealers used rice to keep their powders from solidifying, just like rice in a salt shaker. Frank checked the pockets in Danny's clothes, finding nothing. Not even lint. She was sure Mrs. Duncan turned Danny's pockets inside out before she washed his clothes, and being a smart boy he'd make damn sure there was nothing in them. The rice had probably spilled out of one of his hightops.

"Which god is she with now?" Frank asked, pointing at the bureau. "May I?"

Mrs. Duncan nodded impatiently. She looked like she was trying to contain herself, then she burst out, "Crystal is with *no* god!"

Frank's hand expertly fished through Danny's folded underwear and paired socks, while she kept an eye on his mother, thinking she might start crying. Instead Mrs. Duncan stamped her foot and grabbed her lips in her palm, hissing, "*She's in league with Satan.*"

Mrs. Duncan's histrionics amused Frank but she pretended concern.

"How do you mean?" She frowned, her fingers sliding against something cool and slick under a stack of T-shirts. Frank hid the drawer with her back and lifted the shirts. A *Hustler* and a *Maxim*.

"I mean that girl is *evil*. She got the call. Ever since my great-great Grandmother Green, at least one child in every generation has had the call. It was clear right off that Crissie had it. And she used it for her own ends, soon as she figured out how. I love my mother but I curse her for encouraging that dark seed in Crissie."

"What do you mean she uses it for her own ends?"

"To get her way. To get what she wants. It's always been that way. Only now she calls it *santería*, claims it's a perfectly legitimate religion. Huh," she snorted, "just cause a thing's legal don't make it right. No matter what sort of fancy cloth you dress it in, it's still witchcraft. Plain and simple. She brags she's the most well-known priestess of that devil worship this side of New Orleans. And she got my boy involved in that foolishness. You want to know who killed my son, Detective? My sister did. Plain as you're standing in front of me, my sister did, God help me."

"Are you saying she cut his throat?"

Mrs. Duncan stamped her foot again. In frustration or anguish, Frank couldn't tell, but she went on in a hushed voice, as if someone might be listening to them.

"I'm saying she's directly responsible for him straying from the Lord's path. If Daniel had followed in God's footsteps the way he was raised to, he'd be alive today. But my sister tempted him with material goods, Detective. She tempted him with gods that like women and liquor. And that's not all. She prays to those gods and she made my son bow to them too, and this is what comes of it, my son stretched out in a funeral parlor, barely twenty-six."

Frank nodded. Danny's mother hadn't been holding anything back, so Frank asked bluntly, "What kind of work did Daniel do for your sister?"

"I don't know anything about that," she said, her face rigid with pain. Frank guided her into the easy chair. She perched next to her at the foot of the bed and launched into her good-cop routine.

"I can't imagine your grief, Mrs. Duncan. But I *am* sorry for it. I've been working in this neighborhood for eighteen years and I've seen the damage your sister's done. She's untouchable, Mrs. Duncan. Maybe it's those gods she prays to, I don't know. Whatever it is, we've never been able to stop her. She keeps dealing her drugs and kids keep dying. Good kids. Kids like Danny who started off right, and had dreams and aspirations until they met up with your sister. I want to stop her, and I know you do too. It's too late to save your son, Mrs. Duncan, but maybe we can stop other mothers from going through what you're going through."

Tears slid down Mrs. Duncan's cheeks as she tried explaining, "My son was a good boy, Detective. He never meant anybody no harm. I raised him right, I swear I did. But he just fell in with that sister of mine. I warned him about running with her. But he wouldn't listen. I don't know what he was up to with her, but I know it wasn't good. I haven't talked to Crystal in seven years. My other sister's always talking to her. But I wouldn't. I couldn't. Not with her running with the devil like she does. Maybe Jessie could help you. I just don't know."

She daubed at her face with a wadded tissue, whispering, "Excuse me," then bolted from the garage.

Frank sighed, checking under the mattress and bed frame, under the rug and on top of the armoire, around the tools and potting soil in the garage side. Nothing. Retracing her steps to the kitchen, she stepped through the back door, bending an ear to the living room.

Lewis was saying, "Let me ask you something here, off the record. Between you and me, you see, I know and you know what your aunt does for a living. So it seems strange to me that this boy would be off getting involved with some Nicaraguans he don't even know. I mean if he wants to get into that line of business, it would seem to me he'd be working with his auntie, you know what I'm saying? Why your brother be working with strangers, you know?"

"I don't know what you're talking about."

"Girl, please," Lewis chuckled good-naturedly. "I didn't fall off the turnip truck yesterday, n'mean? I ain't no outsider don't know chitlin' from chicken. Everybody know about your auntie. I been hearing Mother this and Mother that since I was this high, n'mean?"

Frank couldn't see Lewis holding her hand above the floor.

"You can tell me, girl. What was *goin' on* between Danny and your auntie?"

There was a pause. The stiff plastic creaked, and Lewis uttered something quietly.

Finally Kim admitted, "He hustled for her for years. He started spotting corners, then running them. But lately Danny was real unhappy with Aunt Crystal. He said that he took all the risk but didn't get none of the reward. He said he was tired of being treated like a little nappy-headed nigger."

There was a smile in Kim's voice as she added, "He'd carry on something about how Aunt Crystal didn't treat him any better than a slave. He used to call her the White Master, and there was some truth to that. Aunt Crystal always be thinking she better than most folks."

"Is that why Danny wanted to break away from her?"

Frank winced at Lewis's bluntness and the next thing she heard was Lewis asking, "With Echevarria and Hernandez?"

Lewis kept giving Kim answers when she should have been keeping them to work with.

"But I'm not real clear about it all. I didn't really want to know too much about it. You might want to talk to my Aunt Jessie. Danny was pretty tight with her. He'd go hang at her place when Mama got mad at him. But she never stayed mad long. He could always charm his way out of trouble."

Not this time, Frank thought, while Lewis asked about Carrillo.

"I think they were getting the coke from him. He was bringing it up from Mexico or something. I'm not sure."

"Did Danny ever mention flipping script with Carrillo? He ever get in his face?"

"No, not that I know of."

"You said Danny wanted to break away from your aunt. Was he serious or just jawsin'?"

"He was serious. He was tired of holding down corners and getting treated like an errand boy. He kept saying he was his own man, that Aunt Crystal didn't own him. I think he was going to try and undercut her price and lure her regulars into his territory. I told him that didn't sound like a good idea but of course he wouldn't listen."

"Do you think your aunt killed him?"

Frank cringed. Lewis was about as subtle as a runaway train.

"What? Are you *crazy*? She loved Danny!"

Frank stepped into the living room before Lewis could do any more damage.

"Sorry to interrupt."

Frank touched her pager.

"We gotta go. Sorry to bother you again, Miss Duncan. We're just running down every possible connection to Danny's death. I hope you understand that some of our questions might seem ridiculous but we have to ask them just the same."

Frank headed to the door, then stopped to ask, "One last thing. Danny stayed with your other aunt sometimes. What's her name and address?"

Kim told her, shakier now than when the cops had come in. Frank wrote the information in her notepad.

"I know this is a hard time for you and our questions don't make it any easier. We appreciate your help. I hope we won't have to bother you again."

Lewis waited until the car doors were shut, before asking, "What's the hurry? I wasn't done talking with her yet."

"Yeah, you were." Frank smirked.

"What you mean by that?"

35

"Drive," Frank ordered. "We're gonna go talk to Mother Love. I'm going to show you how this is done."

"What you talking about?"

"Watch and learn," was all Frank would say.

Lewis smacked the wheel, but she didn't say anything else.

7

"What you doin' up already, Mama?"

Lavinia had slipped into her mother-in-law's room, as she did every morning, prepared to wake her with parted curtains and a breakfast tray. She was surprised to see Mama Love pinning her hair in front of the mirror.

She laughed at Lavinia, "They a law say I can't get up early?"

"No, ma'am. You hardly ever do, is all."

She slid the tray onto a table by the altar, noticing the freshly congealing blood.

"We got company coming," Mama Love said around a pin in her mouth.

"Yeah? Who?"

"You'll see in a while. When they come, let me know."

Lavinia pulled a chair out and Mama Love took it regally. Lavinia sat in the one next to her.

"Did you sleep good?" she asked.

The Mother nodded, watching Lavinia pour her a cup of milky coffee. She held it with both hands, breathing the steam.

"I finally saw it last night, just as I was getting into bed."

"Saw what, Mama?"

"What's been troubling me the past few days."

Lavinia didn't announce her relief. Mama Love was always quarrelsome, but of late her temper had been quicker than a pistol shot. She knew that happened sometimes before she had a big spell, and knew as well to stay out of her way. Marcus though, he never paid it no mind. Just walked like a fool into a hive of wasps. He and Mama'd go at it then Marcus would come and find fault with Lavinia.

"What is it?"

Mama Love ate a bite of cornbread with fried egg and washed it down with a gulp of coffee before answering.

"It's something, darlin'. Something big. I can't quite name it yet. But I think I'm going to find out soon. This morning, I feel. That's why I'm up and dressed. I'm ready for it. Ain't gonna let it catch me hiding under the covers."

"Is it something good?"

Patting her smooth cheek, Mama Love answered, "If I have my way, it will be. If I have my way."

Lavinia smiled, reassured it was something good because her mother-in-law *always* had her way. Shyly, she asked, "Remember what we talked about?"

Mama Love frowned, "What's that?"

"The bath? Today's the day."

"Well, *of course*, child." She hugged Lavinia, asking, "You've been wearing your hand?"

Lavinia nodded, producing a small cloth doll from her waistband. Inside it were stuffed seven pinches each of jasmine, basil and myrrh, and seven black-eyed peas, pomegranate and poppy seeds. For seven days she and Marcus had abstained, and for seven days she had let a mixture of sea water and molasses, sit with seven pennies and seven sea shells in a watermelon surrounded by seven blue candles. Today she was ready to bathe in the mixture.

"You got the yellow sheets?"

Lavinia nodded.

"I hung mistletoe, parsley, and yarrow over the bed just like you told me to. Tied up with a yellow string."

"Good girl."

"And seven yellow candles like you said."

"And Marcus is ready?"

"He *always* ready," Lavinia giggled. Her mother-in-law looked stern and Lavinia quickly added, "He's been wearing his hand. He's ready."

"Best be. Else he'll have to be waiting again until the next new moon. And you know what to do with the candle wax?"

"I'ma make it quick into the shape of a baby and bring it to you."

"That's right. We'll be waiting next door."

Lavinia's heart galloped. She was pretty sure Marcus would kill both of them if he found out, but she had to ensure her place in the family. She had to make a baby. She'd seen that even before she married Marcus, but still couldn't get pregnant. At her mother-in-law's insistence, she'd collected her husband's seed one morning in the guise of making a pregnancy potion. She'd given the semen to Mama Love who had a doctor waiting for it. It was no good, he'd said. Marcus's sperm were lazy. Lavinia didn't know Lucian had been tested at the same time.

When Mama Love came to her with the plan, Lavinia hadn't wasted time thinking. Mama Love was desperate for heirs and Lavinia knew she would get them at any cost. She knew if she didn't agree to the plan she could be easily replaced. But she'd tasted the sweet life now and wasn't willing to forfeit it.

Lavinia squeezed her mother-in-law's hand. She was scared, but excited too, eager to receive the seed from her husband's twin brother.

8

The detectives stood in an alley facing a vast brick building. In its hundred years the building had been through many incarnations, starting as a granary in the late 1800's, then becoming a sprawling dance hall during Prohibition. It fed a nation during the First and Second World Wars, serving as a slaughterhouse until the railroad industry declined. The structure withstood a fire in the early-50's only to fall into disuse. Winos and derelicts took it over until an aspiring South Central entrepreneur bought the gutted building and rebuilt it, renting the myriad rooms for warehouse and office space.

Eyeing the iron-grated windows and barred steel doors, Frank realized Richard Love was the man who'd restored the building. Looking where Frank did, Lewis asked, "Shouldn't we have back-up?"

Frank shook her head.

"Just want to talk to her about her poor nephew."

"I don't know," Lewis muttered. "This doesn't seem well advised."

"You sound like the Mother. You into fortune-telling now, too?"

A metal grate slid open in the massive door and Frank lifted her ID to it.

"I want to talk to Crystal Love-Jones about her nephew, Daniel Duncan."

The grate slammed shut. Frank knew the Mother was inside. She called less than five minutes ago, pretending to be one of the Mother's clients, and hanging up when she came on the line.

Eyeballing the rust and burn marks, Frank said, "Bet that's the original door from the Twenties. This used to be a speakeasy. Had all sorts of people playing here. Duke Ellington, Count Basie, Charlie Parker . . . all those guys would jam here."

"How you know that?" the younger cop asked, suspicious that Frank knew the 'hood better than she did.

"It's history." Frank shrugged. "You should know it too."

"Hmph," Lewis snorted.

"What?"

Lewis shifted irritably, snapping, "*I'ma* be history if this crazy bitch don't open up soon."

Frank had seen Lewis's testy side—she was already notorious at Figueroa for her knee-jerk response to any perceived racial slight—but this nervousness was curious. Frank had thought her made of sterner stuff.

"The old lady got you spooked?"

"I ain't *spooked*," Lewis spit out. "I just don't like havin' my ass hangin' out in a dead end alley, standing like some two-bit *hustla* in front a crack house that's probably frontin' more firepower than we got back at the station. And this damn witch's wind don't help any," Lewis added, plucking her damp blouse away from her chest.

Frank smiled. Lewis was right. Logistically they were vulnerable, but Mother Love's posse had nothing to gain by fucking with two homicide cops. Frank had seen Mother Love over the years and had heard the talk on the street about the Mother's prowess with hexes and charms. Like most of her colleagues, Frank had thought Mother Love harmless enough. That was until she had established herself as the largest crack dealer in town and protected her interests with a loyal swarm of well-armed followers and highly-paid lawyers. The Mother didn't have to bother with characters like Frank and Lewis.

"Don't you get scared?" Lewis hissed. "I mean, you know, being white an all? I mean just in general."

"Nope. I'm too mean and too ugly. Ain't nobody wanna mess with me."

"Damn," Lewis said, wagging her head. "You got game, Lieutenant."

As Frank said, "Pound on that door again," they heard a series of locks and bolts being turned. The heavy metal door screeched open, revealing two huge, ear-ringed, bald men. They stood impassively, twin black Genies-in-a-Bottle. A third man operated an arm that worked the door.

In a voice like gathering thunder, the genie on the right said, "Mother Love will receive you."

He tilted his head and the other twin led the way across the cavernous, barely lit room. Frank's loafers echoed loudly. Hulks of car bodies materialized against the murk. The place smelled like warm bricks, gasoline, and musty blood. The room's chill was in keen contrast to the outside temperature. Frank shivered, aware of the Beretta's bulk against her ribs. She picked her way around oil spots, very aware of Lewis and the twin behind her.

The genie ahead of her stepped through a door, ducking a little. He emerged into a narrow brick hallway lit with bare bulbs, and stopped behind a closed door. He waited until his twin entered the hall, sandwiching the cops between them, then continued to lead Frank and Lewis through a maze of hallways and flights of stairs. Finally he stopped. His bowling ball fist knocked lightly on a door.

Frank was caring less and less for her position in the cramped corridor and was relieved when she heard a woman's voice announce, "Come."

The genie pushed the door, tipping his head at the opening. Frank stepped inside, surprised to be in a jungle. Palms and ferns reached over rubber plants and dumb canes. Flowering vines crawled over all of them, aspiring to a row of skylights. Behind her, the genie closed the door. Frank felt trapped. She peered through the shadowy foliage, trying to see Mother Love, or whoever it was that had said "Come."

Her eyes lingered on an altar. The white cloth covering it was as streaked and dotted as a Jackson Pollock canvas.

Gotta tell Picasso that, she noted automatically. Picasso was Bobby Taylor, who held a fine arts degree, and appreciated artistic description. The thought passed as she studied a dozen candles burning on the altar. Their flames were sure and straight, yet feathers stuck in the cloth around them fluttered softly. Frank glanced for a fan or air vent but didn't see any. In fact the room was warm and swampy. The swaying feathers and motionless candle flames nagged at her while she searched for the person that had said "Come."

As if reading her mind, a smoky voice intoned, "Over here, child."

A flame seared the gloom and Lewis flinched. Frank stepped toward a table hidden by the greenery. Behind it, the Mother cast a quick look from the shadows. Frank watched as she lit an assembly of black tapers.

Well into her fifties, the Mother was an imposing woman, slim and elegant. Flares of white at her temples set off beautiful, high cheekbones. They jutted like mountain peaks over a strong chin and full, wide, burgundy lips. The slight hook to the nose, and deeply set amber eyes reminded Frank of birds of prey. The Mother watched Frank as if she were indeed prey.

Frank could hear her heart beating. The air felt supercharged and crackly, as if lightning were about to ground. A light draft slid across the back of her neck and Frank's hair stiffened. Her mind

43

didn't know what it was yet, but her body sensed trouble.

What is it? she worried, casually flashing her ID. Frank's senses prowled the room as she introduced herself and Lewis. The Mother dismissed Lewis with a quick glance and Frank's prior confidence in Lewis evaporated—Mother Love would eat that girl alive then pick her teeth with the rookie's bones.

In a thick, low voice, the Mother started their conversation.

"I know you," she claimed.

The two older women stared hard at each other. Frank realized the advantage she'd given the Mother by confronting her on her own ground. The Mother studied Frank behind hooded lids. She tilted her head, stating more than asking, "You're quite the warrior, aren't you? You took on your own institution. Turned on one of your brothers."

The Mother clucked her tongue, smiled teasingly, "That was shameful."

Frank didn't know if she meant Ike's behavior or her ratting.

"I know you too," Frank said, seizing the moment. "There's not a cop in South Central who doesn't. But frankly, that's narcotic's business. I'd like to talk about your nephew, Danny Duncan."

Nodding, suddenly doe-eyed, the Mother agreed, "A tragedy."

She flattened her hands on the white tablecloth, flexing long, red nails like bloodied talons.

"Do you know who killed him?" the Mother asked.

"No. We were hoping you might be able to help with that."

"I wish I could," the Mother answered. Frank had seen her shift effortlessly from an initial wariness, to disdain, then sadness, and now weariness. She was good. Very good.

"His sister tells us you were close to him, that he spent a lot of time here."

"Danny was a good boy," she offered. "He ran errands for me, helped with the church. It's a tragedy that he should have been taken so early."

"Yes it is. When was the last time you saw him?"

"I'm not sure," the Mother considered, smoothing the tablecloth. "Maybe last weekend. I couldn't say for sure."

"Oh. Your niece said he was here last night. Around . . . ?" Frank knew very well what time, but prodded Lewis, "What time did she say?"

"Around eight o'clock."

"That's right. Eight o'clock."

Frank let that hang there. The Mother shrugged innocently.

"I don't know what happened. I never saw him."

"You must have missed him somehow," Frank offered. "Where were you around that time?"

"The church," she said easily. "He must have come by while the boys and I were preparing for Saturday's service. I don't suppose you've ever been to our church, have you, child? Saint Barbara's Spiritual Church of the Seven Powers? Hmm?"

"I don't believe I have. You, Lewis?"

"No, ma'am."

Frank continued, "We'll have to drop by sometime. Now, who are these boys you were with last night?"

As the words came out of her mouth, a powerful *déjà vu* swept over Frank.

She was watching the Mother over the table, the plants and the gloom thick upon her. She'd just asked the Mother a question. The Mother laughed, candlelight glinting off gleaming white teeth. She looked like an animal about to devour something warm and still moving. Frank watched, curiously repelled and fascinated.

The certainty of the scene, the sense that Frank had already lived this moment, was strong enough to make her dizzy. She forced herself to concentrate on the Mother's words, refusing to validate the odd sensation. The same went for the thin tentacle of dread reaching towards her heart.

"Those boys are my sons. Lucian and Marcus. They showed you in. They're very devoted to their religion." With the merest hint of menace, she added, "They're very devoted to me."

Nodding, Frank redirected the conversation.

"I guess that's how you missed your nephew. Do you have any idea what he might have been stopping by for? I mean, I'm surprised he didn't track you down at the church, seeing as he helped out there so much. What was it you think he might have been coming by for?"

"I'm sure I don't know, child."

Frank bobbed her head like it was an apple in a barrel. She stepped closer to the Mother, picking up a sweet, flowery scent. It was like the smell that came out of the bodega next to the station mixed with incense and herbs . . . and something else. Something indefinable, but old. Timeless. Again the hairs tingled along her flesh, and the tentacle of dread near her heart thickened.

"I hate to bring this up, but it's something you might be able to help us with. Your niece, Kim, she mentioned that Danny was getting involved with some Nicaraguans . . ."

The candlelight was bright enough for Frank to see what she'd been looking for. She continued easily, "Boys' names were . . . ?"

Without taking her eyes off the Mother, Frank cocked her head to Lewis.

"Tito Carrillo, Alejandro Echevarria, and Porfiero Hernandez."

"That's right. Do you know them, Mrs. Jones?"

"Danny had a lot of young friends," she observed, her eyes steady on Frank's. "They don't sound familiar, but I might recognize them if I saw them."

Frank admired the effortless save.

"Seems like Danny was looking to hook up with them, get a little action going on the side."

The Mother waved a hand, dismissing the notion as nonsense.

"I don't know anything about that."

"Hm. That's funny. That's not what Kim said."

The Mother smiled tolerantly, as if at a foolish but endearing child.

"What else did my niece tell you, Lieutenant? Maybe I can straighten out these misunderstandings for you."

The Mother had volleyed smoothly, but Frank had what she

46

wanted. For now.

"That's about it. Just that she was worried about the friends he was hanging around with, worried about what sort of trouble he might be getting into."

Frank made a show of reflecting inward, a subtle manipulation signaling she'd taken control of the conversation. Abruptly she said, "Look, we've taken enough of your time. I know you're very busy and I appreciate your seeing us."

Frank placed her card at the Mother's fingertips, careful not to touch the gory nails. She reeled off the standard request to call if she thought of anything, no matter how trivial it might seem. The Mother picked up the square of paper. She tapped it with a lacquered nail, smiled at it.

"Come back sometime for a reading, Lieutenant. You might be surprised how accurate I am."

"I bet I would be."

She turned to make her exit, but the Mother said, "Lieutenant?"

A hint of a smile curved the Mother's generous mouth. Her eyes reflected the yellow candle glow.

"Yes?"

"Look out for a red dog."

"A red dog?"

"Yes, child. A red dog."

9

Working their way back through the network of halls, Lewis mumbled, "I don't care for this place. It's kind of strange, don't you think?"

"Wouldn't put it high on my list of favorite vacation spots," Frank agreed. She paused at a T in the maze.

"Right or left?"

"Right," Lewis said without hesitating.

"You sure? I think it's left."

The rookie grumbled, "Then what are you asking me for if you're so sure?"

"Lewis, you're a bona fide pain in the ass, you know that?"

"I been told."

Frank twisted a door handle in passing. Locked. She tried another. It yielded. Frank peeked in.

"What are you doing?" Lewis complained.

"Just checking things out while we're here. We're lost, right?"

Light from the hall illuminated what looked like a collection of old appliances. A dank, moldering odor drifted out. Frank closed the door. The next one she checked was locked. And the one next to it. Moving into a new hall, Lewis said, "We should have left bread crumbs."

Frank tried another handle and it turned. She pushed on the door and the room erupted in shrieks and flapping noises. Frank swung the door shut, then slipped her hand through to feel for a switch plate. Finding it, she eased inside.

Hens in crowded cages squawked at the sudden light. A black rooster jumped on her leg. Frank swore and threw it by its neck. The bird landed near a crate of pigeons. They thrashed against the bars in a panic. Living birds trampled dead or dying ones.

The rooster shook itself off and raced back over to Frank. She kicked it away. It trotted back but maintained a wary distance.

"Damn hoodoo freaks," Lewis complained tightly, "we ought to call Animal Control on these nasty mothers."

Frank stepped carefully around a few loose animals, an eye on the rooster. Feathers lifted around her as she walked to a table piled with boxes. She pulled out a bottle.

"Palm oil," she read from the label. Pulling a jar from another box, she hefted it and said to Lewis, "It's honey. What the hell's all this for?"

"What? I'm supposed to know just cuz I'm black what all this crazy-ass shit's for? How am I supposed to know? I wasn't raised in no mucketty swamp mixing up little bottles of love potion number nine, mumbling spells under my breath. Damn! I don't truck with none of this back-woods bullshit."

Lewis had mounted her politically correct high horse for a ride up and down Frank's spine, but Frank said, "Just calm the fuck down. I thought maybe you were smarter than me, but now I see you're not."

Lewis huffed but kept her mouth shut. The birds settled down while Frank poked around in more boxes. Holding a bottle out to Lewis, she turned and saw Spic and Span looming in the doorway.

"Took a wrong turn," she explained quickly. "This is some interesting shit. What do you do with all these birds? Eat 'em?"

Frank held her ground as if she had every right to be snooping through the Mother's private property.

One of the genies growled, "I thought Mother Love told you to leave."

"We're trying, but you took us through so many doors we got lost. If you want us out of here you gotta show us the way."

He made an inarticulate rumbling sound at the twin glowering next to him. Lewis squeezed past and Frank followed. Again they walked for a long time between the big men. Frank thought they were deliberately leading them in circles and Frank said to Lewis, "You were right about the bread crumbs."

"Shut the fuck up," said the genie behind them. At length he paused at a door and opened it up to sunshine. The genie's massive torso blocked their exit but he stepped aside and Frank moved past him. He gave her a shove that made her neck snap but Frank ignored it and kept walking into freedom. When she was safely out, with Lewis beside her, she turned and lifted a hand.

"See ya around," she said cheerfully. Under her breath she muttered, "Magillas."

Getting into the Mercury, Lewis whispered, "*Damn!*" then, "What's a magilla?"

" 'Member Magilla Gorilla? The cartoon?"

Lewis frowned and shook her head. "So you're calling them gorillas cuz they're black?"

"Jesus," Frank swore. "You gotta get over this black thing. I called them magillas because they're big and stupid. They could be fucking purple for all I care. They're still big and stupid."

"Hmph," Lewis snorted.

"Hmph," Frank snorted back, relieved she was finally out of the Mother's goddamned Hansel and Gretel rockhouse.

"Damn," Lewis swore softly. She twisted the AC button and warm air whooshed from the vents. "Where we going?"

Frank intended to visit the Mother's other sister, but she wanted to think about the morning.

"Breakfast?" she asked Lewis.

"I wouldn't mind."

While she directed Lewis to the Norm's on Pacific, Lewis argued, "I still don't see why you wouldn't let me handle her. I'd have done all right."

Keeping her earlier thoughts to herself, Frank smiled at the rookie's unfounded confidence.

"She's way too big for you to cut your baby teeth on."

"How would you know if you don't give me a chance?"

"Trust me," Frank assured. "I know."

She didn't add that her handle on the Mother had been slippery enough. Lewis seethed beside her, her eagerness pleasing Frank.

"Whoa. Slow down," she said, staring out her window.

"What?" Lewis asked, trying to see what Frank was looking at. A slim woman in a tangerine skirt and cream colored hat sashayed along the sidewalk.

"Girl, you look good," Frank sang out the lyrics of a popular song, "won't you back that ass up!"

Lewis stiffened and the woman stopped. Making a brim with the flat of her hand, she beamed when she recognized Frank. Singing back, "Bitch who you playin' wit?" she wiggled her ass dramatically toward the car.

Frank's smile was genuine, and in a deep, sultry voice, the woman purred, "Officer Frank, where you been at? I ain't seen you, Lord, on into a month of Sundays."

It didn't matter if they were a detective III, a captain, or the chief of police—on the street all cops were officers.

"Been busy, Miss Cleo. How you been?"

"You tell me," the woman pirouetted.

"It's not right," Frank admired. "I get older and uglier, and you get younger and prettier."

Miss Cleo gushed, "You just gotta know how to work it, sugar."

Frank introduced her to Lewis, amused when Miss Cleo dangled a white-gloved hand out to her. Lewis took the fingertips, saying, "Pleased to meet you, ma'am."

"Ma'am," Miss Cleo laughed. "Isn't she sweet? Now what can I do for you, Officer Frank. It's hotter than seven hells standing out here."

"Don't mean to keep you. What's the word on Mother Love-Jones?"

"Whoo-ee, that old thang?"

Miss Cleo fanned herself.

"Now you *know* I don't involve myself with that kinda traffic. I do my business, on my own side of the street. You know that."

"I know. Just wondering if any of your customers might've dropped a word on her. Her nephew going down and all."

"Oh, isn't that awful," Miss Cleo responded in a deep voice. "I heard he had his you-know-what cut off and stuffed in his mouth. Is that right?"

The rooster found with Duncan had been a holdback, a piece of evidence not released to the media. Still, variations on the truth swirled in the rumor mill.

"Not quite. What else you hear?"

The woman checked up and down the street.

"I heard he'd been going around behind the Mother's back, and this is what come of it, you know what I mean?"

"How going around?"

"Like hustling his own brand. You can't disrespect that old woman like that. If you ask me, that boy was handing out calling cards to trouble."

"Was he grinding ounces or weight?"

"What I heard, that boy was moving *keys*. Right under her nose! He ought to have known he couldn't get away with that sort of business."

"What else?"

52

Waving one of her gloved hands, Miss Cleo said, "I really don't know much more. All I heard was some of them goofers what hangs out at her corner mart talking about it."

"Which goofers?"

The woman offered a couple street names and Lewis wrote them down. Frank ran Danny's associates' names by her and Miss Cleo recognized Carrillo.

"He thinks he's a boss baller. He'd best mind he don't end up with his you-know-what you know where."

"Anything else?" Frank asked.

Miss Cleo hefted her slim shoulders. Frank gave her a twenty and told her to buy a new hat. Tucking the bill into her blouse the woman laughed wide.

"I can see it's been some while since you bought a new hat, Officer Frank."

"You be careful out there," Frank said, motioning Lewis on.

"She's a piece of work."

"He," Frank nodded. "Miss Cleo's real name is Clarence Carter. He's been on the hoe stroll since before dirt was invented."

"Damn," Lewis marveled.

"Yeah. Looks like the genuine article, huh?"

"Better'n you and me put together," Lewis laughed.

"You can't see the scars under his make-up. A rookie tried to bust his cherry on him then went ape shit with his D-cell when he felt under Miss Cleo's skirt. Bobby and I responded. He was almost dead when we got there. Had a big old crack in his skull."

"What happened to the rookie?"

"Last I heard he was up in San Mateo. Working vice."

"Damn," Lewis said through clenched teeth.

Frank kept her window down, letting the hot air outside compete with the slightly cooler air inside.

"So tell me. How would you have handled the Mother?"

Lewis pushed out her lips, studying the question.

"First off, I'd have been respectful, then I'd've asked where she was Wednesday night. Depend—"

"Nope. Right off you've fucked yourself. Right away you've put her on the defensive by wanting to know where she was during a murder. In something like this, where we don't know the level of involvement, it's best to approach them from the standpoint of the bereaved relative or friend. Get them talking about the vic and give them the chance to say something you might be able to bury them with. Once they're talking and comfortable with the story they're telling you, then you can start introducing the questions. Start with something innocuous like, 'What sort of mood was he in? Who was he with?' That makes them give you details you might be able to trip them up on later.

"Try to make every question open-ended. Don't ask, 'Were you with Danny Blank that night?' That just leads you into a yes/no response. Always ask in a way that forces a more detailed answer. Ask, 'When was the last time you saw Danny?' That way you're pinning her to specifics. Instead of, 'Was Danny here last night?' ask, 'Where did you see Danny last?' Never give them the answer. Force them to come up with their own. You see?"

Lewis nodded, slowing at a light.

"That's another reason to breast your cards," Frank continued. Her arm dangled outside the Mercury and she took a perverse pleasure in the searing heat. She absently deciphered the graffiti hieroglyphics sprayed on a crumbling building.

On the sidewalk in the building's shadow, a heap of clothing came to life. A dusty head poked from the bundle and Frank tried to determine if it was male or female. A face that seemed to have weathered countless suns lifted itself to hers. Bluish white eyes stared at Frank. The lips split into a fat grin.

The car started rolling and the grizzled head followed it, the blind eyes and wet smile still trained on Frank. She craned her neck out the window until the relic disappeared.

"Yeah?" Lewis prompted.

"What?"

"What's the other reason to breast my cards?"

What the fuck was that all about?

It felt like that thing with the poached eggs for eyeballs had not only seen Frank, but recognized her.

"Well?" Lewis demanded.

Even as she silently chastised that she was getting as goosey as Lewis, the hair remained erect on her arms, despite the hundred-degree heat.

"What were we talking about?"

Lewis sighed, "You said to never give anyone an out. Make them give it up. And to breast my cards, whatever that means."

"It means don't show them your hand," Frank answered, relieved to be back on familiar terrain. "You want to have something to surprise them with. Watch somebody long enough and their actions'll usually tell you more than words. Did you notice me get closer to the Mother before I asked her about Echevarria and Hernandez?"

Lewis shook her head.

"I wanted to get close enough to see her pupils. Right as I said Danny'd been hanging around some Nicaraguans, they dilated. It was a slight and completely involuntary reaction, and it gave her away. She didn't even know she was doing it. She tightened her lips and her eyes narrowed too. Just a fraction, but enough. When you drop something on them they don't think you know about, they can go through dozens of involuntary reactions like that. All the way from pupils dilating to shitting their pants."

The image of the old beggar faded as Frank talked.

"And pay attention to what they call you. Notice how she went from calling me child to Lieutenant and then back to child? In the beginning she was in control and I was child. Then when she got a little rattled I was Lieutenant. When we were leaving and she told me about the red dog, she felt she had the upper hand again and called me child. Did you notice that?"

"No," Lewis pouted.

"You will," Frank reassured. "It'll all come with time."

Frank checked the world moving by. A nail salon and a cell phone store. Metal works. A discount store. Two long-haired girls pushing strollers. A young man in a Walkman funked out toward them. Everything was normal.

"I was listening to you with Kim this morning. You gave her all the answers. Don't do that. Let them think you're clueless. Makes them think they know more than you do. Makes them feel more comfortable, confident, and that's what trips them up."

"Yeah, but she was cooperating. She was being up front with me."

"Happily or reluctantly?"

"Reluctantly," Lewis admitted.

"Yeah, like you are now. And if I push too hard you're gonna cop that famous Joe Lewis attitude on me and clam up. What would happen if I treated you soft and respectful-like?"

"It'd make it easier to talk to you."

"Yeah, you'll open up to me. What if I beat you over the head with what I think you're doing wrong?"

"I'ma be in your face," Lewis chuckled.

Frank nodded.

"If you make some suggestions and let your wit come to the conclusion you lead him to, then he feels like he's got some power in the conversation, some control. Makes him feel pretty good, then he'll want to keep sharing. N'mean?"

Lewis grinned, "You just did that, didn't you?"

Frank returned the grin.

"You're gonna be all right, Lewis."

The sun felt good and Lewis was pleasant company. Frank had written off the odd déjà vu at Mother Love's even as it happened, and already she was ascribing the blind stare as nothing more than the old fuck in the blankets recognizing the nostalgic purr of a Mercury engine. By the time they got to Norm's, the unnerving incidents were forgotten. But not for long.

10

The Mother laughed. Her daughter-in-law and sons looked up from their plates.

"What's so funny?" Marcus asked. He'd been pissed all day. Tired of being ordered around like a fucking nigger. Do this, do that. Maybe Danny'd been right.

"That girl coming around here this morning. Loo-te-nant Franco." The Mother danced the title around. "Makes me laugh, is all. My daddy used to say, that dog don't know what it's bit into."

"Maybe you don't know what you bit into," Marcus mumbled around a piece of bread.

He didn't see the knife leave her hand. It hit Marcus in the temple.

"Goddamn!" he sputtered, bread flying from his mouth like snow.

"Don't you ever doubt me, child. Not while you're in my house, sleeping under my roof. Do you understand that?"

"Yes, ma'am," he sulked, dabbing his head for blood.

His mother stabbed at her chicken breast.

"Word," she grumbled, "you two are just like your father. Him"—she lifted her head at Lucian—"frettin' all the time, and you sulking the whole day. Uh-huh. You got his temperament, all right."

Yeah, and you little Miss Fuckin' Sunshine, Marcus thought. He shoveled rice and green beans into his mouth faster than a crack-head could hit off a rod. He couldn't wait to get out of this ugly, dark-paneled room. His mother think she living in fucking England or something?

"It seems funny, is all, that girl. She's younger than I thought she'd be. And a fool, too."

That was just like his mama, be thinking everyone a fool. Well that bitch hadn't looked like no fool snooping around in the supply room. What else had she gotten into before he and Lucian caught up to her?

His mother broke her bread and leaned toward him. As if she knew what he was thinking, and often she did, she confided, "You see, son. That's what I was laughing about. This ain't about police business. It ain't about that at all. It's *bigger* than that."

Her grin iced his blood.

"That Loo-tenant? She don't even *know* what this be about. That's what's so funny."

Marcus didn't like the sound of that, wondering what world of trouble his mother was getting them into now. He turned his head from her to his empty plate. Like a ten-year-old, he asked to be excused.

11

The next night Frank held a double Scotch in the air while she worked her way through the melee of the Alibi. Snagging an empty chair, she twirled it next to Noah's and straddled it. She leaned into his ear, asking, "What's your wife doing tomorrow?"

"I don't know. Why? You gonna run away with her?"

"Nope. She's too smart to have me. Think she'd have time to go shopping with me?"

"*Shopping?*"

"Yeah, I gotta find something to wear to the opera."

"*Opera?*"

"Yeah. The opera."

"*The opera?*"

"What are you, a fucking parrot?"

"Give me a break," Noah laughed. "Since when are you a fucking *opera* buff?"

Noah kept saying the word like he was choking on it.

"Mag liked it. I got into it from listening to her play it all the time."

Noah's eyes slitted and he asked, "You goin' with the doc?"

"No fooling you, Detective Jantzen. So you think I could call her? See if she'd help me find something?"

"Sure. Markie's got practice at 2:30 and I think Les's is at 1:00, but we can work something out. Jesus," Noah said wonderingly. "You dressed for the opera. Will you take pictures for me?"

Frank ignored him and leaned across the table.

"You talk to any of Danny's homes?" she shouted at Lewis.

"Yeah," Lewis yelled back. "Echevarria and Hernandez."

Noah said, "Smokin' Joe Lewis, here, called 'em the most sorrowful excuse for men she'd ever seen. At first they're giving us the three monkey routine—see no evil, hear no evil—then I lay it on 'em that they're looking like our prime suspects. That they cut Danny Duncan out of the business to keep overhead down. Then they just caved. Started crying, blubbering in Spanish, snot runnin' all over. Man, they were just pitiful."

Noah gave Lewis the nod and she picked up the story.

"Yeah. Turns out they *didn't* want to be in business with Danny anymore, not because of the money but because of auntie. They're afraid of her. Especially now with Danny dead. They claim she's a witch and that she's been planting curses on them. The one dude, Hernandez, he found a black cat hanging from his porch one morning, then a few days later he steps on this little sack under the door mat. He said he paid his neighbor to throw it away for him."

"What was in it?"

"Damned if I know. He didn't even want to touch it. A week later someone had laid powder all around his house. He said it was dirt from a graveyard and that if the person it's meant for steps in it he'll die within the week."

"So's he still alive?" Frank scoffed.

"He didn't step in it. His wife saw it first, had a heart attack.

They're scared. That old Mother Love's got 'em pissing in their pants. They got two Rottweilers in the yard and can't figure out how someone's puttin' all this shit around without settin' the dogs off."

"Did you see any of this stuff?"

"Just some of the powder by the side of the house. Why?"

"Go back and get a couple clean samples from around the house."

"For what?" Noah asked incredulously.

"Just to have. Make sure chain of custody's clear on it."

"Oh, let me see. First it belonged to some dead guy in a cemetery, then MLJ dug it up at midnight, then she turned into a bat and sprinkled it around their house, then we got it. That's pretty clear."

Frank ignored the sarcasm.

"What else did these three stooges say? And did you get to Carrillo?"

"Carrillo's in Mexico, supposedly. Left the day before Danny went down. Evidently Echevarria—I'd say he was the bolder of the two, wouldn't you?" Noah asked Lewis.

"Yeah," she chortled, "he only went through one box of tissues."

"Evidently he went to Mother Love's after Danny ended up gutted in Carrillo's driveway. Told her they meant no disrespect and kissed her ass a couple times. They promised to be good boys and it's been quiet since then. No dead cats or graveyard dirt."

Frank asked, "So what do you think?"

Lewis looked to Noah and he was about to speak, but Frank said, "Lewis. It's your case."

She swiped an embarrassed glance around the table.

"We know from his sister, Echevarria, and Hernandez, that the vic was planning on going into business on his own. Not only would that be cutting into his aunt's profits, but it would be disrespecting her right on the street. She couldn't let that go down. It seems to me like Mother Love's our best suspect. There's nothing else pointing us another direction."

Frank raised an eyebrow at Noah.

"What she said," he answered.

"All right. Let's ride this pony. But carefully. That woman's kept her nose clean this long because she knows what she's doing. We've got to have a full arsenal before we hit her with anything."

Noah interrupted, "And even then she'll probably still slither out of the charges."

"Maybe, maybe not. If we give the DA enough material, they might be able to do their job."

"For once," Lewis grunted.

"This bad attitude I'm hearing? Mother's not psyching you out, is she?"

Lewis shook her head and Noah answered, "No, but you've gotta admit we don't exactly have a stellar conviction rate for her."

"Harvey Keitel's got a great line in *Thelma and Louise*," Frank said to her glass. 'Brains'll only get you so far and luck won't last forever.' Keep the faith. Sooner or later she's gotta fall. May as well be on this sword."

Frank grinned at Lewis, knowing right where to drop the bait.

"That'd be a helluva feather in your cap, huh?"

"Want us to run an interdiction on Carrillo?" the rookie asked.

"Can't hurt. I'll ask the doc when we can expect the post."

"Yeah, catch her in between arias," Noah cracked.

Frank punched his shoulder. Hard.

Next morning Tracey Jantzen flew across the mall into Frank's arms with the force and emotion of a SWAT team taking a rock house. Frank laughed as she wrapped her arms around Noah's wife.

"For Christ's sake," Tracey cried, "Where the hell have you been?"

Holding her at arm's length, Frank pleaded that work was the culprit.

"That's no excuse and you know it. I'm starting to think you don't love me anymore, now that I'm big and fat."

"Impossible. That day'll never come."

Tracey smiled up at her, saying, "I'm so glad to see you."

"Me too."

Linking an arm through Frank's, she commandeered her toward the Nordstrom entrance.

"Come on, girlfriend, we've got shopping to do! So the opera, huh? That's pretty hoity-toity."

"I don't want to get all glammed up, I just want to look . . . nice."

"Nice, huh? Like gold lamé with a thigh-split and plunging neckline?"

"A little more modest."

"You know," Tracey teased, "I'm awfully jealous. I thought *I* was the only woman of your dreams."

"You are," Frank insisted, "but you're taken. What am I supposed to do?"

"You're right," Tracey agreed sensibly. "It's time for you to move on."

She paused to feel a flimsy neon-pink blouse and Frank said, "I was thinking something a little more sedate."

"Not for you," Tracey chided, holding the blouse up, "for *me*."

Frank nodded approvingly, but Tracey put it back. She tucked her arm into Frank's, steering her through the store with practiced assurance.

"So tell me about you and this coroner. Noah says she's a babe. When do I get to meet her?"

"We should have dinner. Invite us over. I haven't seen the kids in months."

"Yeah, we'll do that, but what's she like? You've got to tell me all about her."

"Like what?" Frank stalled.

"*Everything.* You must be gaga for her if you're going to all this trouble."

"You gotta look nice for the opera. It's the Pavilion. Opening night."

Tracey planted herself in front of Frank, arms crossed, and one brow arched high.

"*Everything*," she demanded. "How am I supposed to dress you if I don't know what your objective is?"

"I'm not busting a Colombian cartel," Frank laughed. "I don't have an *objective*."

"Of course, you do," Tracey insisted. "But you probably don't even know it yet."

"Well, then why don't you tell me. You and No always seem to know what I'm doing before I do it."

"How serious are you two?"

"I haven't asked her father for permission to marry her, if that's what you mean."

"You're evading the question."

"You'd have made a helluva trial lawyer. Too late for a career change?"

Tracey glowered, tapping an impatient foot.

"We can stand here all day or you can answer a simple question."

"Maybe it's not so simple."

"For you, I'm sure it's not. Do you love her?"

"Jesus, Trace." Frank looked for the hole in the ground she could dive into. "It's only been a couple months. How am I supposed to know that?"

Tracey tapped a nail above Frank's left breast.

"This'll tell you."

Frank knew that was true. And she knew more than she could admit to. Some words were still just too hard.

"I like her a lot. Okay?"

"Now, see? That wasn't so bad. And does she like you?"

"Yeah, but I piss her off."

"*No*," Tracey mocked. "I can't imagine."

"What?"

"Honey, I love you, but I can't imagine *being* in love with you."

"Why not?" Frank asked, somewhat hurt.

"You can be as sweet as the day is long—*I* know that—but you come with a lot of baggage."

"I'm working on it."

"You still seeing that shrink?"

Tracey could get away with the question for two reasons—she was her best friend's wife, and she was a psych tech; Frank knew nothing was implied.

"Nope. But I'm . . . I see things different now. It's okay. The stuff that bugs her, it's the stuff that would bug any civilian. You know how it is. The shit we see. Human and otherwise. Rubs off on us after a while. Gail was raised in Berkeley. Ultra PC. She's got a sensitivity that I lack." Frank paused. "She thinks I drink too much."

"You do."

"Think so?"

"I know so."

That wasn't the answer Frank expected.

"So when can we get this shopping over with?"

Tracey took Frank's arm again, pulling her deeper into the stylish racks of clothing.

"Like I said, you're a piece of work. But I love you. If she hurts you, I'll kill her."

"I don't think that'll be necessary," Frank assured, letting herself be towed along.

When the sun had purpled the skyline and the city lights winkled like so many diamonds and rubies and emeralds, Frank met Gail at the door.

The doc sucked in her breath.

"*Ohmigod.*"

"Too much?" Frank grinned.

The doc shook her bob.

"You look *stunning*."

After some not very serious attempts to get Frank into gowns and lace, Tracey had judiciously selected a pair of black silk trousers and a matching silk shell held up with rhinestone spaghetti straps. Frank had wagged her head in disbelief, but the salesgirls had oohed and aahed, dashing off for rhinestone earrings and shoe clips. She'd accepted a black clutch with a rhinestone clasp, but drew the line at a pair of frighteningly high stilettos and a make-over.

She'd let Tracey drag her into the salon for a French twist and laughed when Tracey put her arms around her, purring, "If she doesn't want you after this, you just come runnin' back to mama, you hear, girlfriend?"

Frank thanked Gail, telling her, "You're lookin' pretty fly, yourself, Doc."

The ME wore a simple crème-colored turtleneck tank, but it clung seductively over Gail's ample hips and ended above her knees, leaving plenty of great leg showing. A few large pieces of gold jewelry dramatized the effect, as did some artfully applied make-up.

When Gail chuckled, "Am I dope?" something shook loose in Frank's gut and went flying up to her heart. Right where Tracey said it'd be.

"The dopest," she said sincerely. "You look wonderful."

"Do I look okay, really? You know . . . symmetrical?"

Frank took Gail by the waist, inspecting the soft rounds under her dress. The right breast was real, the left, a perfectly matched prosthesis.

"Can't tell which is which. They look the same. Both fine."

"Okay. I'm just checking. There's only so much I can tell from a mirror."

Frank reassured, "You look perfect. Every inch of you."

Stopping and starting their way downtown, Gail asked, "Did you send anyone to Camp Lockdown this week?"

"Camp Lockup," she corrected, then answered, "One," recalling Jill's bizarrely cleared shooting. "And Lewis got her first case. Guy with his throat slit. Sitting in his Caddy with a chicken in his lap."

"A chicken?"

"Yeah. Headless. Turns out the vic's aunt is Crystal Love-Jones. Ever heard of her?"

"Sounds like someone who advertises in the personal section."

"She's a crack dealer. Pushes tons a year. Keeps an assembly of lawyers on retainer. Narco's never been able to touch her. Anyway, it looks like the Colonel was bled dry. I'm wondering if he was dead or alive when it happened."

Gail frowned, "He was a Colonel?"

"That's what No's calling him. You know, the chicken? Colonel Sanders?"

"Ah, gotcha, that ineffable, indefatigable police humor. How'd Lewis do on her first solo?"

"All right. Made a couple mistakes but mostly 'cause No prodded her into them."

"Why are you all so hard on her?"

"Boot camp," Frank shrugged. "Everybody goes through it."

"Sounds like a frat house hazing," Gail argued. "Inane and senseless."

"Naw, there's a reason. If she can't take a little shit in the squad room she won't be able to take it on the street. I'd rather know now than when my back's against a wall. It's not a big deal."

"It's just so juvenile."

"We like to call it that ineffable, indefatigable po-leece humor. When do you think you'll get to the Colonel's post?"

"Oh, God, we're so backed up right now. Handley's sick. Jacob and I've been in court all week. And I should be at work tonight instead of going to the opera. A slit throat, obvious cause of death, we'll be lucky to get to it by Monday. I don't think I put your boy high on the rotation."

"No big," Frank said. "I was just wondering."

Trailing her fingers under Gail's dress, she added, "I don't think you can tell us much more than we already know."

"Better stop that or we'll miss the opening act," Gail murmured.

"That wouldn't be so bad."

"At these prices, yes it would."

During the opera, Frank studied Gail's rapt profile. She had to admit she was having a hell of a lot of fun with the doc. But she hadn't lied to Tracey; it was complicated. The doc was bright and generous and sexy, but living alone all her life had spoiled her. She held Frank up to standards she wasn't sure she could meet.

Still, Frank was game. Having loved and lost, she was willing to make concessions. She had to admit it was scary as hell, but it felt good to care about someone again. And be cared for.

She slipped her hand into Gail's, rewarded by a bright, quick smile. Tracey's tapping finger echoed against her heart.

12

Monday afternoon Frank slouched into Ike's old chair and draped a long leg over the arm.

"What's the good news?" she asked.

Jill shook her head, so Johnnie answered for her.

"People are scared, man. They don't want to talk about Danny or any one connected with Mother Lo-ove-Jo-ones," he drew out. "Like the ground's gonna open up and swallow 'em or somethin'. They're all spooked, huh?"

He looked to Jill for corroboration but she only made a disgusted sound. She made a lot of those lately.

"What?" Frank encouraged.

"I don't like this," she blurted. "I don't like this case."

"Yeah, she's spooked, too," her partner teased. "Thinks she's gonna get a spell put on her or somethin'."

"Johnnie, shut up," Jill snapped.

"True?" Frank asked.

"I just don't like talking with any of these people. I don't like their vibes."

"What vibes?"

"Just creepy. Weird."

"Come on, you gettin' soft on me?"

"I'm not soft," the detective defended, "They just creep me out."

"That's how those cults operate," Noah chimed in. "They pull a rabbit out of their hat and make everyone think it's magic when all it is is tricks and illusions. They make you *think* they're powerful, and then once you believe that, you're afraid of them. And then they've got you. That's their power, the ability to make you afraid."

Waving his hand, he advised, "It's all superstition and mumbo-jumbo. Don't worry about it."

"Easy for you to say," Jill muttered.

Frank looked at Diego.

"What do you say, Taquito? Horseshit or real?"

Diego shrugged.

"I don't know," he shrugged, surly. "Maybe it's true. Maybe it's not. My grandpa used to tell stories about *brujos*, witches and stuff. How they could turn into coyotes or snakes, make people do things. I don't know."

"Lewis, I know you believe it," Frank mocked.

"Nuh-uh! I don't believe they can change into animals or make anybody do something they don't want to do. It's like Noah says, I think they can make you believe certain things. And then once you believe that, they make you believe other things."

"It's just a form of brainwashing," Noah interjected.

"Yeah, like that. It's all that mind over matter, power of suggestion foolishness. That's all that voodoo stuff is—but mind you, it can work. I'm not saying it's magic or nothin', but that doesn't make it any less effective. Like Noah says, they make you believe their nonsense. You *think* it works so therefore it does. It's a placebo religion, that's all."

"Aren't all religions?" Noah asked, provoking Jill's Catholic ire. She cut him a look, but Frank said, "Darcy?"

He sat back from the report he was typing and measured his answer.

"It's a complicated question. There are a lot of permutations to consider."

"*Permutations*," Johnnie said mincingly to Noah.

His old partner snickered, "You ignorant bastard. You probably think that's a fruit going bad."

"Like what?" Frank asked.

"Like whether you're talking about simple hoodoo, or something more complex. Like voodoo."

"What's the fucking difference?" Johnnie said. "It's all just ignorant dirt-water bullshit anyway."

"Not really," Darcy drawled, his accent faint. "There's a big difference, and both of them can be very complex."

"How so?" Frank pressed, intrigued as always by the man's incongruities. Barrel-chested, bandy-legged, and thick-armed, he drove a Harley, chewed Skoal, and had more tats than most of the bangers he locked up. He kept his own counsel, never joined his colleagues for drinks after work, and rarely joined in conversation unless asked. Off-duty he wore diamond studs in his ear and biker leathers. He looked like a Hell's Angel who'd rather stomp someone in the face than talk to them, but when he opened his mouth a blind man would think he was talking to a tweed-wearing, pipe-smoking professor. The biker façade concealed a man with a sharp eye for details and anomalies at a crime scene, a keen understanding of criminal predilection, and, if the incident with the hidden .44 was true, an uncanny instinct.

Darcy picked up an empty Dr Pepper can. He squirted a thin stream of tobacco juice into it before answering, "Hoodoo's basically folk medicine. Surprisingly effective medicine. It's based on Old World healing principles and incorporates a large botanical pharmacopoeia while working on the same principles as faith healing. The root doctors—that's what we called them in Louisiana—they have some repute for wizardry, but they're not true mambos or priests like you'll find in voodoo. They can make concoctions and juju's for practically every domestic malaise you can think of: How to keep a husband from straying, how to get him to leave, how to come into money, how to get pregnant. You name the problem and I guarantee there's a root doctor somewhere that will know the right combination of herbs and powders to produce satisfaction."

Darcy's audience was attentive, so he continued.

"Now voodoo, that's actually a religion. I guess I should say an American bastardization of a religion. It developed in this country when Haitian slaves were introduced into Louisiana. It was based on the vodun religion that the slaves practiced back in Africa. Haiti was a Catholic island and the slaves there were all ostensibly converted to Catholicism. What actually happened, was that they syncretized their African gods with the Catholic saints. When the slaves were praying in front of an altar to Saint Barbara they were actually worshipping one of their old gods that had a lot of Saint Barbara's attributes. The Catholic masters looked on approvingly and the slaves practiced idolatry right under their noses.

"American slaves didn't have that opportunity. Except for French Louisiana, most slave owners practiced some variation of Protestantism, so the slaves didn't have the opportunity to co-opt their gods to the dominant religion. American slaves were forced to take their religious practices underground, and as they splintered off among the various slave holders, they lost touch with their priests and priestesses. They practiced secretly—what they could remember—but as their old beliefs faded they were be replaced by the prevailing religion of the area. The use of the traditional herbs and medicines—and their faith in them—that remained. That's what we call hoodoo."

"How the fuck do you know all this shit?" Johnnie interrupted. "They teach you this in Coon-Ass 101?"

Darcy ignored him and Frank appreciated that that was how he had decided to deal with Johnnie's juvenile animosity.

"You know anything about a Saint Barbara's Spiritual Church of the Seven Powers?" Frank asked.

Stroking his longer-than-regulation moustache, he mused, "I'm not sure. Spiritual churches are big in the South. They're hard to define. Kind of an amalgamation of southern Baptist, Pentecostal, and spiritism, all rolled into one complicated ball. They use séances to call down the dead, all in the name of Jesus. And the Church of the Seven Powers. To the best of my knowledge it's an offshoot of the Church of the Lukumi. That was the first officially recognized church of *santería* in the United States."

"*Santería*," Lewis interjected. "That's Cuban, right? That's what those sickos in Matamoros believed in."

Darcy said, "Yes, they were sickos all right, but they weren't practicing true *santería* any more than Timothy McVeigh was practicing true Christianity. They took a basically benign theology and ran riot with it. They twisted it to their own sick ends. And yes, it's an island religion. Remember how I said Haiti was predominantly Catholic so the slaves were allowed to syncretize their African gods? The same thing happened in Cuba and throughout the Caribbean. Brazil too. That's how *santería* and *palo mayombe*, *candomble*, all the Afro/Latino religions came into existence."

"So Mother Love-Jones is practicing *santería*?"

"Well, I couldn't say for sure," Darcy drawled. "I'd say with a 'spiritual' in the name of her church she's probably incorporating some form of ancestor worship in her services, and with the Seven Powers and Saint Barbara tacked on, it sounds like some derivative of *santería*, yes."

Jill spoke as if she'd tasted something bad. "Don't they sacrifice animals?"

Darcy nodded, "That was one of the obstacles in legalizing their church, yes."

"What kind of animals?" Lewis asked.

"Usually fowl. Sometimes a pig or a goat if they need to make a particularly potent offering."

"Larger the sacrifice, the greater their power?" Frank asked.

"Something like that, yes. The animals are usually drawn over the supplicant's body to draw out whatever sickness or problem is plaguing him. The theory is the animal will absorb the trouble and then it's killed and offered to whichever god they're propitiating. And different gods have different preferences."

"What about people?" Noah asked. "They ever sacrifice people?"

Darcy spit into his can and shook his head.

"Only in Hollywood."

"And Matamoros," Jill added.

Following Noah's line of thought, Frank asked, "How do they kill the animals?"

All the detectives were silent while Darcy considered Frank's question. Holding her blue eyes with his own, he finally answered, "They slit their throats and bleed them. Then they offer the blood to the gods."

The squad was silent until Jill said, "That's it. I'm going home."

Jerking the sports coat off the back of his chair, Johnnie said, "I'm right behind you."

Frank looked at Lewis. The rookie hung her head and muttered, "Shit."

Noah cackled and clapped her on the back. "Better get some garlic and wooden stakes, partner."

"No, you need silver bullets," Johnnie said. "Or maybe a priest, like in *The Exorcist*."

Frank shot her rumpled detective a look. He was blithely ignorant, but the skin on Frank's arms rose as she pictured Father Merrin in front of his stone demon.

Johnnie went on, "Isn't that right, Swamp Boy? Isn't that what she needs? Or maybe one of those powders *ya'll* concoct out of snake skin and gator teeth."

Darcy didn't even bother looking up. Johnnie bent his big frame over the smaller detective.

"I'm talkin' to you, boy."

Darcy put his pen down, considering the face inches above his.

Frank said, "Johnnie. Go home."

"I'm talkin' to Swamp Boy here. Just tryin' to have a friendly conversation only he's not being so friendly. Where's that southern hospitality, boy?"

"Conversation's over," Frank said. "Go home."

"Since when can't I talk to my colleagues after work?" Johnnie argued.

Frank's eyes iced up and she said, "Don't make me say it again."

"Fuck."

"Come on," Noah said, putting his arm around Johnnie. "I'll buy you a beer."

"Fuck off," Johnnie answered.

Frank stayed where she was until he left the squad room, then withdrew to her office. Darcy followed.

"I don't need you to defend me," he complained.

Frank checked a sigh.

"And I don't you need you losing your temper and pulling a Sandman on him."

Darcy had been demoted from Venice Division to Figueroa for planting his supervisor's face into the beach, through which action he'd become known as the Sandman.

"I wasn't going to do that."

"Good. Johnnie's got a short fuse at the end of the day and I was tired of it. Do you have a problem with that?"

Darcy chewed the inside of his lip.

"No," he mumbled before turning around, squeezing past a flustered Jill outside Frank's door.

Now what?

Frank wondered if she'd run into Johnnie on the way out.

"I thought you left."

"I did. Can I talk to you for a minute?"

"Sure."

Jill closed the door and Frank waited while she dragged a chair closer to the desk. Maternity may have suited Jill, but working a full case load didn't. She looked pale and tired. Big circles under her eyes were vainly covered with make-up and her hair looked dull and brittle. Frank remembered it being thick and deep red. They used to call her the Fire Truck because of her flaming hair and quick response to a hot man.

"I need to ask you a favor."

Jill twisted her hands in her lap and Frank braced herself for the resignation speech.

"I know it sounds silly, but I want off this Duncan case."

"How come?" Frank asked, relieved.

"I'm just not comfortable with it. I know it sounds ridiculous. I can go into a roach-infested tenement and have maggots crawl out of a two-week-old corpse and up my leg, but I don't want to deal with this devil worship shit. Not now. Not with a baby to look after."

"What devil worship shit are we talking about?"

"What Johnnie said. For once he's right. People don't want to talk about Love-Jones. They're scared of her. You can see it. One man I talked to yesterday, he's retired from Caltrans, a straight up fellow, and he went *off*, telling me not to mess with her if I knew what was good for me, that she was a witch, she could make things happen. He almost slammed the door in my face!

"Then one of my CIs—I didn't even call her, she called me, she lives near Love-Jone's place on Slauson—she told me about some really bizarre things that go on there. Granted she's not the most reputable source, but for her to call me out of the blue and tell me she's seen lightning flashing over that place without a cloud in the sky, and red lights on at all hours of the morning?"

Jill's voice climbed as she added, "And her boyfriend? She says he fights pit bulls and none of them will walk by that building. She said they start peeing and whimpering like puppies whenever they get near it. And to top it all off, she tells me the dumpster in front of their place is always filled with dead chickens and pigeons. There are even goats sometimes! I just don't want anything to do with it. I'm asking you to take me off, Frank. Please."

, "No problem. I was going to put everybody back on regular duty anyway."

Jill was visibly relieved and Frank leaned forward.

"Let me ask you something. Personal. I don't mean any disrespect, I just don't know. If you believe in God, and have a strong faith like you seem to, then wouldn't you feel protected from evil? From characters like Mother Love?"

Jill's head shook vehemently.

"Oh, no. Evil's everywhere, and it's insidious. I have tremendous faith but I'm not perfect. The thing about the devil is he uses any chink in your armor, any weakness in your belief as a foothold to claim your soul. It might start out innocently enough, but Satan's persistent. He digs in and has all eternity to undermine your faith, until you finally, without even knowing it, have crossed to the dark side. He's patient and clever. And he's dangerous. Don't underestimate him, Frank."

"No. I won't," Frank reassured. She'd never seen this evangelical side to Jill and was slightly unnerved.

Jill stood, all tired pride and defiance. "Anything else?"

When Frank shook her head no, Jill smiled weakly.

"I know I probably sound like some crack-pot zealot, but I'd rather be safe than sorry. This just feels all wrong to me."

She seemed to consider an idea, then added, "Be careful, Frank. And take care of Cheryl. She's so green. Don't let her get hurt."

"I won't," Frank promised.

Jill left Frank stinging with the memory of Kennedy bleeding out in her arms. That had been Frank's fault. No. She wouldn't let anything happen to Lewis.

13

The Slauson exit was coming up. Frank was on her way home, but she wasn't in a hurry. The only thing waiting for her tonight was the impassive steel in her weight room. She swung onto the off ramp, crossing back under the Ten, not at all curious about why she was going to the Mother's headquarters. It was close to 5:00 PM and traffic was heavy on the east-west artery. That was good. Frank parked across the street from the brick complex, her old Honda indiscernible amidst all the other cars.

For an hour she watched, and waited, for what she didn't know. Frank was enjoying her secret proximity to the Mother. She'd always liked surveillance and thought she would have made a great spy. She had a fine view of the entrance fronting Slauson and noted three people go inside, stay a few minutes, then leave. The first was an old black woman, followed by a well-dressed Hispanic woman, then a nervous middle-aged black woman. A thin blonde woman came out fanning herself. None of them looked like cluckheads and Frank guessed they were some of the Mother's hoodoo clients.

Debating whether she should go in or not, she saw a ragged figure shuffling towards the building. Despite the heat, a wooly gray head poked from layers of uniformly tattered and dirty old blankets. Frank couldn't tell if it was a man or a woman. She got the uneasy feeling it was the same beggar she'd seen when she'd been riding with Lewis.

Frank watched the figure inch its way toward the door of the slaughterhouse. It wavered about twenty feet short, seemingly unable to travel any farther. The grimy bundle settled against the warm brick wall and sank to the sidewalk. Its blankets puffed around it like a toadstool. The figure remained still for a long moment, then slowly lifted its head.

The face was leathery, the eyes clouded and sightless. The gray head pivoted, noting its surroundings like some ancient, lumbering reptile. Satisfied, it stopped, its face square to Frank's. Through the rush of cars and trucks, Frank saw the pink mouth widen into a grin. The dead eyes were straight on her.

Frank stared at the ruined visage. It was impossible, she told herself. Just coincidence. A trick of the light.

She held the relic's leer. There was no way it could see through the thick film over its eyes, yet it stared. Right at her. Despite the broiling sun, Frank shivered.

The relic grinned. Suddenly its chin dropped to the blankets, like someone had yanked the plug on it. Frank watched a minute longer, half tempted to roust the old fuck and find out what its story was. But she didn't. Instead, she started the car, expecting the relic's eyes to fly open and fix on her. It didn't move. Frank eased into traffic, careful not to look back.

After work the next day, like a kid determined to walk by a haunted house to prove she's not afraid, Frank cruised by the impassive brick building. No one loitered out front and the thing in rags was nowhere in sight.

Continuing down Slauson, she angled southwest toward the Mother's church. Frank recognized her vintage, cherry-red Cadillac parked at the curb. Admiring the finned drop-top's showroom condition, Frank wondered what she was doing here.

She'd come as if on autopilot. She had nothing to confront the Mother with and the woman was far too savvy for Frank to run any type of bluff on. Bludgeonings, poisonings, drownings, shootings, shovings, shakings; electrocutions, defenestrations, exsanguinations, eviscerations, disarticulations, immolations—there wasn't an "ing" or a "tion" Frank hadn't seen. The Mother's alleged homicide was only slightly artful, yet Frank had to admit that after almost two decades of dealing with mentalities that natural selection had somehow overlooked, she was intrigued by the Mother's guile and ability. Was she really that good a con? Did she have connections in the system?

Maybe she put good luck spells on herself, Frank mused. Curiosity drew her from the car. The engine ticked behind her as she stepped across dead, yellow grass. The lawn was dried out, but neatly trimmed. Beds of flowers flanked the entrance to the simple, white-washed building. There was no graffiti on it and the church's name was high above the door where taggers would really have to work to get it.

The large, double door was locked. Frank stepped around the side where a smaller door stood open. Pushing her RayBans onto her head, she peered inside. She quickly noted a rectangular, windowless room, painted scarlet and banana-yellow. Plants splayed from clay pots. Fronds and vines were trained over a sky-blue ceiling. Rows of white benches were lined symmetrically on both sides of the center aisle. They stopped a respectful distance from a small pulpit.

One of the Mother's twins was watering plants and the Mother was adding greenery to the pulpit. She paused, turning toward Frank, even though Frank had entered without a sound.

"You said to drop by."

"Well, here you are, then," the older woman replied with a sweep of her bangled arm. "Welcome to my church."

Frank walked to the pulpit, while the Mother eyed her from soles to crown. Frank was aware of the twin cautiously returning to his work. She took in a life-size black Jesus crucified on the front wall and two child-sized plaster saints at its feet.

"Who are they?" she asked, more to make conversation than out of curiosity.

The Mother looked at the statues, appearing amused.

"They are Saint Michael and Saint Barbara."

"So this is a Catholic church?"

"Not quite," the Mother flashed a bright grin. "But some of the saints are associated with the gods of my faith."

"Which faith is that?"

With the same air of bemusement, the Mother replied, "You have a lot of questions, child."

"That's 'cause I don't have a lot of answers." Frank took in the room, asking, "So what do you do here? Save souls or something?"

Now the Mother laughed outright. It was a high, clear sound, like a bell tinkling, and Frank smiled, willing to be the rube.

"I can't save anybody's soul for them. We save our own souls."

"You don't wash them in the blood of the lamb and all that jazz?"

The Mother stared as if Frank was teasing her.

"No, I'm serious. How do you run this place? What do you do for the people that come here?"

"I am a bridge between the people and their gods. The people are here, the gods are here. Sometimes they just need help coming together."

"So you're like a spiritual matchmaker?"

"I guess you could call me that."

Mother Love hit Frank with a dazzling smile, her intensity mesmerizing. Frank searched the keen amber eyes, understanding how the Mother could had such loyal followers. She broke from the Mother's charismatic tug to examine a framed document on the

81

back wall. A stamped and sealed certificate ordained the Mother as a spiritual minister. Three other frames showed a business license, the church's articles of incorporation, and another ordination certificate recognizing Crystal Love Jones as a priestess of the Church of Lukumi.

"This Church of the Lukumi," Frank said. "That's *santería*, isn't it?"

The Mother scoffed, "*Santería* is a Latin corruption of the ancient African religion. What we practice in the Church of the Lukumi are our ancestral beliefs."

"So *santería's* Latin and Lukumi's African?" Frank pressed.

"Lukumi is pure. It doesn't have the mix of Catholicism that *santería* does."

Waving at the saints, Frank contended, "Seems like you got some taint going on here."

The Mother's eyes lit up and Frank realized the Mother wouldn't brook challenge.

"It's for them," the Mother said with a finger toward the door. "The ones who don't accept the true faith. I don't need these false gods, *they* do. Many of my worshippers have been with me since I started the spiritual church. I didn't want to alienate them when my faith turned down a new road. The saints are easier for them to understand than the African deities, and because the deities correspond to the saints, I use them here. This satisfies *all* my worshippers."

"I see. They make your brand of paganism easier to swallow."

"I'm assuming"—the Mother etched her words with acid—"that you didn't mean to offend me but are simply showing your ignorance."

"Please assume that," Frank said with a show of humility. "I just meant paganism as opposed to conventional Christianity."

"The Church of the Lukumi is based on African beliefs older than any white belief system. If anything is pagan here, it's Christianity."

"You don't have to preach to me," Frank protested. "I don't care one way or the other."

"Child, of what faith are you?"

"Lapsed Catholic," Frank lied, uncomfortable admitting she was of no faith. "You wear quite a few hats. Minister. Priestess. Fortune-teller."

The Mother surprised Frank by laughing, "Oh, I wish I could tell the future. I have a gift, child, that's all. Sometimes I can see things before they happen and I often make accurate predictions using the *diloggun*. Those are cowry shells," she explained patronizingly. "The deities speak to me through them."

Though the offenders Frank dealt with rarely considered anything more complex than how to get laid and where to score, Frank nonetheless enjoyed seeing how a criminal mind worked. The Mother was giving her a toy store to play in. The woman was obviously bright, but short on humor; wary, yet boastful. Frank quickly pegged pride as a major gap in her defenses. Especially after such a long run of consistently defying the odds.

"Are you like a channeler or something?"

"A channeler, a priest, a psychiatrist, a doctor. Child, I'm all of those things."

"A doctor?"

"I heal people. Sometimes all they need is someone to listen; unburdening their souls is half the cure. Other times they require teas or balms. When their ailments are more serious, I call on the gods to intervene on my clients' behalf."

"And how much do you charge for these services?"

"It depends." The Mother lifted her shoulders.

"On?"

"The severity of the problem. How much time it will take to effect a cure. The materials I use."

"What materials do you use?"

She shrugged again.

"It depends."

Frank monitored the Mother's reaction as she asked, "Do you sacrifice animals?"

"Sometimes," was the offhand reply. "Again. It depends on the nature of the problem."

"Give me an example."

"All right. A client comes to me—"

"—are your clients the members of your congregation?"

"Sometimes. Not always," the Mother answered, annoyed at the interruption. "They come to me with a problem. It could be something as simple as a client's lost her wedding ring to a case as serious as someone's boy got shot in the heart four times. Sometimes I can find the ring using the *diologgun*. The gods suggest where to look for the lost item. To thank them we offer their favorite food and drink. For something as complicated as saving a life, larger sacrifices are required. A life for a life."

"Is that what those chickens and doves at your house are for?"

The Mother nodded.

"Do you ever use bigger animals?"

The Mother held Frank's gaze easily.

"Sometimes a goat or pig. Once I sacrificed a bull"—her white teeth flashed—"but that was such a bother I'll never do that again."

When humans are so much easier, Frank finished for her.

"How'd you get into this? The spiritual and Lukumi stuff."

"You're born to it, child. Someone in my line's always had the gift. Usually a female child but sometimes a boy. My uncle Ekuban had the sight. He could heal. My mother had it. She passed it on to me. I learned how to heal from her. From my grandmother too. They were steeped in the Spiritual Church and I followed that for a time.

"Then a client introduced me to *santería* and I realized that my true path was to follow the ancient gods. I studied to be an *olosha*, a priestess, and in 1994 I was ordained by the Church of the Lukumi Babalu Aye."

"You see your clients—do your healing—over at Slauson?"

84

The Mother rearranged some flowers on the pulpit, purring, "That's right."

"Who's that beggar that hangs around outside your place? The old one wrapped in the blankets?"

The Mother threw an eye at Frank.

"I don't know who you're talking about."

"Got cataracts, gray hair, wears about half a dozen blankets, even now, in the heat."

"There are many beggars in this city. Am I expected to know all of them?"

"This one hangs around your place a lot," Frank pushed.

Fussing with some pots around her arrangement, the Mother asked, "Why do you want to know?"

"I know a lot of them, but I don't know this one. I was just wondering if it was a client of yours."

When the Mother didn't respond, Frank continued, "So you see clients at home and this is where you do church stuff, right? The singing and preaching. All that."

The Mother laid a hand on Frank's bare arm. Her touch was cool and dry and Frank was reminded of a snake shedding its skin.

"If you're so curious, why don't you come to a service and find out. There's one tomorrow night at seven o'clock. Even better"— the Mother leered—"come to a *bembe*. You'll *really* see something there. I'm having one two weeks from this Saturday. It starts at five-thirty. At my home. For a client's daughter."

As if leaving, Frank turned away from the Mother's touch.

"What's a *bembe*?"

"It's an initiation ceremony into the faith. It's where the initiate is chosen by one of the gods. I don't usually allow outsiders, but I'll make an exception in your case."

"The initiate is chosen by one of the gods to do what?"

"Why, to serve!"

The Mother bared her teeth in a shark's smile. Frank ignored the shiver crawling up her spine. With an effort at nonchalance, Frank answered, "I just might show up."

14

Anthony Dalton had married a woman younger than his first granddaughter and was feeling like his mojo needed freshening up. Mother Love agreed, fixing him up with a new hand and a prescription for Uncrossing salts and High John the Conqueror oil. She guaranteed that before the week was out he'd be restored to his full manhood. He believed her; his sweet little girl had balked at marriage until he'd visited Mother Love for a magic potion. By the end of that month his sugar was Mrs. Anthony Dalton

Isabel Salia had love trouble too; her husband had left with another woman. Mother Love told her she had to get her husband to drink a glass of sweet wine with some of her own cat juice mixed into it. That would make her man come back and stay. She recited a prayer for Isabel and dressed a black candle in Crossing Oil. Isabel had to carve her rival's name into the candle, light it, and repeat the prayer over the flame for nine nights, as well as sprinkle Hot Foot

Powder across the woman's front door. That woman would leave and never come round again. Isabel had been doubtful about visiting this Mother Love, but her sister had convinced her, swearing she'd been promoted *and* found her lost diamond ring within nine days of Mother Love's cleansing her for good luck and fortune.

Rita Kincaid wanted to know if the man courting her was serious or just milking the cow for free. The Mother patiently cast the cowries, making repeated notations in a thick ledger. The upshot was that this man only spelled trouble for Rita. Mother Love fixed her up with a spell kit to attract the right kind of man and Rita happily laid $100 on the table.

Meanwhile, Eddie Mae King had been waiting. When it was her turn to see Mother Love, she transferred her great bulk from the waiting room into the plant-cluttered office. Eddie Mae didn't like it in here. It was too hot, too dark, and too crowded. She always felt like she was going to suffocate and collapse and they wouldn't be able to drag her big body out of there. She perched one buttock over a rickety little chair, fanning herself with a stubby hand. She started to cry, telling Mother Love her son had been stabbed in his belly and was dying up to Drew/King.

Mother Love got into Eddie Mae's face, scolding, "Does he have a chicken scratch or is that boy carved up like a Christmas ham?"

"He's in the ICU since last night," Eddie Mae sobbed.

The Mother relented, claiming, "We'll have to make *ebo*."

Eddie Mae nodded. Her four chins nodded too. Mother Love scratched something on a piece of paper while Eddie Mae explained the circumstances about Tyrell. Lucian appeared after Mother Love pressed a buzzer. She handed him the paper and when he left Eddie Mae sighed, "I wisht my boy had come out like your Lucian. He's such a darlin'."

"Your boy'd a come out right if you'd a knocked some sense into his head," Mother Love answered coldly. "You always spoiled them children, Eddie Mae. Didn't I warn you 'bout that?"

"Yes," Eddie Mae had to sigh. Lucian returned with a box and

Eddie Mae recognized the offerings for Saint Lazarus. Babaluaye, is what Mother Love called him. That was his African name. Eddie Mae didn't much mind what name they used, as long as she got results.

Mother Love propped a crutch and straw broom into a corner next to a small table. She started singing, one of those African songs that made Eddie Mae feel proud. And a little afraid too. She knew what was coming. Mother Love smoothed a square of yellow satin over the table. On it she put a Saint Lazarus holy card, a clay pot with a perforated lid, and two plastic dogs. She surrounded them with seventeen yellow candles.

Stepping back, she surveyed the table. She must have liked what she saw, because she gave a short nod, saying, "Now we'll feed Babaluaye."

Eddie Mae's four chins quivered nervously. This was the part she didn't like. She offered a silent prayer to Jesus, hoping He wouldn't mind. She meant no harm, only wanted her son to be healthy. He could understand that, couldn't He?

Mother Love dipped a perfectly manicured hand into the box Lucian had brought. She unwrapped a square of cornbread and put it on the table next to an orange, a banana, and an open jar of coconut butter. A bottle of 151 rum complemented the food. Eddie Mae hoped she had enough money to pay for this.

Mother Love studied the table again.

"I'll make beans and rice tonight, but for now this'll have to do."

Scratching sounds came from the box and Mother Love pulled out a paper bag. Eddie Mae squirmed, enduring a scornful glance as she crossed herself. Mother Love sang her African song again and drew two pigeons from the bag. She held them over the table by their legs. Eddie Mae closed her eyes, but not quickly enough. With swift ease Mother Love twisted the heads off. She shook their blood onto the table, placing the drained bodies alongside the other offerings. She sang again.

Mother Love's low voice, Eddie Mae's faith in her, the sticky heat—they all combined to make Eddie Mae drowsy. She watched sleepily as the Mother washed a rope of black and white beads in the blood, didn't protest when she folded the sticky strand into her hand.

"Take those to Tyrell," she ordered. "Put 'em on him. Don't let no one take 'em off. They got Babaluaye's power now. You take 'em offa him, I can't tell what'll happen."

Eddie Mae's chins waggled their understanding. Mother Love barked, "That'll cost you two hundred dollars, Eddie Mae. And cheap at that."

"Lord, don't I know it."

Eddie Mae pulled a wad of wet, crumpled bills from her cleavage. She smoothed them out against her thigh, laying them gently, one by one, into the Mother's bloodied palm.

15

Driving home one late night, Frank had heard a telepathic spy on a talk show share his vision of the world's end. He saw the jet stream swooping down close to earth and wreaking havoc with agriculture. He predicted mass starvation, particularly in Third World countries. Even more gruesome, he warned that as this time approached, it would be heralded by an unprecedented number of children killing other children.

Reading the *Los Angeles Times*, she wondered if the end was indeed nigh; the Santa Anas had been bellowing wildfires for a week, and another high school kid had decided to settle a pubescent score by shooting half his classmates and a teacher.

Sprawled half naked on a chaise lounge, Frank found the almost empty Corona in the chair's shade. The sun was hot, the beer was cold, and the news was always bad. World without end, amen, Frank thought, but if it ended today she was going out a happy woman.

Dinner was ready—pink shrimp in avocado halves, sliced ruby tomatoes from the farmer's market, fresh bread from the Old Town Bakery, all accompanied by an icy bottle of pale Fumé—and Gail would be here any minute to share it with her. Frank shook the newspaper into place, amazed she'd actually admitted to, and accepted, being happy.

She came in from the patio for a fresh beer, just as Gail burst through the front door. Her entrances were fast, breathless, and usually scared the shit out of Frank.

"Hurricane Gail has made landfall," she greeted.

"That's me," the doc laughed. "All awhirl to see you."

Gail dropped her fat briefcase onto the tile floor and hurled herself at Frank, who found the doc's physical enthusiasm as unsettling as it was charming. In her office or cutting in the morgue, Gail's passion for her work was obvious, but she maintained distance from the cops and detectives she worked with. Maybe because she'd never thought to, Frank had unwittingly bridged that distance. She'd accepted Gail's friendship, and then diffidently, her courtship. Frank's hesitance wasn't related to Gail, but rather to her own doubts about being a lover again.

There'd been the fling with Kennedy but that was just what it was—a fling; something they had both needed at the time, but which was never meant to last. It felt different with Gail. Less urgent, more thoughtful. She felt like she wanted Gail rather than needed her. That was reassuring, in that it lulled Frank into a sense of control over her emotions.

They cooled off later in the shower, still unwilling to part. Wearing only loose robes, they ate the plump avocados on the patio and satisfied the last of their hungers. Settling into one of the side by side lounge chairs, Frank poured the last of the wine, luxuriating in the peace that comes with perfect satiation. Gail's hand rested on her thigh. Frank stroked it, asking, "Think you'll get to the Colonel tomorrow?"

"The Colonel?"

"Lewis's slit throat," Frank reminded her. "I know you're back-logged. Just curious."

"Ahh, right," Gail nodded dreamily. "Barring any unforeseen disasters, we'll probably get to him tomorrow. I can't cut him for you though. I have to chain myself to the desk in the morning, then have lunch with Sartoris, and there's the Health Department meeting after that. Isn't your Colonel just a slice and dice?"

"Don't know."

Frank explained about Mother Love, after which Gail murmured through her drowsiness, "She sounds nasty. You should be careful."

"Don't tell me you believe in that sort of hocus-pocus."

"Well, I do."

Frank waited for the punch line. When it didn't come she craned her head to see if Gail was joking.

"You serious?"

"I just think you should be careful. You could be getting into something much bigger than you think."

Frank laughed, "You sound like Jill. She's terrified of all that mumbo-jumbo. Me? I'm pretty confident I can hold my own against an old woman with dead cats and graveyard dirt."

"Laugh now, but still, watch your back. Let's go to bed."

"Wait a sec. You're a medical doctor. A rational, twentieth-century woman trained in scientific method and you're telling me you believe in the Psychic Hotline?"

In a fairly decent Jamaican accent Frank imitated the TV commercial, saying, "Call now, fuh yuh free readin'."

Gail scowled. "All I'm saying is that if someone's truly intent on hurting you, they can. That's all."

"How do you figure? Mother Love's going to make a doll with blonde hair, dress it in a miniature Armani suit and stick pins in it?"

"Who knows? Not that the pins in the doll would work but the intent she harnesses might."

"I'm not tracking."

"All I'm saying is don't be too cocky. There's energy in the world

—some of it's positive, some of it's negative—and I think it can be channeled for good or bad purposes."

"So you think she can put a spell on me? Turn me into a toad?"

"Don't be silly. I just think she can tap into negative energy and apply it with mal intent. Good God, don't we see enough of that every day?"

"I don't think what I see on the street is evil. I think it's stupidity. People get carried away by greed and jealousy. Anger. They're not evil, just ignorant. Or chemically imbalanced." She shrugged.

"What about a guy like Delamore?"

Frank flinched at the name, but quickly rationalized, "He's not evil. He's sick. He didn't develop normally. At some point kids learn compassion, but if they're never taught it, then they grow up to be quote/unquote evil. I think what you call evil is a profound developmental and/or physiological failure. The Delamores never learn how to relate to anyone other than themselves."

"Do you deny that evil exists?"

"Why do I feel like I'm being cross-examined?"

"Do you?"

Concealing her exasperation Frank answered, "Yeah. I don't believe Satan's sitting in a fiery cave at the center of the earth eating lost souls any more than he's hangin' out at the corner of Florence and Normandie."

"Do you deny the existence of good?"

"Yeah. Good is just like evil. If a child is treated well, and taught goodness, then he or she grows up to do good things. They get perks and rewards and feedback that encourages the positive behavior just like a neglected child creates the sick perks and feedbacks that keep him in his loop. It's all they know. Nice, not nice, it's all learned behavior."

Gail swung her feet off the lounge chair to turn and face Frank.

"What about kids like that eleven-year-old who disemboweled his baby sister? By all accounts he came from a wonderful, loving home."

93

"Organic," Frank explained, tapping her temple. "Something didn't come out right as he was developing. The right gene didn't get turned on. Or off."

"What about luck? You're always saying you need some luck on a case. How do you explain that?"

"Luck is just . . . circumstance and timing. A chain of events that can turn out well or badly. Besides, how'd we get off on this theosophical debate? I thought you wanted to go to bed."

"I do," Gail answered, "but humor me. I'm curious to know where you stand on all this."

"I stand deeply, madly, head-over-heels, insanely crazy about you. That's where I stand," Frank declared emphatically. She tried pulling Gail up, but the doc wouldn't budge.

"No really. I want to know."

"Know what?" Frank weaseled.

"You really don't believe there's any sort of force or power in the universe, do you?"

"No. I don't."

"You can't even admit it's a possibility?"

"I suppose it could be. Just seems that if there is something somebody would have proved it or seen it by now."

"What would God look like to you?"

"God? He's a guy in a white bathrobe with a long beard who sits around with his feet up reading *Playboys* all day. Every now and then he looks down and laughs at all the tiny people scurrying around beneath him, blowing each other up in his name. He gets a good chuckle out of that then goes back to his *Playboy*. Tells a curvaceous angel to bring him another beer and a fresh cigar."

Gail smirked. "It sounds like your god's Hugh Hefner."

"Not *my* god," Frank countered. "That's the dude *you* all believe in."

"And you have no dude?" Gail persisted.

" 'Fraid not. There's just what I touch and feel today. And right now I'm feeling you and I'd like to go fall asleep with my arms around you."

"You really don't believe in *anything*?"

"Just you," Frank said. She tried to kiss the top of Gail's head, but the doc reared back.

"I find that so sad. That you don't believe in *something*."

"I believe in hard work and trying to make a difference while we're here."

"But then what? What happens when you die?"

"Then I'm dead. End of story. Cleared case."

"What about your soul?"

"Haven't you noticed?" Frank joked. "Ain't got no soul. That's why I can't dance."

"Tell me you believe you have a soul."

"I believe I have a soul," Frank dutifully repeated.

Gail studied her lover.

"You don't, do you?"

"Nope. I'm just blood and guts and when my heart stops pumping"—Frank spread her hands—"Game over."

"That's the saddest thing I've ever heard," Gail said.

"Aw, Gay, don't get all melodramatic on me."

"I'm not. I mean I know people don't believe in God, but it just seems . . . lonely. So disconnected from everything else around you. So unrelated."

"We're all the same species, with the same problems," Frank offered. "We all have that in common."

"That's human." Gail waved her off. "Human concerns are so insignificant in light of the bigger picture."

"And what's the bigger picture? The World According to Gail," Frank disparaged.

"Look at the stars," the doc retorted. "They've seen centuries come and go. They've witnessed billions of us coming and going, yet they persist. How can you look at a star and not believe in God? Or oak trees. The ones on your street were there when Cortez came through. He and his men are all dead now but the trees are still there. You can touch them and touch a tree Cortez might have sat under while he charted his course. Where do those stars, those trees, where do they come from? Who made them?"

"UAW?" Frank guessed. "Should I go look for the union label?"

"You're serious, aren't you?"

"About the label?"

Gail kept studying Frank.

"I don't see you hopping out of bed on Sundays to get to church."

"You don't have to go to a church to believe. And when I need a church I head out of this god-forsaken city and into the mountains. That's where my church is. Where I can see what God's made. Not what people have made."

"All right. You win. Can we drop this?" Frank cajoled, her hand out to the doc. Gail took it, but not happily.

"If it'll make you feel better, I'll believe in something. Tell me what you want me to believe in and I will."

Gail squawked, "I can't *make* you believe! That's got to come from *inside* you. It has nothing to do with me."

"So how do kids learn to be good Methodists or Jews? Don't they get taught? Don't they go to Sunday school or temple or whatever? You want me to be a tree-hugger, show me how. I'm a quick learner."

"That's different, Frank. They're children. You're a grown adult. I can't foist a belief on you. You should have your own values, your own beliefs."

Frank followed Gail inside, countering, "I do and you don't like them."

"Working hard and making a difference isn't a faith, it's an ethic. There's a big difference."

"Does that make me any less of a person?"

"No," Gail admitted. "I just . . . I don't know. I know you claim to be an agnostic, but I always thought underneath it all, bottom line, that you'd have something to cling to greater than yourself."

"So why's that so sad?"

"It seems lonely. And it makes it impossible to share what I believe in."

Locking the patio door, Frank answered, "Not at all. I love it when you talk about the trees and stars. And that grove in Berkeley that you used to hike to when you were a kid. You light up when you talk about that stuff. You're beautiful. Just because I don't believe in it doesn't mean I can't respect that you do."

"It's just such a comfort to have faith in something greater than myself and my fellow stumbling, bumbling human beings. It's a wonderful sense of tranquility to believe I belong in the world; that I'm part of a design, even though I don't know what that design is. I don't know how to express it. You'd have to feel it yourself and that's the part that makes me sad. That we can't share that tranquility. It's not an option for you."

Frank kissed the top of Gail's head.

"I'm tranquil when I'm with you. That's all I have right now and it'll have to do."

"But I'm only human, Frank. I'll fail you."

"And God hasn't?"

"No," Gail said, twisting out of Frank's arms. "Never. Things might happen that you don't like but they happen for a reason. Fate, God, Karma, call it what you like, everything happens for a reason."

"Ah. The Divine Plan."

"Exactly. Just because you don't know what it is doesn't mean there isn't a reason."

"There was a reason you got cancer," Frank argued.

"Yes! I believe that every time we're faced with a choice we can make a good one, a bad one, or a mediocre one. How you choose affects the results. If we keep making poor choices, ones that concentrate on our lower, more base instincts, then we keep getting the same poor situations until we learn to respond to them with love and move beyond them. So for me the breast cancer was God's way of shaking me and getting me to take a look at how I was living my life.

"I worked from six in the morning until eight at night. I ate shitty food, got no exercise and slept horribly. All I had was work and the cats. Then when I had to face the very real possibility that I might die, I realized how much I was missing. How much time I've wasted in my life, how much love I've missed. It was so wonderful to be around my mom and sisters and to just appreciate how much they loved me. And how much I loved them. I'd never realized it, never really felt the depth of my passion for them until I was so close to losing them. And you know what? I might not die today or tomorrow, hell, I might live another fifty years, but the point is, I *am* going to die. Someday. Yet I've lived like I had all the time in the world to waste. The cancer showed me I *don't* have that time to waste. It was a gift in that it opened my eyes to all the goodness that I can have in my life."

"So now that you realize all that you'll never get cancer again?" Gail sighed.

"Now that I realize all that it doesn't *matter* that I get cancer again. I have the best life imaginable. The best work, the best family, the best lover, the best friends. I finally feel like I'm not missing something."

"I'm still not sure how God figures into all this bliss."

"Because my body will be gone, but my soul won't. The core of me, the essence, the energy I have created—either good or bad— will go on without a corporeal vehicle. I don't know if it's reincarnation or angels or what, but I will take the lessons I've learned and apply them elsewhere. The fundamental goodness of me will persist. Just like the stars. I don't know what shape I'll take but I believe there are realities we can't sense, that we're not supposed to sense because our poor little pea brains couldn't comprehend their magnitudes. There's a joy in the mystery, in the not knowing. It's exciting. When I die I'm going on a huge adventure, like a cosmic Disneyland. I don't know what the adventure is—I don't have to know—all I *do* know is that it's out there."

Frank didn't say anything. God meant nothing to her and dead was dead. If there was a god, she'd reasoned when she was still a child, he wouldn't have taken her father and left her to care for a woman with one foot wedged in the nuthouse door. When Maggie died, she had irrefutable proof that there wasn't a god. She allowed people their beliefs like an indulgent parent allowed their child an invisible friend. Besides, she had so many of her own crutches she couldn't very well kick others' out from under them.

Still, she found it amusingly human that people persisted in believing in soft and warm and fuzzy. It was so much easier than admitting there was nothing out there, nothing waiting when your ticket finally got punched but oblivion. Frank didn't really think oblivion would be all that bad. Some days she felt it would be her reward for the hell she walked through now. So if Gail wanted to believe in trees and stars, and Mother Love Jones wanted to believe in chickens and hexes, then who was Frank to judge? It was still a free country.

"Look," Frank said, trying to put an end to the interrogation. "My dad was Catholic and he went to church once a year. My mom tried on religions like they were shoes. I had an aunt who was a devout Catholic and I've never seen a more pious, more bitter woman. My uncle hated the church and slammed it every chance he got, usually in front of my aunt just to drive her crazy. I didn't have any good role models for organized religion. Or unorganized religion for that matter. I learned that at the end of the day, all I could count on was me. And I haven't seen anything in forty years to change that."

"How do you explain miracles?"

Frank frowned. "Random circumstance."

"I don't believe this," Gail marveled, "I'm in love with a raving atheist."

"Ah, ah," Frank corrected, shaking one finger. "Agnostic. *I* don't believe in a god but I don't care if you believe in one. For all I know there might even be one and *then* won't I be in trouble. Now, can we drop this and go to bed?"

Gail followed Frank into the bedroom, grumbling, "A drunken agnostic. How can I ever take you home to meet my mother?"

"You'll just have to play up my other attributes."

"Remind me what they are."

"Brilliant detective, superior commander. Exquisite lover. Gourmet chef and chief bottle-washer."

"Not to mention smooth talker."

"Not to mention," Frank agreed, pulling Gail to her and hugging her oh-so-tightly. Tight enough that if there was a god, he couldn't take this woman too.

16

All Frank could see was the mouth gaping wide, with rows and rows of teeth. Sharp, glistening teeth. And laughter. The Mother's laughter, pealing like bells. And behind the laughter, bells did ring. The war was over. But Frank knew that couldn't be right. This war would never be over. Not between these two. Not now. Not ever.

The Mother was still laughing, but farther away. She stood against a red sunset, trailing black and red and white gauze. The wind flapped her wrappings, unraveling her like a mummy. The Mother held a bloody sword above her head and a hand stretched to Frank. Blood dripped from the sword into pools at the Mother's feet. She laughed, beckoning Frank.

Behind her, a soldier stood amid the rubble of a ruined city. Around him, singly and in heaps, dead men stretched to the horizon, their artifacts strewn carelessly by the eternal desert wind.

Lip-smudged photographs and letters torn at their folds blew restlessly from corpse to corpse.

Vultures flapped indifferently among the abandoned relics, feasting easily from gaping wounds.

Ragged beggars and women in chadors scurried to collect gold fillings and wedding rings.

An ancient crone knelt at a body. She stared at the soldier, her eyes milky blue, like Aegean shoals after a storm. She wrenched the dead man's neck, then dangled a crucifix, cackling.

The soldier turned away, his helmet under his arm. Sand filled his hair and blew over his boots. Still he stood. He had been here before. He had never been gone. He had always been a soldier. He scanned the desolate horizon. It was silent, empty but for the rising moon.

He listened to the steady snick and crunch of jackals feeding. They ate without snarling. No need of that tonight. There was plenty for all.

The moon cleared the earth. It lit the dead sleeping in their shadows. The dogs slipped stealthily between them.

She woke slowly, floating up from the dream into the solidity of her bed. Canceling the alarm, Frank rolled into Gail. She kissed her shoulder, pressing into the doc's flank, wanting to wake her and get lost in the sweet, ephemeral refuge of desire. But Gail didn't stir.

Frank resigned herself to a scalding shower, then dressed in the clothes she'd laid out the night before. When she flipped the light on in the kitchen, the coffee was hot in the pot. She poured it into her travel mug while the twin gods of Routine and Order maintained harmony in her world.

Frank sipped her coffee at the sink. Bobby was probably going to be in court all day, and Darcy would be on his own. They were next up on rotation so if a call came in she'd send Darcy out with Diego. Noah and Lewis would—

Frank whirled, her eye catching a flash of white. She instinctively dropped her mug, reaching for the Beretta she hadn't strapped on yet.

"Jesus fucking Christ!"

Gail stood wide-eyed and startled in a long T-shirt. Frank swore again, ripping off a handful of paper towels and swabbing the spilled coffee.

"*Jesus*. Give me some warning next time you sneak up on me."

"I wasn't sneaking up. I just woke up to pee and figured I'd say goodbye. Fuck you too."

Frank threw the soggy paper into the trash can, snatching Gail's elbow before she could leave the kitchen. She apologized.

"I'm just a little edgy."

"A *little*? Christ, I'd hate to see a lot."

"I wasn't expecting you to be up traipsing around. You were sleeping like one of your customers a minute ago."

"Well, I think I'll just *traipse* on back to bed."

"Come on," Frank said, shifting Gail toward her. "You just surprised me. Guess I'm still jumpy. Had a weird dream."

"What about?" Gail asked.

"Can't tell you 'til I get a kiss."

Gail gave her a sulky one.

"I was a soldier, and there were dead bodies all around me. It must have been World War II because there were letters and black and white pictures blowing around. And the uniforms looked like they were from then. And the helmet under my arm, too. It all looked like World War II, but it felt like it could have been any time. It was weird. I was dressed like a GI, and so were the corpses, but I felt like I'd been there before. Like I could have just as easily been a Roman soldier standing there with a leather helmet instead of a metal one. And beggars were looting the corpses. Women in robes . . . veiled, like in the middle east. They were scurrying from body to body like cockroaches. It all felt like it could have been centuries ago or yesterday. It was . . . eerie, but real familiar too. And the wind was blowing, getting sand all over everything. Covering the dead men's faces. And it smelled like blood. Fresh blood. Lots of it. It was sad, but at the same time it felt. . . ."

Frank searched for the exact word.

"Like I was supposed to be there. Like it was my destiny or

something. Like I couldn't have been—like I'd *never* been anywhere else. I didn't want to be there—I was sick and tired of the whole thing—but it was where I *belonged*. It didn't feel like I had a choice. And it felt like it was just one more battle in a long campaign."

"Sounds creepy," Gail mumbled into Frank's neck.

"Yeah," Frank agreed, but it hadn't been creepy. Just . . . inevitable.

Frank kissed Gail and said, "Go on back to bed."

"When do I get to see you again?"

"Tonight? Dinner?"

"Med-line meeting," Gail said, crinkling her nose.

"Tomorrow then."

Swinging in a locked embrace against Frank, she pouted. "You going out with your children first?"

"Of course," Frank smiled.

"Will you be too drunk to make love to me?"

"Have I ever been?"

Gail considered.

"No-o. But let's not have a first, okay?"

"Deal. I gotta go," Frank said, disentangling herself. "I'm gonna be late."

"Ohh!" Gail gasped in mock horror. "The trains will stop running and the wind will stop blowing!"

"You," Frank said, leaving her with a quick kiss, "who can't even conceive of being anywhere on time, have a lot of nerve. You're gonna be leaving Saint Peter or the Devil waiting twenty minutes for you someday."

"Hey!" Gail cried as Frank grabbed her briefcase and crossed the living room, "I thought you didn't believe in those guys."

"I don't," Frank called back, "but *you* do."

17

Frank was just about to grab a *torta* for lunch when a call came in from one of the HUD scattered housing sites. Folks in the Projects didn't much care for the police, so Frank headed out with Darcy, Diego, and two backup units.

Flanked by the uniforms, the nine-three detectives walked behind the apartment manager up bullet splintered, piss-stained stairs. Neighbors huddled outside a door. The one who'd called the station repeated what he'd told Darcy over the phone—the girl across the way had knocked on his door to tell him she'd suffocated her kids. She'd said it as calmly as if she were saying it was going to be a sunny day.

The cops knocked on her door and a small voice said, "*Venga.*"

She was sitting on a stained mattress, two boys and a girl neatly arranged behind her. They looked like they were sleeping. The detectives touched the little bodies. Each was cool and starting to rigor. Darcy knelt in front of the mother while she pulled at a hang-nail.

"What happened?" he asked, his voice soothing.

"I kilt 'em all," she confessed, matching his solemnity.

Darcy nodded as if he understood.

"How come?"

"I didn't want 'em to suffer no more. They's always hungry. The little one"—she indicated a baby that couldn't have been more than six months old—"she's crying all the time 'cause I didn't have no more milk."

She assured Darcy, "It's better this way. This way they can't know no more pain. They're happy now."

Darcy studied the girl a long time. Frank wondered if he was going to pull a Sandman on her. The girl tugged at the hangnail while he stared. Ripping the offending flesh from her finger, she watched the long tear start to bleed. So low Frank could barely hear him, Darcy asked, "There's another baby, isn't there?"

The girl looked at him with big, trusting eyes. She nodded.

"Where?"

"The garbage. I wrapped him in a towel. It was too bloody. I couldn't do it that way. I couldn't see him like that no more."

Diego and Darcy went downstairs to look for the boy. While they were gone, the woman confided, "He was my oldest. I kilt him first so he wouldn't see what was happenin' and be scared."

"Very thoughtful," Frank murmured. Behind the greasy, stringy hair, the teenager smiled at Frank's praise. Jack Handley showed up from the coroner's office. He shook his head and went to work on the tiny corpses. Frank went after her detectives. They were coming back into the tenement as she was going out.

"Find him?"

"Right where she said he'd be," Darcy said, dusting his slacks off. Two uniforms were taping off a row of dumpsters. Not to protect evidence, but to keep the curious crowd back.

"Handley's upstairs," she said to Diego. Darcy started to follow, but Frank touched his sleeve. A scraping sound distracted her. She glanced around at the onlookers, sourcing the sound to a bent metal cane sweeping the ground in front of crusted, swollen feet.

"How'd you know there was another kid?" she asked.

The scraping grew louder and Frank jerked her chin, indicating they should back up toward the stairs. Before Darcy could answer, Frank was stunned to feel a hand clamp onto her wrist. She turned to stare into filmy, sightless eyes.

What in the fuck?

The leering pile of rags held her in a death grip. Frank tried to pull away as its mouth gaped wide. Frank almost gagged. She'd smelled the vilest putrefaction, but nothing compared to the stench reeking from this . . . *thing*. The mouth stretched wider, thick strands of spit connecting the top and bottom lips like jail bars. The cracked lips split. Blood welled from the rents. Behind, in the dark maw, crumbling stumps jutted from puffy gums.

Frank was sickeningly fascinated, but still thought to yank her arm free. The hand only tightened on her wrist. She wanted to punch the reeking mass but it wouldn't do to hit a homeless person in a crowd of witnesses.

The thing cackled softly, staring straight into her eyes even though its own were cauled with cataracts.

"You don't recognize me," it accused in a rough whisper. Frank immediately noticed that the words had no accent, no inflection. It had to be someone she'd sent up, maybe when she was in uniform, coming back now to blame her for how miserable his life turned out. Or hers. Frank scanned the face for a clue to the thing's gender, but it was like studying a strip of rawhide.

The thing laughed again, louder.

"Too long for you to remember. But I remember. I never forget. No," it crooned. "I never forget."

Spit flew into Frank's face. She tumbled back, finally jerking her arm loose. The relic stumbled too. It almost fell against Frank, but she sidestepped the fetid breath and curving, yellow nails. Frank's

107

nemesis recovered itself, rapping its twisted cane on the concrete. The obscene head swiveled toward Frank, the eyes impossibly seeing her. It nodded, acknowledging the ludicrous. Then it turned, leaving as it came, metal rasping against the sidewalk.

"Friend of yours?"

Frank jumped. Darcy's eyes were steady on her. She followed the shuffling bundle until it was well away. Frank wanted a long hot bath to wash the stink off. She shuddered, completely flustered.

"What?" she barked at Darcy, probing her with quiet eyes.

"Nothing."

He retreated into the building and Frank pulled herself together. The usual onlookers, curious and unconcerned. Another kid in a dumpster. No big. Yellow tape. Coroner's van. Black and whites. The peeling Mercury. Beretta snuggled into her ribs. Sun shining. Everything okay. All as it should be.

Frank followed Darcy. The stairway was invisible after the bright sun and Frank tripped on the steps. Darcy turned at the top. Behind him, a lone bulb burned in its wire basket. Frank couldn't see Darcy's face, only the soft glow around his head. She wondered how long it would be before she could get herself into a tub and open a bottle of Scotch.

Back at the office there was a message from Gail. She'd finished Danny Duncan's autopsy and Frank could page her if she wanted. Frank did; it was a good excuse to hear Gail's voice.

"Hey," she answered when the doc called back. "Got your message."

"Hi. Paul did your Colonel. I was busy counting how many times a man stabbed his wife because she served him cauliflower with dinner."

"How many?"

"More than I could count," she yawned. "At least ten on her head and neck, thirty to her chest. Not to mention defensive cuts. I'm bushed. Thank God he confessed and I can let it go at that. I've still got to type it up, though. Ick."

"I thought you were gonna be chained to your desk all day."

"We drew coffee stirrers for this guy. I lost."

A thin smile eased the strain on Frank's face; she liked a boss that shared in the grunt work.

"What'd you find out about the Colonel?"

"Probably nothing you don't already know. He exsanguinated due to penetration of the carotids and jugulars."

Frank heard her shuffling papers.

"I don't have his report yet. I'll let you know as soon as I do."

"Who was at the post?"

"Lewis. She's nice. I like her."

"How'd she do?"

"Fine, I think. She seemed all right."

It was common for new detectives to ghost on their first autopsies. The overly ripe, gamey smell of a freshly opened torso; the sound of skin being stretched from fascia; the first glimpse of an exposed brain hunkered like an obscenely large pearl in an oyster—those were only a few of a dozen sensations that could send them spinning from the morgue. If the cutter knew a rookie was watching, they could be excessively gruesome.

"Was Noah there?"

"No. Just Lewis."

"Alive or dead when he was cut?"

"I'm sorry. I forgot to ask. Does it matter?"

"Probably not. Might give us a little more insight into his last couple minutes."

"I'll get Paul to finish his prelim first thing tomorrow. How's your day going?"

Frank was determined to forget the incident at the projects.

"From a civilian's perspective—tragic. From a homicide lieutenant's—productive. Four closed cases. The captain'll be a happy man. You should have gotten them by now. Three boys and a girl."

"Oh, God," Gail groaned.

"Yeah, Mommy pulled a euthanasia. Stabbed the oldest with a

steak knife then decided that was too messy. Smothered the rest of them with a pillow. Thought they'd be better off that way. Maybe she's right."

"Did you get up on the wrong side of the bed today, or what?"

Frank almost snapped something, bit it back.

"You headed out on rounds?"

"Pretty soon."

"Why don't you stop by on your way home? Let me kiss you goodnight."

"How can someone so cynical and so embittered be so romantic?"

Frank rubbed her eyes.

"I'm not embittered. I'm world-weary."

"That's very poetic. I think I'm rubbing off on you."

"Yeah? That'd be awful nice."

When Frank hung up she was an hour closer to that bottle of Scotch.

18

Frank was leaving a note for Darcy when Noah and Lewis strolled in. Noah slid into a chair like he'd just lost all his bones.

"Guess who's back in town," he said.

"Elvis?"

"Not an Anglo."

"Hendrix?"

"Not black."

"Pancho Villa?"

"Not as nice a moustache. Tito Carrillo. Guess the border boys missed him."

"Did you talk to him?"

Contributing to the conversation, Lewis settled her muscled bulk onto a chair that looked like it was about to become kindling.

"Not yet we haven't. I stopped at Hernandez's—"

"She forgot to have him sign his statement," Noah snickered.

Lewis flushed, nostrils flaring like a bull's before a charge. Frank wondered what her blood pressure was like. Mad-dogging her partner, Lewis continued.

"I stopped by Hernandez's place and he told me Carrillo was back in town. He seemed awfully tense and it finally come out that Carrillo still wants to do business with him and Echevarria. I don't know *why*," Lewis snorted. "There ain't no way I'd want those two backing me. Nuh-uh. But he's determined to go through with his plan, despite what happened to Duncan and despite all the warnings they got. Hernandez said Carrillo said that he ain't scared. That some old lady isn't gonna tell him what to do."

"Find him," Frank said. "Talk to him."

Lewis nodded.

"I went by his crib but he wasn't home. His old lady said she didn't know when he's coming back. I figured I'd drop by again on my way home. But the—"

"Sister Shaft," Noah rode Lewis. "Don't you ever sleep?"

Frank backed her rookie, asking Noah where he'd been while Lewis attended the post.

"Now I knew you'd be pissed about that," Noah defended, "but wait'll you hear this. Oh God," he laughed, clutching his stomach, "You're gonna love this. Johnnie, listen up. This is rich."

That was all the prompting Johnnie needed to sit back and prop his feet on the desk.

"Okay, so I was going through Belizaro's murder book this morning—waiting for Smokin' Joe," he acknowledged his partner, "to do whatever the hell she was doing in the girls room—and I notice he was busted a couple months ago for jackin' that butcher shop on 69th. And it dawns on me, I was talking to Mrs. Belizaro a couple days ago, and she mentioned something about how she never knew she had such wonderful neighbors. *Even the butcher.*"

Noah smiled, rocking his chair back on two legs. A slow grin lit Frank's face and she shook her head. Noah nodded.

Lewis looked puzzled, prodding, "Yeah?"

"Yeah," Johnnie echoed, "for those of us who aren't into that Vulcan mind meld shit like you two."

Noah continued, "Mrs. Belizaro says, 'I never go to him, but he brought me a bag of meat. Isn't that sweet?'"

"Nice," Frank said.

"And," Noah continued, dropping the chair back down, "that cold case of Nook's, 'member, about nine months ago? Male black with his guts emptied out behind the Pik-Rite and chunks carved off of him? Jacked that same *carniceria* nine days before he was picked off. I called his baby muhvuh and asked if a butcher had come by offering condolences. 'Yeah, she says. He even brought us a bag of meat.'"

"She-et," Lewis said, disgusted, and Johnnie laughed. Noah did too, but managed to say, "No wait. This is the best part. The baby muhvuh says"—Noah laughed, wiping his eyes—"she says, 'He was the *nicest* man. He knew we were Muslim and he even made it *kosher*.'"

"Ya'll sick mothers," Lewis said, stalking over to her desk. Johnnie was still laughing as Noah said to Frank, "I figured you'd rather I worked on the search warrant."

"What a fucking job," Frank said. "Mrs. Belizaro have any of that meat left?"

"Why, you wanna have a barbeque?" Johnnie choked.

"I already got it. Put it on ice. I'll send it to the lab tomorrow, see what we get."

Frank said to Lewis, "Heard the post went well."

"It was all right, I guess. It didn't tell us much more than we already know. Seems like our boy was still alive when his throat was slit. The doctor didn't find anything unusual."

"Did he say much?"

"Naw, he didn't talk hardly at all. I had to keep asking him things."

Frank glanced at Noah and he lifted his hands in the air, knowing she was peeved Lewis had to work with Paul Seuter alone.

Seuter was a skilled pathologist, but extremely shy. Talking was as comfortable for him as chewing razors. Because of that, and his pasty skin, the detectives called him Boo Radley. Frank wondered what the novice detective had missed and hoped she could spot it in Seuter's prelim report.

"Anything else?"

"Yeah," Noah piped up. "What else did Sister Shaft do today? Close all our opens, catch Jack the Ripper, and still get to soccer practice on time?"

Lewis glared at her partner.

"Do you *mind* if I finish?"

"A'ight," Noah rapped, "I'ma head for the door, I'ma give you the floor. Y'all wanna speak, then *talk* to Le Freek."

When it came from anyone other than Noah her nickname had a nasty edge, but Frank applauded his rhyming skills.

"Shit," Lewis whined, "why I gotta work with some crazy-ass O'Malley think he Busta Rhymes?"

"Hey, I ain't no O'Malley. I'm a Jew."

"Jewish, Irish, shit, y'all look the same to me," Lewis zinged back. Frank was pleased to see her holding her own, not getting her back up too much.

"Now let me finish," Lewis continued. "We leaned on Hernandez some. Jack Lord here," she said, tilting her head to Noah, "he ran the 'you're the best suspect' number on him again. Hernandez did his crybaby thing then allows as how he was *at Carrillo's* the night Duncan's murder went down. Not only was he *there*," Lewis gloated, "he and Carrillo *saw* one of the twins get out of Duncan's car after parking it and drive off in another car. Looked like a gray Benzo, sedan model."

"That's the good news," Noah interjected. "Now tell her the bad news."

"Ain't no way he's gonna cop to it in court. He knows Mother Love'll kill him. He messes his pants just thinking about her."

"Well, at least we're on the right track," Frank said. "Keep looking for Carrillo. We need him. I'll check with Fubar, see about some witness protection for Hernandez. Might be more inclined to turn if we can get the Mother off his back."

"I doubt it," Noah said. "He's a punk ass. And besides? Which twin are you gonna pin? Lewis say's they're identical."

Noah's pessimism was his way of venting. Frank knew there wasn't a lead he'd pass up, no matter how improbable. She ignored him, letting Lewis add a few more details, until the phone rang in her office. Frank dashed for it.

"Homicide. Franco."

"Narcotics. Kennedy."

"S'up sport?"

"Got the info you requested. There's a boat load. Want to swing by on your way home?"

"That'd work. Until then, give me the gist of it."

"Gist of it is this lady's got some fat pockets and knows how to keep her ass out of a sling. *Twenty-three charges*, mostly all related to felony possession, and *not one* conviction. This Betty knows how to fly below the radar. And who to fly with."

Kennedy named a preeminent L.A. law firm, citing a cadre of attorneys the Mother retained there.

"Another curious thing is that a lot of her associates tend to have ugly accidents. Rico Dali, Honduran coke peddler, fell off a roof in 1983."

That was Joe Girardi's frigidaire.

"JoJo Johnson, he was evidently a player in the Rollin 40's and a turf rival. He apparently electrocuted himself in his bathtub. Billy Daniels hustled for the Mother in the early '90s. Somebody doused him with gas and set him on fire in his own bed."

"Whoa," Frank said, making furious notes. "Who handled that?"

Kennedy's papers whispered together.

"Newton," she answered, referring to the LAPD division just east of Figueroa. "But wait, there's more. You get all this for only nineteen ninety-nine, plus, we'll throw in free, extra, at no charge, a pair—you heard right—a pair of Panamanians *also* with their throats slit."

"A double?"

"That's right. But if you act now, we'll throw in a pimp and rising ghetto star burned to death inside his car."

"What year?"

"Looks like '88."

Gough's cold one.

"Impressive, huh?"

"Back to the Panamanians. Who caught that?"

"That would be . . ." Her papers rustled again. "County. In '89."

"You done good. I owe you a Cherry coke and fries."

"That's all? A coke and fries?"

"I don't even want to know what else you have in mind."

"Aw come on, now, I know you're putting the squeeze on Doc Law, and dang don't I know you're a one-woman gal. I was just thinking dinner and maybe some gin afterwards."

Frank recollected how previous gin games had ended in the bedroom. Darcy leaned into her office, holding up the note she'd left. She waved him in.

"All right. You're on. But let me get back to you. I gotta go."

Kennedy talked to air as Frank swung the receiver into its cradle.

"Have a seat," she told Darcy and closed the door.

"How'd you know about that kid in the dumpster?"

He shrugged.

"It was like the .44."

Resettling into her old chair, Frank said, "Just another picture in your head?"

"Kind of. This was more like a feeling that there was another kid, but that he was missing."

"A feeling?"

Darcy nodded without giving anything else up.

"What are we talking here? ESP, premonitions?"

"I can't bend spoons or make doors slam," he smiled, "but I guess you could call it that."

"What do you call it?"

"Just a utilized talent. I think everybody's capable of receiving extrasensory information, but most people don't develop the requisite awareness."

"And you have?"

"Obviously."

Frank sat back with her hands behind her head.

"What about all this voodoo shit? Do I even want to know?"

Darcy's smile widened.

"My ex-wife's a Mambo priestess."

"A Mambo priestess," Frank repeated. Darcy's complexity amazed her once again. "The only thing I know about mambos is the Perry Como song."

"When you grow up in Louisiana it's almost impossible to avoid learning something about the culture. History permeates your life as surely as mold. Then when you marry into it . . ."

Aware she was opening herself up to a dissertation, Frank asked, "So what would it mean if somebody hung a black cat on your porch, left a little sack under your door mat, and sprinkled some kind of dirt all around your house? All this while your two dogs were loose in the yard."

Darcy smoothed his moustache while Frank tried to imagine him with a Mambo priestess. He was good-looking, short but powerfully built, attractive if one liked the strong, silent type. Brown hair—defiantly past regulation limits—set off baby-blues that didn't miss much. As Darcy mulled the question, she admired his self-assurance. He radiated a quiet strength and Frank thought he'd be a good man in a crisis. Despite her earlier misgivings about his temper, she was increasingly glad he was on the team. When she'd asked him on his first day if he planned on punching her out like his last supervisor he'd thought it over, answering, "Only if you're as dumb an asshole as he was." Frank had checked a smile, deciding Darcy James the Third might fit in well at Figueroa. So far, so good.

"It would appear," he answered at last, "that someone was fucking with my head. First of all, the black cat, that's a powerful hoodoo symbol. The thing about a black cat is it's universally recognized as an ill omen. The term *mojo* originally meant a bone from a black cat. It's come to mean a hand, or gris-gris—small bags, traditionally made of red flannel, filled with whatever ingredients the conjurer deems necessary. Mojos are usually worn under the clothing for good luck, but as in this case, they can be filled with bad things and left somewhere near the victim to emit their properties."

"What sort of bad things?"

"Oh, that's quite a list. The graveyard dirt you mentioned. Coffin nails. The victim's own hair or dried skin. Bodily fluids. Snake parts. The list goes on and on."

"So basically pretty benign stuff."

Darcy raised a finger. "Benign to you and me, but wonderfully potent to the believer."

Frank made a concessionary motion.

"Now the graveyard dirt, that's a large part of what's called laying down tricks or crossing someone. You sprinkle a prepared powder like Goofer Dust or Crossing Dust where your victim has to step on it. The theory is the powder then imparts its power to the victim and he succumbs to whatever hex the conjurer has placed on the powder."

Frank interrupted, "A prepared powder? You buy this stuff somewhere?"

"Any good *botanica* should carry it, yes. It's probably harder to find out here, but in Louisiana you can find powders in drugstores. I suspect you can order it on-line nowadays."

"Do you mix it with anything else or just straight powder?"

"That depends on the conjurer. Some of them won't even use the prepared mixes. They'll make their own, especially if they need it in quantity, so there can be anything in it."

"Like what?"

"Well." Darcy went back to stroking his moustache. "My guess would be you'd start with something like graveyard dust or lodestone dust, add some cayenne, ground up black cat bone, snake skin. Add a little salt, maybe some sulphur. I'm sure it varies depending on the locality."

Darcy fixed Frank with his pretty blues, asking why she wanted to know all this.

"Just trying to get a handle on the Mother. See where's she's coming from so I know what we should be looking for."

She explained about the powder in Hernandez' yard and was wondering if it might be traceable back to the Mother.

"You'd have a hard time proving that."

"I know. Circumstantial at best. But every link helps. Right now she's our best suspect but how the hell do we prove it?"

"Maybe you'd better get some Just Judge Powder." He grinned.

"They make something like that?"

"You bet. It's supposed to get the judge on your side."

"I'll be damned. You're just a walking voodoo compendium."

"Hoodoo," Darcy corrected. "Voodoo, that's something else. But I have to admit, I found it all pretty intriguing."

"Do you believe in it?"

The moustache pull and pause.

"To some degree, yes. The mind's a powerful tool. I wouldn't discount what it can do."

"So you think it's all based on power of suggestion."

"That's certainly a crucial element but I wouldn't limit it to that, no."

"What else is there?"

Darcy's smile was enigmatic.

"That's the million-dollar question, isn't it?"

They exchanged a slow, steady stare, two cops steeped in the realities of blood and bone.

"All right." She settled back. "Anything else I should know?"

Darcy rose with slow grace. Like a big jungle cat, Frank thought. He paused, seeming to juggle his thoughts before telling her, "I wouldn't underestimate this Mother Love."

She stifled her irritation, replying to a memo she'd picked up, "I try to never underestimate anyone."

Frank had expected more objectivity from Darcy and was fast losing patience with everyone's misplaced awe of a conniving old drug dealer. As he was leaving, he added, "I'd appreciate it if it didn't get out about my ex."

"Why do you think I closed the door?" she said without looking up.

"And hey," she called after him.

Darcy popped his head back in.

"Get a haircut."

19

No longer male or female, sexless, it had even forgotten what it used to be. Once the bones had been fleshed, but now they carried only creased skin. It ate very little and until lately, was always cold. It felt as if it had been cold for generations, but recently the red rage had started a final resurgence through its ravaged, yellow bones. That lovely, self-sustaining anger was the only thing that could warm it anymore and the heat was greatest when it was near either one of them.

After so long a time, it was delirious to feel that warmth again and it tried to stay near one of the two. The dark one was consistently warm, dependably so, but the other one . . . oh what an intense heat came from that one! A heat so bright, so white-hot, it could feel it sitting here against the brick wall, far from the source. Yet—it cocked its head—that blinding, beautiful sun was getting closer. Its eyes were useless, true, but yet it saw and its mouth cleaved in a toothless, puerile rictus.

They were coming together. At first their heat had touched it as tentatively as a spent wave reaches the shore, but the surges had begun to mount. Hotter and stronger now, deliciously warming, the waves lapped steadily against it, day and night.

No, the storm wasn't far off. But just as a moth couldn't think about the outcome of diving into a flame, the relic couldn't contemplate the inevitable clash of darkness meeting light. It orbited closer and closer to the center of the flame.

20

After talking to Darcy, Frank fired off a quick call to an acquaintance at the County Sheriff's department. Robbie Harris, a.k.a. Bartlett, wasn't in. She was just as happy to leave a message and bypass his endless recitation of quotes.

Done with that, she made nice to Lieutenant Tremont at the Newton Division. He assured her Billy Daniel's murder book would be waiting for her when she came by. But before that, she wanted to drop in on the one person who might know the Mother best.

Jogging down the stairs Frank glanced at a commotion in the lobby. A dreadlocked man with a striking resemblance to Dirty Old Bastard was trying to take on a knot of cops. Muñoz and Romanowski were patiently talking him toward the door, the older cop placating, "Come on, Peter. Be a good boy, now. Don't let's piss off the nice policemen, okay? 'Member what happened last time you did that?"

Frank smiled, glad Peter wasn't her problem. No one knew who he was, but he'd been coming into the station since Frank was in uniform, daring the cops to kick him out while he flashed whoever was on the desk. Hence the name Peter.

Driving out of the lot, she turned into the traffic on Broadway. She passed the mini-mart and deli, the bail bond shops and *botanica*. She saw the pedestrians without really seeing them, until one made her stand on the brakes.

"What in the goddamn hell?" she said lurching into Park. The car was still rocking as she jumped out.

From its huddled heap on the sidewalk, the thing in rags grinned up at her.

Frank groped for an arm through the blankets.

"All right, buddy. You want to follow me around? Got more to say to me? That's fine. We'll talk. Let's go upstairs."

She jerked the old thing up and it scrabbled to its feet. It scuttled after Frank like a crab. She half-dragged it toward the Honda, guiding the reeking mass into her back seat, using the back of her hand as buffer between its matted head and the car roof. She felt contaminated again, overcome with the urge to soak in a hot bath.

Executing a U-turn she headed back to the station, wondering how long it would take to get the stink out of her car. Not the brightest move, she conceded, but she'd had it with this fucker. She should've cuffed it when it grabbed her outside the tenement, but the truth was she'd been too rattled. Now she wasn't rattled, just pissed. And curious. Unless it was a trip to jail or the ER, homeless people didn't usually travel too fast or too far. Especially blind and crippled ones.

Frank reclaimed her parking spot, hustling her passenger into the station past the holding cells. Upstairs she shoved the stinking bundle into an interview room. Darcy's voice startled her as she locked the door.

"Who've you got?"

"Cousin It. That bum that grabbed me the other day."

"Oh yeah? What for?"

"Just want to talk. See what his trip his."

It was too embarrassing to admit that this thing made her nervous, that its sudden appearances were giving her the willies.

Frank took her time in the bathroom, washing her hands, splashing a little water on her face. As she patted herself dry in the mirror, her higher brain argued with her lower, *it's just some old bust with a grudge*. But her lower brain wasn't buying it. She knew even as she dismissed it, that she was ignoring the primitive, irrational, information system that had evolved to keep her alive while her intellectual mind ran around on its fool's errands.

"Well, this time you're wrong," she whispered to the waiting, watching self in the mirror. "I'm just letting this thing wig me out."

Wadding up the paper towel, she hooked a rim shot over her shoulder into the garbage can. She ran into Donna from downstairs shuffling up the hall with a sheaf of papers. She handed a ream to Frank, sighing, "Inventory. You need to go through every item assigned to you and verify its condition. If an item's missing, broken, or obsolete, you need to fill out"—she showed Frank a form—"one of these."

"And you need 'em back tomorrow," Frank guessed.

"Wednesday." Donna smiled tiredly. "Have fun."

The support tech lumbered on, her two-hundred-odd pounds looking as painful as they must have felt. Frank dropped the stack off in her office. Darcy was writing at his desk and Bobby and Jill were chewing the shit. She thought to remind Jill that she was late with a half-dozen follow-ups, but she knew.

Before stepping back into the box with Cousin It, Frank peeked through the surveillance window. She looked around the tiny room. It was empty. Ceiling, corners, under the metal table, all empty. Frank stepped inside. The room was empty. She held the door open and tested the lock. It didn't open from the inside.

Frank ran back to the squad room.

"Did you let that bum out?" she demanded of Darcy.

"No," he said, surprised. "Why?"

"He's not there. You see a pile of rags walk by?" she asked Bobby and Jill.

They both shook their heads, following Frank into the hall.

"Bobby check up here, the men's room. Jill get the women's room and help Bobby. Darcy you go look downstairs. I'm gonna look out back."

She trotted down the stairway, fuming over who'd let her detainee out. In eighteen years Frank had seen that happen a number of times and always over a miscommunication. There was no misunderstanding here, no colleague to assume or misinterpret whether they should keep him, it, *whatever*, in the box, no one to make a mistake with. Someone had deliberately opened that door. When Frank found that someone she was going to chew them a royal new asshole. With gusto.

The good news was that it couldn't go too far. Not on those feet. She checked the holding cells, asking the occupants if they'd seen anybody go by. Couple cops, that was all.

"You missed the guy in the blankets?" she asked.

"Weren't no one in blankets," a Hispanic man claimed.

Frank stepped into the afternoon sunshine, sweeping the parking lot. A rooster crowed and she jogged to the entrance on the side street. It was the only way in or out other than through the station. She scanned the short street. It was empty. She sprinted to the corner. There were plenty of people on Broadway, but no one shambling around in rags. The 12-Adam-22 car was coming into the station. Frank flagged it and bent to the driver's side. Sergeant Haisdaeck was behind the wheel and the 36-24-36 new boot rode shotgun.

"Haystack, you see an old wino on your way in? All bundled up in blankets?"

"Only thing I saw," the old uniform boomed, "was a six-pack and an easy chair."

Frank shifted her eyes to the rookie who answered, "No ma'am."

She slapped the top of the car and it rolled on.

"What the fuck?" she wondered.

Frank backtracked, checking between each car on the side street. She glanced into the lot. Bobby and Jill were near the back door.

"Did you find him?" she yelled.

Jill shook her head and Frank swiveled at a sound in the bushes. It was a scrabbling noise, like someone clawing in the litter of old cellophane and dead leaves. Frank crouched, trying to see into the dark greenery. She reached to part the branches, instinctively pulling back when she heard the low growl. But too late. She saw the pit bull's square head the instant she felt the flare in her arm. Frank's left hand folded and smashed into the dog's tattered ear. The blow made her grunt in pain, but didn't faze the dog. Its teeth were buried in her wrist.

Frank dropped her weight onto its thick chest, but the dog nimbly pivoted. She swung an ineffectual kick then tried prying the jaws apart. She only impaled herself deeper. Frank thought about shooting the dog, simultaneously gauging her backdrop, the chances of shooting herself, the paperwork involved in firing her weapon, and the prospect of an IAD investigation. She pulled at the jaws again, unable to believe she couldn't get free of this fucking mutt.

She heard the feet and saw the legs. Bobby, Jill, and the boot had run over from the lot. Haystack puffed up behind them. Bobby tried to get a kick in, missing as the dog wheeled around the fulcrum of Frank's wrist.

"No!"

Bobby yelled and Frank glanced up to see Jill pointing her pistol.

"Hold still," she shouted at Frank.

"Don't shoot!" Frank shouted back. "Don't shoot!"

Frank saw the boot—what the hell was her name?—pull a 2x4 out of the back of a pickup. It ripped through the air into the dog's back. The dog yelped and spun to confront its new attacker. Frank felt the teeth give and tried pulling free. Her movements made the dog forget the pain in its spine. It locked down on her wrist, eyes snapping back onto hers.

"Hit it again!" Frank bellowed. The uniform swung again, harder. Frank winced at the shock of the blow, but the dog let go. Frank scrambled back on her ass and the legs around her jumped beyond the reach of the chain. Frank saw the hole the dog had made under the fence, wondering what would have happened if a little kid had walked by instead of her.

She grayed out a little, thinking it was Haystack who said, as if from a distance, "That's a lot of fucking blood."

Jill, equally distant, screamed for an ambulance. Frank tried to protest, but was stunned by the ferocity of a sudden memory. The remembrance was so vivid it cleared her head and erased the fire in her arm. The dog lunging on its chain, the pain in her bloodied arm, the feet shuffling around her, Jill screaming for the ambo—she was reliving it over again.

"I've already done this," she said to herself.

Jill bent next to her and the déjà vu vanished.

"What'd you say?"

"Nothing," Frank mumbled. She was watching the dog. It danced on its rear legs, slavering and barking wetly. Its jaws were slick with drool and blood. Her blood.

"It's red," she said.

"What?" Jill asked, lifting Frank's mangled arm over her head to slow the bleeding.

"The dog. It's red."

"Yeah, Frank, it's red."

Frank's vision darkened and tunneled inward. She felt queasy. The Mother's honeyed voice teased, "Watch out for a red dog," then Frank heard laughing.

The Mother was still laughing, but farther away. She stood against a red sunset, trailing black and red and white gauze. The wind flapped her wrapping, unraveling her like a mummy. The Mother held a bloody sword above her head and a hand stretched to Frank. Blood dripped from the sword into pools at the Mother's feet. She laughed, beckoning Frank.

Bobby was asking her if she could stand.

"Yeah," she answered, but didn't try. She thought she was going to puke.

"Let's just wait for the ambulance," Jill said.

"I think we should get away from this dog," Bobby maintained. "He pops a link we're in trouble."

Frank felt hands under her arms, tried to help raise herself. Couldn't.

"Give me a sec," she whispered. Her cops ignored her, dragging her across the street.

"Wait. Wait," Frank tried again, fighting the nausea and grayness. They hesitated and she breathed, "Let me sit a sec. I'm okay."

She slumped onto a fender and dropped her head between her knees, rushing the blood to her brain. Jill told Bobby to go get something for her arm. Jill was trying to support it in the air and at the same time keep Frank propped against the fender. Seeing the blood smeared on her pants and the arterial stream plopping steadily onto her shoes, Frank thought, *I'm gonna have to throw these away.*

People from the station crowded around. Frank kept her head down, hoping she wouldn't hurl. By the time Bobby raced back the shock had lessened. She was able to sit up with her good arm braced against her leg. Frank focused on the pain. It was deep and sharp, like her ulna was being forged of molten steel.

Bobby tossed Jill a towel and a pack of gauze. Jill glared at her old partner.

"Do you think I could get a little help?"

Darcy had joined the knot of people and he grabbed the gauze. Frank bit against her teeth as he unrolled the spool around her wrist.

"If we had some Saran Wrap we could package this up and sell it as hamburger."

He grinned at her and Frank asked, "Did you find him?"

Darcy shook his head. "No one saw him. He just disappeared."

Frank corrected weakly, "People don't disappear."

"This one did."

He wrapped her arm in the towel but the blood soaked through even before he was done. Looking into her face, Jill asked, "How you feeling?"

"Fine," Frank lied. "This is gonna fuck up my range marks."

"You should put your head back down. You're really pale."

But Frank insisted, "I'm all right," even as she felt herself slide onto the road and into darkness.

21

Yawning, Frank padded barefoot into Gail's guestroom, which was really her home office. The doc twisted from her computer, pulling her glasses off.

"Hi, poor baby. How do you feel?"

"Pretty good, considering."

Considering it had taken the emergency room surgeon three hours to sew her wrist back together.

"Have you taken any Vicodin yet?"

Frank shook her head and bent to kiss Gail, holding her arm well away. It throbbed, and hurt if she flexed her hand, but over all the pain wasn't bad. She had some minor nerve damage, but nothing that wouldn't heal with time and therapy.

"I don't like it. Makes me feel flat."

"Well, you take it if the pain gets bad. And if you want I'll get you something else. It's a fact that people heal faster when they're not in pain."

"It's a fact, huh?"

"Don't get flip with me. Oh. I've got a surprise for you."

Gail rummaged through the chaos on her desk, finally placing a stack of faxed pages into Frank's left hand. It was Danny Duncan's preliminary autopsy report. The doc made a face, saying, "It looks like he was still alive when they bled him."

Frank scanned the first sheet. Death was attributed to exsanguination due to a single incised wound. The anatomical summary listed obvious pallor and evidence of exsanguination, and one incised wound to the neck, resulting in gross transection of the left and right carotid arteries as well as gross transection of the left and right internal jugular veins.

"Are you hungry?" Gail interrupted. "Can I make you something to eat?"

"Coffee?" Frank asked.

"That's all?"

Frank nodded and Gail admonished, "Your diet's atrocious."

"Don't start," Frank warned, making herself comfortable on the guest bed. She skimmed the generalities: External examination revealed the normally developed body of an adult black male weighing 167 pounds and measuring 71 inches in length. Decedent appeared muscular and well-nourished. Rigor mortis was present and generalized; livor mortis fixed and posterior. Tattoos, abrasions, and scars were duly noted, as well as continuous, circular contusions around each wrist and ankle.

Frank took the mug Gail handed her. Pointing at the remarks about the bruising, Frank asked, "Did Paul say anything about this?"

"Uh-uh," Gail scanned quickly. "Do you think he was bound?"

"Appears that way."

Frank put the mug down and pushed the papers in her lap until she found the body sketch. Paul had only indicated the contusions with a slash mark. She checked the clothing and valuables section for anomalies, then scanned the systemic review.

But for an absence of blood, Duncan's insides were unremarkable. The trauma was localized to his neck. There, Frank read to Gail, "A deeply incised wound starting from the left sternocleidomastoid muscle stretches seven-point-five inches to the anterior border of the right sternocleidomastoid muscle. The wound is smooth-edged and gaping, exposing the larynx and vertebral column. The incision passes cleanly through the thyrohyoid ligament and hypo-pharynx and point-five inches into the C3 vertebrae.

"Translated"—Frank looked up—"that means whoever cut Duncan was one strong motherfucker."

"Do you have to talk like that *here*?"

"Sorry."

"Not only is he strong, but he's probably left-handed, too."

"So it's highly unlikely that someone the Mother's size and age could slice so cleanly and deeply through a grown man's throat that she goes half an inch into his neck bone."

"Highly unlikely," Gail agreed.

The opinion section of the report concluded that due to the incision's cleanness, smoothness, and regularity, the decedent was likely immobile during infliction of the fatal neck wound. The lack of blood in his body indicated his heart had still been pumping when he was cut, but he probably lost consciousness within seconds, if he wasn't already out. That would explain the immobilization, Frank thought, squaring the papers with one hand.

Gail spied over the edge of her glasses.

"Does that help?"

She was wearing shorts and Frank admired her legs.

"Some. What are you working on?"

"I'm finally getting back to my friend in Canada. I told you about her, didn't I? Tempe Brennan? The forensic anthropologist? She's a neat lady."

Gail had a wide network of associates and colleagues. She'd put a lot of effort into her career, unlike Frank, who'd had it thrust upon

133

her. Joe Girardi had taken her aside only three few months after Maggie died, outlining her advancement to command. Frank hadn't wanted to climb the LAPD ladder; Detective Grade II was good enough for her. But she'd numbly accepted Joe's tutelage, partly to fill the black hole inside her, but more to please Joe. He'd been her angel and she couldn't let him down. In retrospect, he'd probably known that was exactly what she'd needed to distract herself from an alcoholic oblivion or swallowing a bullet.

Frank patted the space beside her.

"Come here."

Gail filled the indicated spot, carefully wrapping Frank in a hug. "You know something?"

"I know a lot of things," Frank said against the flat plane where Gail's left breast used to be. She kissed the scar through Gail's shirt as her good hand found warm skin underneath.

"I was worried about you last night."

The doc pulled back to look at Frank.

"It surprised me. I've never felt like that before. I felt so protective. I don't want anything bad to happen to you."

Frank was ready with a flip answer but Gail's earnest expression stopped her. She nodded instead.

"Do you ever feel that way about me?"

"All the time," Frank admitted.

They touched in the gentle and private way that lovers do when words are too much or not enough. This was so different from Maggie. Maybe because Frank was so different. She felt older, more stable. There'd always been so much excitement with Maggie. Big melodramatic fights ending with one of them stalking out, then sheepishly coming back, and lots of great make-up sex. They learned a lot along the way, but with Gail it felt like Frank was taking what she'd learned and putting it to use.

Gail murmured, "What would you say if I said I was falling head over heels in love with you?"

Frank continued caressing the warm skin. It was such a lovely distraction from the fear fluttering inside her chest.

134

"I'd say that was a wonderful thing."

"But you wouldn't say you were falling in love with me," Gail fished.

I *couldn't*, Frank wanted to say. Flirting with the thought was so much easier, and safer, than admitting it, than actually saying the words. Frank remembered Tracey tapping her on the chest.

"Maybe," she hedged, "I've already fallen."

Gail didn't press for specifics and Frank was grateful. It was so much easier to *show* the doc how she felt. They made love softly and slowly, feeling each other's heartbeat when they returned to words.

"How's your hand?"

"Fine."

Frank kissed the head against her chin, marveling at the range of emotions she'd had in less than twenty-four hours; her anger and curiosity as she picked up the thing in rags, the subsequent alarm and puzzlement when it disappeared, the shock and pain of the dog bite, relief in the hospital, and finally safety in Gail's bed. And again now in her arms. Safe harbor after rough passage.

And *that* was the thing Frank was dancing around. It wasn't the dog mauling her or the stitches nor the considerable blood loss. That was rough but not extraordinary. What made her want a safe haven was what she'd seen while she was sitting on her butt staring at the frenzied pit bull. The vision of the relic laughing in the Mother's voice had been frightening enough, but the *clarity* of the déjà vu that followed was inexplicable and bordered on terrifying.

In the hospital she'd dismissed it as a brief but intense hallucination brought on by shock and stress. The explanation had worked for a little while, but Frank ultimately had to admit it was no hallucination. What she'd seen and heard had been real, as real as Gail in her arms. Not only that, the moment had felt as familiar as coming home at night and stepping into her house. That sense of *normalcy*, of time unfolding in its ordinary pattern was jarring. It scared Frank that a moment so intellectually alien could be so physically real.

Frank murmured into Gail's hair, "What's predestination?"

"Hmm?"

"What's predestination mean? Like in psychic phenomena or religion."

"Gee, let me think. I'm not used to theology quizzes in the midst of my afterglow."

"What *are* you used to?" Frank grinned, tilting Gail's lips up for a kiss.

"Something more along those lines," Gail said rolling onto her elbows. "Well, the Christian definition is that God has ordained the future as well as the past. Everything that's happened to you, and is going to happen is writ in stone. Even who gets to be saved and who is damned."

Gail said "damned" with an eerie conviction.

"Do you believe that? About being damned?"

"No. Being damned is committing the same senseless actions over and over again. We do that right here on earth. People that don't grow and learn from their mistakes, that keep repeating them over and over and stay mired in their misery, *that's* hell."

"What's heaven?"

"Love," Gail said instantly.

Frank smiled, tucking the doc's bob back behind an ear.

"Everything's so simple for you."

"It is now but that doesn't mean it didn't take me a while to get here. Why are you asking about all this?"

"I don't know," Frank evaded. She hadn't told Gail about the freakish occurrences during the dog attack and didn't plan to. "So basically predestination is fate. Do you believe in fate?"

"Actually fate was the Greek version of predestination. I think there were a couple goddesses responsible for determining human destiny. See? There's another word for you. Predestination, fate, kismet, karma—a rose by any other name is still a rose. Every culture has their belief in divine rule."

"So you believe all that."

"To a certain extent. I believe we choose the lives we're going to

136

live and the choices we'll be confronted with. If we choose loving choices we grow and evolve. If we choose safe, comfortable choices, we stay stuck in our quagmires. They may be perfectly comfortable quagmires, too. A lot of us don't even know we're in them. I didn't, before the cancer."

Another subject Frank was less than eager to talk about.

"You ever had a déjà vu?"

"Yeah," Gail nodded. "Is that what this is all about?"

"They're kinda weird, huh?"

"I think they're fun. I can count on one hand how many times I've had them, but they're always so bizarre. It's like a veil gets pulled away and until it's dropped back into place we're seeing a world we're not supposed to know anything about."

"What is it you think we're not supposed to know?"

"What happens when we die and before we're born."

"Why aren't we supposed to know?"

"I don't think we're emotionally or intellectually capable of dealing with it. We're too enmeshed in our corporal comforts. I think cosmic truths go against our biological imperatives for survival."

"I love it when you talk dirty. Could you say that in English?"

"Meaning our body and mind have evolved to keep us alive. Physically safe. It's a temporary situation, and inevitably we all lose. We all die. Our biological drives are counterintuitive to what our souls know—that our bodies are only *temporary* structures. They die, but our spirits don't. Our bodies are just rentals our souls use to drive from spiritual lesson to spiritual lesson."

Frank had to laugh, asking, "Why did I even open this can of worms?"

"I've been wondering that same thing," Gail said.

The conversation shifted to mundane matters and for a while longer Frank was safely anchored at harbor.

22

Her family still teased her about marrying a man named Helms, but Jessie's sister never took part in that foolishness. Crystal was long on vision but short on humor, as serious most times as a bullet to the brain. The only time she loosened up was when she sipped tea in Jessie's cramped, sunny kitchen.

With a sharp eye Crystal watched Jessie add pinches of valerian and skullcap to the chamomile. She poured boiling water over the herbs and pushed the brew toward Crissie. Fussing with the strainer, as if that would make the tea steep faster, Crissie said, "Marcus told me that poh-leece woman come by here."

Always uncomfortable with words, Jessie just nodded. She marveled how one minute her sister could sound like a lawyer and the next like some old do-rag off the street. Crissie'd always had a way with words, easily mimicking her clients to put them at ease or testifying in front of a jury as if she had a PhD from a back-east college.

"What she axe about?"

Jessie lifted a shoulder in answer.

"I wasn't home. Wardell talked with her."

Her sister's face clouded.

"Wardell!" she bellowed. "Come in here right now!"

A moment later Jessie's husband loomed over the kitchen table. A big, loose-jointed man, he was as affable as his wife and sister-in-law were stern.

"Woman," he sighed, "why you holler at me like that in my own home?"

Crystal demanded, "You talk with that police woman?"

"Yeah, some," he nodded. "She axed about you."

"And what you tell her?" the Mother snapped back.

He raised his big hands.

"Nothin', Crissie. Just talked mostly about ol' times, is all. Wasn't nothin' to it."

"Wardell Helms you ain't got the sense Spirit done give you and you tell me ain't nothin' to it."

The Mother shoved a chair away from the kitchen table, jerked her head at it.

"You set right down and tell me every word that passed between you two."

"Aw, come on, Crissie. The game's on."

She flapped a hand.

"I don't care nothin' 'bout no foolishness on the TV. Now sit down!"

It was his house and Wardell Helms was a big man, but he left his beer warming by the recliner and took the hard chair pushed toward him.

23

The bar was busy for a Sunday afternoon, most of the patrons sitting with their heads tilted up at the TVs. The Raiders and Broncos were brawling it out and as much as Frank wanted to watch the game, she had to concentrate on writing her notes.

Bored with resting and being nursed, albeit by the loveliest of nurses, Frank had run out to Eagle Rock hoping to talk to the Mother's other sister. She'd been initially disappointed that Jessie Helms wasn't home, but her husband, Wardell, was pretty talkative when he realized Frank didn't have a grudge with him. He'd offered her a beer—she'd demurred—and he'd settled back into his easy chair keeping half an eye on the morning game.

Turned out he grew up with the Mother in a little suburb outside of Compton that got buried under the Artesia Freeway. She let him talk about growing up, gently leading him where she wanted him. They all four of them, Crissie, Jessie, Olivia and Wardell, used to hang together catching crawfish and frogs in the ditch behind their house and chasing dragonflies with mayonnaise jars. They hung out in the same gang, the Black Swans.

"Nothing like the gangs today," he'd chuckled. "Lord, the things we did back then."

That's when the Mother had really started making her mark, mojoing rivals and hexing their girls. Crissie was arrogant and strong-willed, and Olivia whetted her budding piety on her sister's transgressions. Jessie, the quiet one, went her own way, and while not as good looking as her sisters, she was kinder.

"She a *good* woman and I'm still proud to have her on my arm."

Wardell had sipped on his beer, continuing, "Now you take Olivia. There's a woman whose love of the Lord has turned her bitter and close-minded. And Crissie, she started off with religion, their folks raised 'em right, but she took off on her own path."

He'd heard stories about her on the street. What she did in that church of hers. Dark things. Things he wouldn't listen to anymore and didn't want to believe were true.

"Like what?" Frank had asked

"Naht—" He held up a meaty palm. "I don't mess with that. Jessie don't tell me nuthin' and I don't ask. I do not want to know," he stressed.

"How come?" Frank pushed, looking perplexed.

"I hear, rumors, a'ight? 'At's enough for me. At's more 'an I wanna know."

"How 'bout her business?"

Helms shook his big head.

"Crissie married into money. 'At's all I know. How she runs her affairs ain't no concern a mine."

"She married into money?"

The big man nodded, taking a long pull off his Coors.

"Right outta high school." He smacked his lips. "Married Old Man Love. Her daddy was dead by then. He'd a never stood for that. You know ML Laundries? Off'n Manchester and another to

141

76th, 77th Street? Those were his. And that old warehouse she livin' in? He won that in a game a *low-ball*. Can you believe that?"

Helms shook his head again, as if awed by the inequities in life.

"Pretty lucky guy," Frank agreed.

Helms snorted, "Not *that* lucky. Old Man died before his and Crissie's first anniversary."

"What'd he die of?"

"Old age? I don't know. Said it was natural causes. Natural enough a man his age couldn't keep up with the likes of a gal Crissie's age."

"How long before she remarried?"

Helms thought hard.

"It was some while. Before she took up with Eldridge, she was with a fella named Roosevelt. Lincoln Roosevelt. I always remembered him 'count of he was named after the presidents."

"Nice guy?"

"Linc? He was tight. Kinda close-mouthed like Crissie. She got that church from him. He was a preacher too, if I recall correct. But she didn't bring him around too much before he went off to Kansas or someplace like that."

"He just gave her the church?"

"Yeah, I don't know." Helms waved a big hand. "You'd have to ask Jessie about that. All I know was he was gone and she got the church. And that fine Cadillac she *still* driving. That's a good car, Cadillac, uh-huh, way they made 'em back then."

"So who'd she take up with after Roosevelt?"

"I don't know that there wasn't anybody serious 'til Eldridge. Crissie *fell* for that man," he chuckled. "I mean *hard*. And God Almighty what a hustler he was. They was a perfect match those two. Mean as a nest of baby rattlesnakes and twice as hungry. Both of 'em. 'At's when she fell in with those Panamanians."

Helms tensed, his face locking into the mask of someone who realizes he's said too much. Frank didn't want to lose him so she eased into another area.

142

"Did she marry Eldridge?"

"Uh-huh," he said, tracking a shovel pass on the large screen TV.

"That's how she became Jones?"

"Uh-huh."

"What about her boys? Who's the father?"

"That'd been Eldridge," he answered. "They're good boys. Rough, but respectful."

"Yeah, they seem pretty devoted to their mother."

"Uh-huh."

"What do they do?"

"For work you mean?"

Frank nodded.

"Little a this, little a that. They mostly help Crissie run her businesses."

"Did she have other kids?"

"Just the twins. Didn't want no more after that."

"What happened to their father?"

"Eldridge?" Helms wagged his head again. "He got sent up to 'Dad. Got himself shanked in there. Aryan Nation done it, what I heard. Made a circle around him to keep the guards out long enough for him to bleed to death."

"Crissie"—the name felt strange in Frank's mouth—"she musta been pretty upset."

"Nah, she'd left him by then. Had no more use for that snake."

"She pretty mad at him?"

Helms grinned at her.

"Leave it to say I'm glad I wasn't Eldridge."

"Let me guess. He left her bank too?"

"No, he was different from the other ones. He didn't have much to start with. Worked the streets some, drove an old Lincoln, but he didn't have much to leave behind."

"She married him for love?"

"Much as that woman can love, yes, I believe so."

"So why'd she boot him?"

Helms chuckled again.

"You gotta understand, Eldridge was a *player*. Crissie couldn't keep that boy chained to her bed too long, see?"

Now it was Frank's turn to shake her head.

"What'd he get busted on?"

"Oh, he wasn't no good, old El. Got caught with five pounds of coke in his trunk. Uncut. Sent him up for dealing the stuff."

Satisfied with what she already had, Frank gambled, "And it was probably Crissie's all along."

"I ain't sayin'." Helms shrugged.

"Don't have to. Your sister-in-law's record's longer 'an your arm. What about that fortune-telling stuff she does? How long she been doin' that?"

"Oh, a *long* time. Crissie been doing that since we was kids. Always good at. She has her mama's talent. It runs in the Green women's blood, you know."

"She read the tea leaves for you?" Frank joked.

"She definitely has a gift for prophecy," Wardell mused. "She can see things before they happen. Between you and me," he confided, "that business makes me nervous. Jessie does it too, some, and I tell you, I don't like it. Makes me nervous."

"What about that church of hers? Do you ever go?"

"Lord, no," he chuckled. "I ain't much of a religious man and even if I was I don't think I'd be going to *that* church. Uh-uh."

"Why's that?"

"Not my cup of tea, Lieutenant."

"Does your wife go?"

"Not her cup, neither," he sniffed.

"What exactly goes on there?"

Wardell's head swung from side to side.

"I do not want to know," he emphasized again. "But I don't think it's anything good."

"Why do you say that? I mean, if you've never been?"

"I hear things. They ain't good things."

144

Frank could sense Helms entrenching himself so she fed him easier questions.

"Like devil worship? That kinda thing."

"On a level with that."

"That's pretty harmless, isn't it?"

The man looked at Frank as if gauging her sanity. Maybe he deemed it questionable because he just sucked at his beer.

"Well, isn't it? I mean, if they're just in there mumbling about the devil and lighting black candles where's the harm in that?"

Wardell remained fixated on his can.

Frank bent her head closer to his.

"That's all she's doing, isn't she?"

"You know, I ain't never been. I really can't say."

"But you hear stuff."

"It's talk. That's all."

"But you believe it."

"Look. Let's just say my sister-in-law has certain . . . talents. Things happen to her that don't happen to ordinary folks."

"Give me an example."

"Just . . . things," he shrugged.

"Well like what?" Frank grinned good-naturedly. "Is she sacrificing virgins on an altar?"

Wardell was suddenly and clearly afraid.

"You know," he said, plunking his beer on the end table, "I promised my wife I'd get lunch started and I haven't done a thing about that. She comes home and catches me in fronta this ball game, they'll be hell to pay."

He stood. Frank had to follow suit.

"You don't really believe Crissie's doing anything harmful, do you?"

Exasperated, he puffed his cheeks and blew a load of air.

"Lieutenant, I don't know what that woman does and I don't want to know. Yeah, I hear things but you know what they say; don't believe everything you hear. I know she's a strange woman, a *power-*

145

ful woman. She can make things happen. Things that I sleep better at night not knowing about. You want my advice, I'd leave her alone."

"You mean things like this?" Frank raised her gauzed hand. "The dog that bit me was red. Your sister-in-law warned me a couple weeks ago to watch out for a red dog."

Helms nodded, "Exactly like that."

"But you don't believe she made that *happen*," Frank argued. "She might have seen it in some weird way, like a premonition, but she couldn't make it happen."

He shrugged again, "Maybe. Maybe not."

"Do you think she could make things happen to her own nephew?"

He stared at Frank.

"I can't say."

"Can't or won't?"

"*Can't*, Lieutenant. Now I really best be getting to lunch."

Frank flipped him a card.

"You seem like a decent man, Mr. Helms. If you think of something I should know, here's my number."

Frank had let herself out.

Now she twirled her pen around and around on the tabletop, losing herself in the pinwheel effect. The Mother had everyone tiptoeing around her like she was enthroned on eggshells. For Frank's money, Mother Love was just another hustler. An effective one, but a charlatan nonetheless.

The odds were good, Frank had contended all weekend, that at some point she'd come into contact with *a* dog. If it happened to be a red dog, all the better for the Mother's prediction. If it wasn't, it was still a dog. An easy enough scam. Because Frank had been looking for the thing in rags when the dog bit her, the relic's image was in the forefront of her consciousness. The dog bit her where the beggar had grabbed her a few days ago so her discombobulated brain had made a logical association.

146

The explanation sounded perfectly viable, and Frank *wanted* to believe it, but her reptilian brain fought her. Thrashing around just under the waterline of her consciousness, it whispered, *too many coincidences*. Reluctantly, she listed them.

Being warned about a red dog, and then a red dog biting her. That thing in rags popping up all over town like a target in a shooting gallery, then disappearing from the station. The intense déjà vus when she'd been bitten; the one before that when she was in the Mother's office. The freaky dream that had left her jumpy and rattled. And what about Darcy knowing all that voodoo shit and his wife being a *mambo*?

Separately, there were logical explanations for each incident. Bumping back to back, they made an ugly pattern. It was a pattern Frank didn't want to see, but all her training and instinct told her the line between coincidence and design had broken.

She held a finger up, motioning Deidre to bring another stout.

24

Frank emerged from her office at six sharp and Johnnie crowed, "Hey, look at this—Frank's imitation of Julia Child. Where's the other mitt?"

Noah asked, "What the hell happened to you?"

"Didn't you hear?" Johnnie answered for her. "Frank's taken up pit bull wrestling."

Jill rushed into the squad room and Frank said, "All right. Let's get going. What've you got, Taquito?"

She called on Diego first, knowing he wouldn't razz her or ask questions. She kept the briefing short, motioning Noah and Lewis into her office afterward.

"So what happened?" Noah insisted.

"Long story. There was this pit bull across the street. Dug out from under its yard and nailed me. Punched a couple arterial holes and made a helluva mess before Garcia beat it off with a board. I gotta give her a heads up for that."

"Did you have to have stitches?"

"Forty-two. And a little reconstructive surgery, but it's fine." Frank held up Danny Duncan's preliminary autopsy report. "Couple things Boo Radley failed to mention."

Noah turned to Lewis, marveling, "You gotta love her. Forty-two stitches and reconstructive surgery, but its fine. You're like the freakin' Black Knight, Frank. 'Oh, it's nothing! Just a flesh wound!'"

"Don't change the subject. Lewis, did you see the bruises on Duncan's wrists?"

"No," she answered, embarrassed. Frank handed her the autopsy report and recited it from memory for Noah's benefit.

"Track the body down. If it's been released, get to the funeral home ASAP. I want you *both* to check out this bruising. See if you can find a pattern. Get clear pictures."

"Didn't Boo Radley get pictures?"

"If you'd have been there you'd know that. I just got the text faxed to me. Did you see him take pictures?" she asked Lewis.

"I, uh, well, yeah, he took some," Lewis admitted. "They were peeling this old lady's face back on the table next to me. I must've got sidetracked."

Frank sighed, "When you're with Seuter, question his every move because he won't volunteer anything. Duncan could have had a time bomb ticking inside of him and fucking Boo Radley'd take a picture and sew him up without a peep.

"I dropped in on Jesse Helms. She wasn't there, but her husband gave me some names to look up. Lewis, run a male black name of Lincoln Roosevelt. Used to own the church the Mother's in now. Might trace him through property records. That would have been back in the sixties. Helms said he might have moved to Kansas around that time."

Lewis was making fast notes, bobbing her head.

"Run the second husband, too. Eldridge Jones. He ended up at the 'Dad on felony possession. Got a back door parole. And here's some names Kennedy dug up for us."

Frank passed Lewis a sheaf of papers. She'd called Kennedy to apologize for standing her up Friday afternoon. Kennedy had rightly figured that unless Frank was dead she'd want the notes ASAP so had taken them home with her. Frank picked them up Sunday before visiting Helms.

"How's she doing?" Noah grinned.

"Good. This should hold you two for a while. Now go away."

Uncoiling his long frame, Noah declared, "Well, this talk meant a lot to me too, Frank."

With her left hand Frank awkwardly signed off for personal leaves and overtime. She scanned a collection of 60-days, deciding to send them up to Foubarelle. Let *him* mark the red hell out of them, if he could even tell what needed correcting besides dangling participles and inappropriate use of commas. Thinking her supervisor would have been more useful to society as an English teacher, she reached for a pen with her right hand. Jolting it against the desk made her wince. Worse than that, the leering image of the relic popped up again.

"Fuck you," Frank whispered to it. She concentrated Kennedy's data. The narc had uncovered a nugget that neither Gough nor Joe had dug up during their investigations.

In 1967 Lincoln Roosevelt bought two life insurance policies, both naming Crystal Love as beneficiary. Seven months later, the insurance company identified his bones amid the rubble of an unexplained fire in a St. Louis boardinghouse. The Mother had collected $50,000 from the first policy and a cool $300,000 from the second.

Helms pronouncement, that his sister-in-law "can make things happen," echoed in Frank's head. Too many accidents around the Mother, and unexplained deaths. While her supernatural talents were debatable, Frank decided her maliciousness was not. If all these cases were connected, then Lewis was chasing a career serial killer.

Frank was plotting a time line of the Mother's suspected criminal involvements when the phone rang.

Bartlett, from Sheriff's Homicide, said, "Look here, see. I gotta do this. 'All they that take the sword shall perish with the sword.' Okay, so it's a little trite, but you can't go wrong with Saint Matthew. But seriously, I've thought about this. Stick with me. The first is Wilfred Owen. Great war poet. You gotta love him. Listen.

" 'Let the boy try along this bayonet-blade how cold steel is, and keen with hunger of blood; blue with all malice, like a madman's flash; and thinly drawn with famishing for flesh.' Great, huh? Now listen to this. 'For—' "

Frank interrupted, "So they were both cut. Was it swords or bayonets, Bartlett?"

"Houseman. Another great war poet. 'For when the knife has slit the throat across from ear to ear, 'twill bleed because of it.' "

"English, Robbie."

"Their throats were cut. Both of 'em. It didn't happen where they found 'em though. They were cut, then dumped."

"You got pictures?"

"Sure, I got 'em. Got the whole enchilada here. Whaddaya want to know?"

"How do they look? Kind of tidy or the usual mess?"

Frank heard him flipping pages, muttering something about bloody blameful blades and boiling bloody breasts. She was never sure which irked her more; the endless quotations or his normal conversation, which was more like dialogue from a 40's B-movie.

"Looks normal to me. As normal as guys can look with their windpipes letting the rain in."

"So pretty messy?" she persisted.

"Whaddaya think, Franco? They got their throats cut, for crying out loud."

"Let me borrow the book?"

"Oh, most pernicious woman! Oh, villain, villain, smiling damned villain!"

The murder book was archival. It wouldn't sweat Bartlett to loan it out.

151

"Come on," she coaxed. "I gave you Ackerman." Then she tested a foggy line from a college humanities class.

"We gotta stick together. 'We few, we happy few, we band of brothers we . . . for he today that sheds his blood with me . . . forever shall my brother be . . . ' Close enough, huh?"

Bartlett burst out, "He which hath no stomach to this fight, let him depart!"

Frank pinched the phone against her shoulder and rubbed her eyes while he finished.

"Come get your book, Franco! 'Come cheer up, my lads, 'tis to glory we steer—remarked the soldier whose post lay in the rear!'"

She started to interrupt his next soliloquy, then fell silent, all too familiar with the feel of gooseflesh rising in her skin.

"Say that again," she told him.

"You're a scholar and a gentleman, Frank. I knew you'd appreciate me someday. 'Cry Havoc! and let slip the dogs of war, that this foul deed shall smell above the earth with carrion men groaning for burial.' Shakespeare, my lady fair. The bard himself."

Frank fumbled the phone into its bed, the dog's searing teeth and the dream of the battlefield fresh upon her.

25

Tito Carrillo packed three pieces of heat. A .38, police-style under his arm, a .25 in his boot, and his favorite, a black 9mm Smith & Wesson in his waistband. Carrillo made sure the alley was empty before releasing a stream of piss against the wall. He knew that *bruja negra* was looking for him, but he felt confident. If she wanted a piece of him, she'd have to get a piece of his three friends first. He shook himself and zipped up, catching his shirt in the steel teeth.

"*Mierda*," he whispered. He was so engrossed in pulling at the stuck fabric he didn't see the huge shadows engulfing him. Fingers bit into his arms. He didn't even notice the needle's quick sting. *Los hijos negros*, that black bitch's sons whipped a gag into his mouth. He writhed and twisted, trying to fight, but the *hijos* held him with ease. They shoved him into the car then squeezed in beside him. He kicked wildly, flailing his torso like a whip. Carrillo used the strength and courage that accompany imminent death, but he was still no match for the ebony twins; one held him in a macabre embrace while the other tied his wrists and ankles.

"That ain't necessary," *La Negra* said from behind the wheel.

Translated, the gutsy thought in Carrillo's head would have been something like "The fuck it isn't," but even as he struggled he felt a strange numbness in his limbs. They jerked of their own accord. At the same time he noticed he was having trouble moving his eyes and that his lungs were getting awfully tight.

One of the evil *hijos de la gran puta* looked into his face. Carrillo saw the red lips move. He heard, "It's working," but the words seemed to come from a tunnel. They pulled the .38 from its holster, then he felt the 9mm leave his pants. But they didn't know about his boot. If he could just get to the .25 he'd be okay. Streetlights raced over his locked lids. *Ay dios*, he couldn't move! How could he get to his gun if he couldn't move? Carrillo hadn't cried since he was three, but he wanted to now.

The car stopped. Doors opened. Carrillo's head fell and bumped. Hands grabbed him, pulled him. They moved swiftly against an angry wine-red sky. That was the color of hell, Carrillo thought. That's where he was going.

Then he was rolling over and over, like when he was a boy, down the hill behind their house in León. When the rolling stopped, *La Negra* was looking down at him. A woman was singing soft and far away. Was it her? Hands moved back and forth over his frozen vision. His eyes were dry and he wanted to lick his lips. He couldn't. He knew then he'd never get to his .25. That was enough to make Tito Carrillo a reverent man. He tried to shut his lids, but Carrillo had to apologize to God with the Mother in his eyes. He felt wetness soak the carpet. He prayed it was his bladder, prayed the sharp hiss he heard wasn't a match striking.

Tito Carrillo was still praying when he blossomed into a hideous black and orange flower unfurling itself toward a disinterested moon.

26

Noah flopped onto Frank's couch. Draping his long arms across the back, and sighing for emphasis, he announced, "Tito Carrillo's dead."

Frank rested her chin onto her good hand.

"What happened?"

Noah shrugged.

"Echevarria's wife called while you were in the meeting. She was all hysterical and wanted us to come over ASAP. We get there and there's this cow tongue hanging on her porch, all wrapped up in leaves and twine. Lewis bagged it. We got it off her porch and asked where her husband was. She said he split. Went to Arizona for a couple weeks to hang with a cousin. Since he heard about Tito.

"I said 'What about Tito?' and she looks at me all amazed. 'That he's dead,' she said. Turns out he got lit up in an alley two nights ago. I'm gonna call LAFD, and the Sheriff's, see what I can find out. Did the doc mention anything about a crispy critter?"

Shit, Frank thought, that had been Carrillo. Gail had trailed the job home with her the other night and Frank had complained about the smell.

"She mentioned something about it. It wasn't one of ours so I didn't pursue it. I'll give her a call, see what she's got. Where's Lewis?"

"We thought in light of Carrillo's immolation we should have SID look at the tongue. We might find some trace in it. Who knows?"

"Good. Anything else?"

Noah shrugged. "Lewis is running those names you gave her. I'm still trying to talk to the managers at her other businesses. They all think she's a fucking saint. They don't see her too often. Seems like one of the twins—Marcus, it sounds like—handles most of the business."

"You gonna talk to her sometime? She knows we're asking around about her."

"Yeah, I know." Noah stroked his chin. "But I want to get as much as I can on her before I hit her with anything. This way she's sweatin'. Not sure what we're up to."

"I don't think this woman sweats much. I'm sure she's got her legal team marshaled by now."

"Yeah, but if we can get something tight on her, even God won't be able to help her."

"I don't think that's who the Mother's bankin' on. Hey. You want to go by her church with me? See her in action?"

"When?"

"I don't know. I'd have to check her schedule. See when she does her gig."

"Yeah, let me know.

" 'Kay. Keep me posted."

"Aye, aye," Noah saluted, rising.

"How's Trace?"

"She's good. Kids are good. It's *all* good, baby."

● ● ●

156

Lewis pranced into Frank's office.

"S'up?" Frank asked, irritated at the intrusion into her quiet time.

"That nasty old tongue at Echevarria's house? Turns out there was a note inside. SID lifted a print off it. You ain't never gonna guess who it belongs to."

"How the hell'd you get that back so quick?"

Lewis batted coy lashes.

"I got my ways," she answered.

Frank gave her diamond in the rough a smile.

"Must be the Mother's print."

Lewis deflated like a popped balloon, demanding, "Who tolt you that?"

"You did. Why else would you be bouncing in here? What'd it say?"

"Nothing," Lewis pouted. "Just had Echevarria's name on it."

"That's good," Frank encouraged. "Evidence she knows him and of mal intent."

"It doesn't give us nothing for Duncan though."

"Patience, Lewis. You're in homicide now. Collars come slower. Go home and start working jigsaw puzzles. Find the right pieces, put them together one by one. Eventually you'll get the whole picture. Just a matter of time."

Frank knew Lewis didn't want to hear this horseshit. She hadn't wanted to hear it a decade ago either.

"What else you got for me?"

"I found Eldridge Jones's bunkie when he was at Soledad. Name's Darryl Little. He's up in Bakersfield. I want to go up and talk to him, if that'd be all right."

"Can't do it by phone?"

"I think it'd be better if I talked to him in person."

That was true, but Frank couldn't justify the expense.

"Try the phone first, see what you can get."

Lewis nodded.

"What's Hernandez say about all this?"

"He won't talk to us. Yelled at us to go away. He's got nothing to say. He's freaked."

"We're gonna need him."

"Yeah, I know. He'll be all right. We just gotta let him chill a bit. He'll come around."

"Unless the Mother gets to him first. What can you hit him with?"

"Not much"—Lewis shrugged—"nothing serious. Noah said we should get a priest to bless him. Kind of like do an exorcism on him or some nonsense like that so that he wouldn't be afraid to talk to us." Lewis snorted, "I told him I work for LAPD, not Mental Health Services."

"That's not such a bad idea."

"Puh-lease," Lewis groaned.

"Think about it. There's a lot these boys could be telling us, but they're afraid. This'd be the same as a witness protection program. We guarantee them safety in exchange for information. We don't even have to relocate the bastards. Just sprinkle 'em with holy water. I like it. Check it out."

"You're serious," Lewis gawked.

"Yep. A priest might not work though," Frank said, hunkering across the desk toward her cop. "We might need somebody like the Mother, a priestess or whatever who does this same kind of voodoo shit. Somebody Echevarria and Hernandez believe could counteract the Mother's mojo. Check it out. See if they'll bite."

Lewis's laugh came out like a bark.

"And if they do? Where I'ma find this *priestess*, huh? I'm supposed to look her up in the Yellow Pages. Axe around at the Local Wizards 14?"

When Lewis was done amusing herself, Frank asked, "You forget who writes your evaluation reports?"

The rookie sobered.

"No, ma'am."

"Good. Don't. Anything else?"

"No, ma'am."

Frank pointed at the door.

27

The next morning, on her way to the lieutenants' meeting, Frank cornered Darcy outside the men's room. Making sure no one was within earshot, she said, "Hey. You think your ex would do us a favor?"

"For you," he rumbled, "maybe. But she sure as hell won't for me."

"This guy on the Colonel Sanders case, Hernandez, he knows shit but he won't talk. He's petrified. Thinks the Mother's got curses on him. Noah was thinking we could get somebody like a priest to break the spells. To cleanse him or whatever, convince him he's safe. I was thinking your wife might be equivalent to Mother Love. Maybe we could get Hernandez to go for that. What do you think?"

Darcy folded his arms.

"I could ask her, but if your man doesn't believe in her it won't do any good. So I suppose it's up to him."

"You let me work on him. Meanwhile you work on your wife."

"My ex-wife," he corrected.

"Right. Find out what she'd charge. I'll have to figure how the hell to bury it in expenses."

Frank sat distractedly through the meeting.

What if Noah was right? Maybe they *could* gain Hernandez' trust by protecting him with some bigger, badder mojo. Frank wasn't against humoring a witness if he helped bring the Mother down. It amused Frank to think of turning the Mother's own weapons against her.

It was late when she returned to the squad room; except for Noah and Lewis, everyone else had gone home.

"Hey," Frank said to Noah. "Lewis told me your idea about the priest. You think if we could find another voodoo queen like the Mother that Hernandez'd go to her?"

"Maybe," he considered. "He might be scared enough to try anything."

"Talk to him. Find out."

In her office, Frank found a note on her chair. She read, *X says yes but you have to bring him to her. She won't come up here.*

"Deal," Frank said to the room.

She didn't know what Noah had told him, but Hernandez was eager to meet Marguerite James. Frank was pretty curious too. And surprised.

Darcy's ex greeted them silently at her front door. She was at least a foot shorter than Frank expected and bordering on plump. She was barefoot, in a sleeveless white dress belted with a bright assortment of scarves. Dozens of beaded braids ended above the swell of her breasts and Frank forced herself to look away. The woman's breasts were perfectly round and full and they pressed against her blouse like jail-bound cantaloupes making a run for it, dark nipples sent out as the advance team.

She wordlessly appraised Frank and her witness. She didn't even

160

have a glance for her ex-husband. Hernandez fidgeted, swiping his mouth with the back of his hand. Frank endured a silent appraisal, thinking Marguerite James looked like a woman who knew secrets and wouldn't tell you what they were. Frank had a dozen questions she probably wouldn't ask Darcy until she knew him a hell of a lot better. Marguerite studied her a lot longer than Frank thought necessary, seeing as Hernandez was the client.

"Follow me," she commanded, leading them through a living room decorated with carvings and sequined flags. In the rear of the apartment she let them into a windowless room. It was empty but for a large table with two chairs opposite a flowery altar. She told Frank and Hernandez to sit.

"Tell me about this woman who's cursed you," she demanded of Hernandez. He glanced at Frank and she jerked her head in assent. He nervously told Marguerite about Danny and the hexing of his yard and Echevarria's, and the identical tongue he'd gotten but thrown away. He said he'd been going to Mass twice a day but didn't know if a Christian god could fight these older gods.

Marguerite smiled for the first time. She asked for more details about the hexes. Hernandez was vague and Frank filled in what she could.

"Do you know this woman?" she asked, her blunt gaze on Frank.

"Not well."

"But you've met her?"

"Yeah."

"Describe her for me."

When she'd talked to her on the phone, Marguerite had indicated she knew Mother Love. Reputations evidently spread among the Afro-Caribbean religions like AIDS in shooting galleries. Anyone evincing talent as a priest or priestess didn't remain a secret for long.

"I thought you said you knew her," Frank asked back.

"I know of her," Marguerite snapped. "But we don't travel in the same circles. Tell me your perspective."

161

Frank shrugged, starting with a physical description, but Marguerite interrupted, "No, no, no. What's she *like*? Her personality."

"Like I said, she's not very big, but she's . . . forceful. She seems larger than she is. She's proud. Arrogant. Been used to having things her way for a long time."

"How does she dress?" Marguerite asked. "Tell me about her appearance."

"She's flamboyant. She's got a big personality and she dresses big. She had on a red blouse, silk I think. And big hoop earrings. Lots of bracelets. Very—"

"Does she wear beads?"

Frank peered into her memory.

"Yeah. I thin—"

"What color?" Marguerite barked.

Frank closed her eyes, unprepared for the interrogation.

"I want to say glass. Red. Maybe white."

Marguerite's unexpected smile was as powerful as a searchlight. Turning to Darcy, she asked, "How well do you remember your *orishas*?"

"Not very well."

Marguerite rolled her eyes.

"Which one would be associated with red and white?"

Darcy had to think a minute but his answer was apparently satisfactory, for Marguerite said, "There. You're not as stupid as you think."

"I'm not the one who thinks I'm stupid," Darcy bickered back.

She flipped her hand at him.

"You two leave," she told the detectives. "I will take care of Mr. Hernandez. What I'm going to do," she told him carefully, "is rid you of the spells this woman's put on you. I'm going to give you protection too, like an invisible shield, so that whatever she tries to put on you will bounce right off of you and back to her."

Marguerite took one of Hernandez's hands in both her own. She leaned into his face and asked, "Do you believe I can do that?"

162

Hernandez glanced at Frank again, then back at the woman holding his hand. They waited for his answer. Finally it came in a timorous nod. Marguerite tilted an eyebrow at Frank and Darcy. They returned to the living room where Frank studied Marguerite's art collection. She couldn't vouch for its quality but the quantity was impressive enough. Running her good hand over a beaded fetish, Frank asked, "What was she giving me the third degree for?"

"I don't know." Darcy sulked. He'd been morose all day and Frank had to prod him for answers.

"How long's this going to take?"

"About an hour."

"What's she going to do?"

Pressing his thumbnail into the caulking of the windowsill, he shrugged. "I suspect she'll cleanse him—rub oils on him and smudge him—then she'll invoke an *orisha*. My guess is she'll call upon Shango. That seems to be Mother Love's god. Plus, he's the god who protects against evil. She'll have to set an altar to attract him. The gods are like six-year-olds. They're easily bribed. She'll pray over Hernandez and probably make him a mojo that'll make him feel safe. But like I said, it all depends on how much faith Hernandez has in her."

"What's an *orisha*?"

"One of the African gods. There's a whole pantheon with a specific hierarchy, much like the Greek pantheon. Each god has dominion over a specific natural phenomenon. They each have their own attributes and personalities. It's pretty involved."

Frank nodded at a tall carving of a bent old man.

"She do any of these?"

"No, she just collects them. She's a physics professor."

"No kidding?"

When Darcy didn't respond, she asked, "Where at?"

"UC Irvine. She's a bigwig in plasma physics."

"Plasma physics," Frank repeated. She was thinking Marguerite was as impressive as her ex when a door banged.

"Where's your daughter?"

"She's spending the night at a friend's. I wanted to see her but Marguerite doesn't like the schedule disrupted. She can be a regular bitch."

Frank examined a row of book spines.

"That why you left her?" she ventured.

"It was the other way around." Darcy grunted, then volunteered, "I used to have a pretty bad temper. I came home drunk one night, I don't even remember it, but I guess I hit her. I woke up in the tank and by the time they let me out she'd changed the locks. She packed my things in a couple of boxes and brought them outside for me. Her brothers were with her. She had a big gash on her cheekbone and her right eye was swollen. She told me to expect the divorce papers within a week and that I'd never see Gabby—my daughter—again."

Darcy went Code 2 again and Frank said to the books, "I thought you had custody every other weekend."

"Yeah, we're working it out. It's not as much time as I want with her, but it's better than what it used to be. She wouldn't even let me see her in the beginning, or call her. She had a restraining order. Plus those brothers. But it's getting better. I've just got to be patient and not lose my temper. That only sets me back."

The conversation died in uncomplaining silence. Darcy went outside to spit tobacco and Frank wished she'd brought some work to do. She pulled a book from the shelf, a doctoral thesis on African religious art.

She found Shango in the index but it directed her to Xango. She browsed the indicated entries, discovering he was the god of pride, arrogance, and warfare. He loved all physical sports, often carried an ax or a club, usually made of copper, and his favorite colors were red and white.

As Darcy said, he was associated with all natural phenomena, ruling over lightning and fire. That reminded frank of Jill's informant, who claimed to have seen lightning over the Slauson house.

Even as Frank rationalized that the CI had seen a spotlight or some explicable weather event, her lower brain whispered, *not a coincidence*.

Frank flipped to another entry. Xango was the god to call upon for help with black magic. He had to be propitiated with large offerings, and was especially fond of crabs. A red rooster should be used for sacrifices to Xango, and though he was fair, and often called upon to settle judgments and disputes, he had a fierce temper, often burning those who offended him.

Lincoln Roosevelt torched in a St. Louis flophouse. Billy Daniels burned while he slept. Gough's pimp immolated in his hooptie. Tito Carrillo rolled up and lit like a blunt.

Frank snapped the book shut. Was the Mother appeasing her god and eliminating competitors at the same time? Why hadn't she burned Danny too? Or the Colombians? Because she's smart enough to change her MO, Frank answered herself.

She jumped when Marguerite opened the door. Shelving the book, Frank asked, "All done?"

Marguerite approached without a sound, as if she were trying to catch a spooked animal.

"I'm done with *him*," she emphasized. She crossed her arms and they disappeared under the overhang of her breasts.

"How much contact do you have with Mother Love?"

Darcy started to come in the front door, but Marguerite held up a hand.

"Leave us alone," she said without looking at him. Darcy retreated. Frank was tempted to join him. Holding Marguerite's gaze was like holding a live coal and Frank almost stepped back. She didn't. Besides making her look silly, she realized, it wouldn't do any good. She could be standing across the room and Marguerite James would be just as formidable.

"We're investigating her nephew's murder. He worked for her. She was one of the last people to see him. I've talked to her."

"Just about the investigation?"

165

Frank hesitated.

"Other stuff. She explained *santería* to me. Said she was a healer. Could see things. She warned me about a dog." Frank held up her bandaged hand and gave Marguerite her most winning grin. "I didn't listen."

"That's all? No other contact?"

"No offense, Mrs. James, but why am I getting the third degree? Hernandez is your client, not me."

As if Frank hadn't spoken, Marguerite pressed, "Did she ever touch you, or offer you food or a drink?"

Frank shook her head, then remembered her visit to the church.

"She put her hand on my arm for a second."

"Did you notice an itching or burning afterward?"

Frank had a crude answer, but asked instead, "Is Hernandez ready?"

Marguerite's head tilted to the side, the physicist analyzing data.

"I gathered from the tone of our telephone conversation that you don't have much use for my religion. I don't care about that. I'm not a proselytizer. But like Mother Love I can see things, Lieutenant. And I can see her hand all over you. It's like you're walking in a black cloud and you don't even know it. I can help if you like. Maybe. I've heard much about her. Her hand is very strong."

Frank smiled, "I appreciate your concern, but I think I can handle her. Are you done with Hernandez?"

Marguerite also smiled, but where Frank's smile had bordered on condescension, Marguerite's was wise, the secrets in her eyes hidden in plain view. Frank felt oddly contrite.

"I'll get him," the priestess offered.

Marguerite led a much calmer Hernandez to the front door. She and Darcy exchanged terse custody plans for the following weekend, then Frank paid her fifty dollars cash. Per their telephone conversation, Frank was to pay whatever she felt the service was worth. Frank had consulted with Darcy who'd explained mambos traditionally didn't charge for their work, accepting donations instead. Marguerite took the money without looking at it. She started to close the door.

"Wait," she said, ducking inside. When she came back, she handed Frank her university business card. Her home phone was written on it.

"If you change your mind, call me. Anytime."

28

Hours ago the neighbors had flipped "Closed" signs and pulled iron gates across their doors. The halogens over head were all shot out and Saint Barbara's Spiritual Church of the Seven Powers crouched in the dark. Above it, a thin rind of moon curled against newly blackened sky. It was beautiful. Frank thought about forgetting this. Just showing up at Gail's and locking the door and holding her all night.

Voices spilled from across the street. Frank looked at the moon once more then followed a vague crack of light at the side of the church. She listened at the door, recognizing the Mother's sultry timbre.

"Who got Spirit wid' 'em?" she implored, and Frank stepped inside.

The church was dim with incense smoke and dull yellow lights. The Mother clapped next to the pulpit, exhorting the small congregation. Frank sat in a vacant pew, meeting the eyes she felt all over her. But even a lifetime on the streets couldn't prepare Frank for what she saw in the Mother's eyes. It hit her like a blow to the head, a flare of hatred, so pure and undisguised it was breathtaking. A perfect black-hole of hate.

Frank's bladder swelled. Bullets nor knives or angel-dusted behemoths had ever scared Frank as much as the tiny woman in front of her. No one could hate that much and not kill. Or worse.

Tommy Trujillo bounced into her head. He'd beaten her up on her way home from school one day. She was in third grade, he was in fifth. He wanted her Batman lunch box. He took it after bashing her ear bloody. When she told her father what had happened, he'd slapped her. Frank had been stunned.

"Do you know why I hit you?"

She'd backed away from him. He'd followed, slapping her again. It was a light slap, its unexpectedness more frightening than its sting. He slapped her again. And again, until Frank was furious. Until she slapped back. Then he'd grinned and pulled her to him. Kissed her tears.

"You know why I did that? To make you mad. You know why I wanted to make you mad?"

When Frank shook her head he'd said, "Because mad is better than afraid. Anger you can use. You can fight with it. But fear'll just eat you up. You may as well lie down and die if you're afraid. I'm not always gonna be there to protect you. Your mom neither. You gotta learn to protect yourself. Next time somebody wants to fight you, get mad at 'em. Remember me slapping you, okay?"

The old memory came like a benediction, allowing Frank to rein her fear. She forced a cool smile. To her surprise the Mother bent double, erupting in laughter. She clapped gleefully and capered in circles. Her eyes flashed at Frank, hands cracking like a bullwhip.

"Who's got the Spirit here?"

She cocked an ear at the assembly. Frank looked around, hiding her shaking hands in her pockets. Maybe twenty-five, thirty people were scattered among the pews. About a third were black, the rest Latino. Roughly the same ratio of men to women. They all appeared expectant.

A hand shot up and a woman claimed, "I got the Spirit, amen!"

"She say she got the Spirit! Aché!" the Mother clapped, her s's tangling in their hurry.

"Who else got the Spirit now?" she demanded.

"I do! Praise be, I *do*!" a voice called out.

The clapping increased. Against the walls, toward the front of the church, Frank counted eight men sitting around an array of drums—round ones, cone-shaped, hour-glassed, congas. They sipped from glasses, nodding at the Mother. Frank watched one poke around in his nose then inspect his finger with great care. They were older men with more lines between them than a Rand McNally atlas. Blue incense drifted over their heads.

"Who *else* is filled with Spirit?" Mother Love howled.

Souls cried they had the Spirit. The Mother's hands moved faster. Her flock followed the tempo, clapping, rocking, nodding in time. The Mother bellowed her queries in the same meter, but faster now. Testimonies rang out like rifle shots. The Mother praised each one, chanting a rhythmic sing-song.

"I call down the Spirit—aché!—of the god of the earth! Praise be! I call down the Spirit—yes sir!—of the Lord of the skies! Amen! I call down the Spirit—aché—of the god of all Spirits! Amen! Come down! I call the Spirit—praise God!—to fill our hearts. Come down! Fill us now! Aché!"

The hypnotic litany gained speed. Mother Love equally thanked the wind and sun and rain, ancestors, spirits and saints. Her followers joined in, shouting, "Amen!" and "Aché!"

Frank watched one of the old men touch his drum. He listened intently between pats, his eye following the Mother. He tapped to her rhythm, hesitant until he'd captured it, then he beat the skin firmly. Another man followed him, then one drummer after another picked up the beat. Deep boomings rolled under lighter, faster

170

notes. It sounded like raindrops falling into puddles while thunder rumbled in from an ugly horizon.

The rhythm was hypnotic and Frank had to force her concentration. At the front of the church, the Mother whirled round and around. Ropes of beads on her neck whirled in the same orbit, dizzyingly red and white. The Mother chanted half in English, half in a foreign language. Like Spanish, but not quite, Frank thought. Maybe Portuguese. She whipped her crowd with the mysterious words. They knew the refrain, joyfully shouting it in time. Standing, clapping, they danced and twirled in the aisles. One old man pounded his cane to the beat. His wife wiggled next to him, her arms waving in the air like thick snakes. A young girl writhed in the aisle, her eyes white where there should have been pupils.

The Mother danced and Frank watched. Seeing but not believing. The Mother carried almost sixty years on her wiry frame, yet she whirled with the force of a small tornado. Her red and white skirt blurred to pink. She turned faster than Frank's eye could follow. Bending her head to her toes, the Mother hurled herself backward with inhuman force. Frank was certain bone must have bent and muscle snapped, but the Mother whirled on.

The hair rose on Frank's skin.

The drummers pounded in glassy-eyed fury. Their hands galloped like headless horsemen across the plains of their drums. The Mother twirled faster, arching brutally and impossibly. She leapt like a jungle cat, landing on hands and knees. Then she twisted and rose, continuing the dance, all the while calling down her dark gods.

The faithful fell about in fits. They screamed for Jesus or Saint Jerome to come into them. Some yelled names Frank didn't recognize. The din was mesmerizing. The drums sang an old song, as old as the first moon, and the crowd responded convulsively.

Frank sought Mother Love.

She stood at the pulpit, staring back. A grin twisted her sweating face. Recognition hit Frank like a sledgehammer. Memory replaced present time. She'd already been here. She relived the Mother's triumphal grin, the drums calling her to an ancient home, the rolling eyes and writhing bodies. The incense mingled with sweat, the leafy church, and cries to heaven—it all played in Frank's head with a familiarity that made her dizzy.

The chimera passed as quickly as it had come. Frank drew a hand over her face, unable to look at the Mother. It was enough to hear her keening in the crowd, a wolfish howling that made Frank's blood tingle. Frank stood, clutching the pew in front of her.

The drummers began to slow. The Mother walked among her followers making sure none had hurt themselves in the frenzy. Frank watched the Mother soothe her faithful, bringing them up, down, or wherever they needed to be. The drumming ebbed to a single instrument beating the time of a resting heart. The Mother worked her way to the back of the church.

After drying her tears, Frank's father had taught her how to place a chokehold and lay a chop at the back of the knees. How to roll and block and land a double chin shot. How to jab and hook. Watching the Mother come down the aisle, Frank doubted any of that would help her now.

"I knew you'd come," the Mother said. Her voice was smoky and sweet. "You couldn't resist. You're like a child after candy."

She leaned closer. Frank smelled the flowery bodega scent and sweat and the dust of dry places.

"My church is open," she whispered. "Come join us."

The invitation was sensual and erotic, a lover's desire. Frank had an urge to get up and follow the Mother, to dance with her around a blood-red fire in a place where beasts still stirred beyond the pale. She wanted to cry at the moon then bow low to receive the warm sacrament . . .

Frank was surprised to hear herself say, "Never."

The Mother's wolfish eyes almost closed. In a voice like snakes slithering over each other, she warned, "Don't be so sure, child. Never's a very long time."

172

29

Darcy leaned in after the briefing.

"Can I talk to you?"

"Sure."

He closed the door and perched on one of her chairs.

"Marguerite called last night. She says she's worried about you."

"Me?"

He nodded.

"She says you don't know what you're into, but that it's bigger than you can handle. She wants you to go see her."

"What for?"

Darcy shrugged.

"She says you need a cleansing and some serious protection. She sees bad juju all over you."

"Bad juju, huh?"

Frank grinned, partly out of condescension and partly to

convince herself the Mother's malevolence last night had been routine good guy-bad guy antagonism. Ignoring the reptilian voice asking, *then why were you so scared*, she concentrated on Darcy and how much money he made. She knew he couldn't foot too much for alimony *and* child support and wondered if Marguerite thought she had a fish on the line.

"How much she gonna charge me?"

"I don't know. That's irrelevant. The thing is, she wouldn't call like that unless she had a good reason. Marguerite's very selective about who she works with. New clients all have to be recommended by established clients. She doesn't deal with dabblers."

Her logic crippled, Frank admitted, "Look. I just don't get any of this hocus-pocus, mumbo-jumbo shit."

Darcy shot back, "You don't have to get it. It'll happen whether you believe in it or not."

The only sign of Frank's annoyance was the slight jump in her jaw.

"What'll happen?"

"I mean if Marguerite sees the Mother's influence around you, then it's there. It's like radon. Just because we can't see it, that doesn't mean it's not there doing damage."

"Everybody keeps saying you have to believe in this shit to make it work. How can the Mother hurt me if I don't believe in her?"

Darcy hunched forward. He was about to speak but stopped. Frank gave him the time he needed to pull his words together.

"Remember when you asked me if I believed in voodoo?"

The question wasn't rhetorical, so Frank nodded.

"And what did I say?"

"Somewhat."

"And I told you not to underestimate the Mother, right?"

Frank tapped her watch.

"Where we going, Darcy?"

"To a place you don't know anything about. I know you've got no reason to believe me, but all I can tell you is that I've seen situations that defy practical explanation. Marguerite's cousin was my best friend. I practically lived with him and I spent a lot of time with his family. We used to stay out at his uncle's in Simmesport, go hunting and get drunk, just being boys. This was in the back country, where the old ways are still pretty common. Jeff had a couple, three-four aunts and uncles up there. Understand, the LaCourts had been there a long time. They were part of a pretty tightly knit community. A lot of the women called themselves root workers. Some were better at it than others because they had a talent for it. A gift. Jeff's grandmother, Pearl LaCourt, she was one of those women. All the other root workers came to Pearl when they needed advice or couldn't help themselves. She was tremendously respected. And feared. Hell, even I was afraid of her, and I was too young and stupid to be afraid of anything."

Frank tapped her fingers against the desk and Darcy said, "I know. My point is I knew her fairly well. I didn't just hear stories about her or catch a glimpse of her on the porch now and then. I spent almost every weekend and half as many weekdays up to Jeff's and every Saturday evening we'd go to revival. It was out in a scythed field behind the church which was really just poles and a roof with hay bales and stumps for seats. I know that sounds like a strange way for two hell-loving, hormone-addled boys to spend a Saturday night, but for one thing, Marguerite was there.

"Even more importantly, I *wanted* to go. Jeff too. We only talked about it once, after the first time he took me, and then we never mentioned it again. Jeff couldn't explain what happened. It'd just always been that way. That was all. These people accepted that his seventy-year-old grandmother could suddenly jump up in the air and do somersaults like a girl a quarter her age. They accepted that a bite from a copperhead could cure arthritis. They accepted that Loula Tremaine's husband fell down a well and drowned while she was at the revival praying for God to wash his wife-beating sins away.

"Jeff had a cousin that liked little girls. No one did anything about it because he was a big, mean, son of a bitch and everyone was afraid of him. The last girl he raped started praying at the revivals for vengeance. The women would join in with her, crying and praying. A month after he'd raped her, a car punched out his backbone. He's a quadriplegic."

Frank interrupted, "That's coincidence."

Darcy shook his head. "That's the tip of the iceberg. Things like this happened routinely. It was a matter of course. No one thought anything of it. I could go on, Frank, but I know you don't want me to. The point is, not every question has an answer. When the bounds of coincidence and logic get stretched, one has to accept the inexplicable or go crazy trying to figure it out. Jeff's cousin didn't believe. Loula Tremaine's husband didn't believe. I can name a dozen other examples."

Frank held up a hand.

"So Marguerite's a root worker too? I thought you said she was a priestess."

"She grew up with root workers, in the hoodoo tradition, but it wasn't enough for her. She wanted to learn more and went to Haiti to study Vodun religion. That was when her talents really emerged."

"Like being able to see the Mother's evil influence on me," Frank mocked. "Think she could tell if I'm going to meet a tall, handsome stranger?"

Darcy's answer was slow in coming.

"She knew there was something wrong with Gabby even before she was born. The doctors didn't pick up on it but Marguerite knew. She kept saying Gabby's lungs were heavy. She's got cystic fibrosis."

Frank regretted her flippancy, but maintained a mother could intuit something wrong with an unborn child without being psychic. Sensing her doubt, Darcy added, "It's not just Gabby. She sees a lot of things. She saw the Oklahoma bombing. She was seeing it for about a week before it happened. She had this picture in her head of the building blowing up and scores of people dying. It got stronger and clearer the closer it got to that day. She actually pegged the time of the explosion by an hour. It was that strong. Only she thought it was a building in L.A. She didn't realize where it was. Not that it would have mattered anyway. Who'd have believed her?"

"Did she tell you this *post facto*?"

"No. I was picking up Gabby the weekend before it happened, and she was pretty upset. It was hard for her to keep seeing it, knowing it was coming, and not being able to do anything about it. Then it happened that Wednesday."

"And you just accept all that?"

"I do," he said simply. "I accept without understanding. It happens to me sometimes, too. That's one of the things she hates about me. She thinks I'm lazy, because I have a gift and won't use it. I tried, but it's just not for me. It's not an avenue I want to explore anymore than I already have."

"Great. You're telling me I'm sitting here and you can see what color my underwear are?"

Darcy blushed.

"I'm not that good. I just get glimpses now and then. Like when I saw that kid stashed in the dumpster. I think it's something everybody has. Cops use it all the time, only we call it instinct or a hunch. Some of us just listen more than others."

Frank couldn't argue with that. Listening to her instinct wasn't always logical, but it was usually right.

"She gave me her card. Told me she saw the Mother's hand on me. Like a black cloud."

"What did you say?"

"Told her I could take care of it."

Darcy assessed his boss, then shrugged.

"Maybe you can. But if I were you, I wouldn't risk it."

Frank sat back, sighing. "I gotta tell you, I'm tired of all this superstitious shit. I'm trying to solve murders here and for all I know half my squad's packing silver bullets and garlic necklaces. You'd think there'd be a little more logic to all this."

177

Darcy stood with his palms up.

"Hey," he groused, "don't shoot the messenger. I'm just telling you what she said. Maybe if you weren't so defensive about all this you could see that *logically* you've got nothing to lose by seeing her."

He strolled out, leaving Frank stewing in her skepticism.

30

What the hell, she'd rationalized all the way down the 405. She had questions Marguerite might be able to answer, and she'd been meaning to visit Orange County Sheriff's anyway. She'd called Homicide and set a time to go through a couple of their murder books. Frank hoped they might tie into a series of execution-style hits the nine-three caught in June. Her appointment was at two-thirty. Meanwhile, here she was back in Marguerite James' apartment.

Dressed all in white, Marguerite had led her in with no preliminaries.

"This will be easier and more effective if you take all your clothes off."

Frank folded her arms and stared.

Indicating a chair in the center of the room, Marguerite said, "At least your shoes and socks then. And your belt and everything in your pockets. I want the energy to move through you as freely as possible."

Frank did as instructed, suppressing a sigh. Entertaining this new-age, woo-woo crap was embarrassing. If anybody found out, she'd pull a Sandman on Darcy's ass.

"What exactly are you going to do?"

"Did you ever play with a Wooly Willy when you were a child?"

"A Wooly Willy," Frank repeated. "Was that the bald guy with metal shavings you made hair with?"

"Exactly. That's similar to what I'm going to do. I'm going to draw the shavings off you, then I'm going to put a fresh new set of them around you."

"But I'm not a Wooly Willy."

"No, but you do have an energy field. Call it an aura if you like."

"So you're going to rearrange my aura?"

"Like that, yes."

"Is it going to hurt?"

Marguerite scowled and lifted a brow. It was a look Frank would know well by the end of the day.

"Basically, I'm going to do to you what I did to Mr. Hernandez. I'll cleanse you, then we'll invoke the proper spirits and ask for protection. While we're doing this I want you to picture this woman. Envision a large black envelope flying straight toward her. You're going to send all her negativity back to her."

Frank joked, "How much postage do I use?"

"Lieutenant, I assume you've come here for a reason. Now be silent and let me do my work."

Frank watched Marguerite fussing with jars of herbs and a pitcher of water. She started singing, her voice light and soft. Frank thought the words sounded French, Creole maybe. She came to Frank, still singing, dabbing at her roughly with a rag she kept dipping into the pitcher. Frank closed her eyes. She felt like a kitten getting cleaned by its mother and despite her cynicism, she felt oddly safe.

Marguerite finished and went back to the table. Frank asked, "So what else do you know about Mother Love?"

"I know she's widely respected in certain circles. That she is much feared and venerated."

"Do you respect her?"

Marguerite pursed her lips.

"I respect her abilities but I don't respect what she does with them."

"And what's that?"

"When a person of power uses their gifts for personal profit, it's called working with the left hand. Instead of using her gifts for healing, she uses them for material betterment. I've heard she's a fine healer, but that many of her clients enlist her for protection against criminal activity. It's people like Mother Love that give my religion such a bad image. She's a powerful *sorciere*. Very old."

"What's a *sorciere*?"

"A sorceress. A witch."

"Is that what you are?"

Grinding a white powder with a mortar and pestle, Marguerite clarified, "I'm a *mambo*. I can do the same things as a *sorciere* but I work with the right hand. I do what I do for the good of all rather than for profit or gain. That's the difference."

"Like the difference between a dedicated surgeon and a hack."

"Exactly. Hush now."

Marguerite knelt before Frank. Dribbling the powder between her fingers she drew a design around Frank's chair.

"You said she was very old. She's only fifty-nine."

"Fifty-nine in this lifetime"—the mambo frowned—"but she is an ancient soul. One of the oldest I've ever felt."

"What's it mean if she writes a name on a piece of paper and ties it up in a beef tongue?"

Marguerite glanced at Frank like she was expecting her leg to be pulled.

"Did she do that to you?"

"Hernandez' cohort. Left it on his front door. Wife went ballistic."

"Where I come from, that's how the two-headed women cursed someone who told secrets. They'd write his or her name on a piece of paper and then put it into a slit cow tongue. They'd add pepper, sulphur, and nine coffin nails, then tie it up and leave it where the person it's intended for would have to pass by it. In nine days, the victim would die."

Frank suppressed a sigh. First the Mother killed Duncan, then Carrillo. Did she really plan on offing Hernandez and Echevarria too, or was she just freaking them? She had to know they weren't criminal masterminds, but maybe it was worth the trouble if she could appease her twisted notion of a god at the same time.

"Do these *sorcieres* make human sacrifices?"

"Everything's possible," Marguerite said.

"Likely?" Frank pushed.

"I couldn't say. I only know my own business. Just because I would never do such a thing doesn't mean she won't. But you have to understand, most tales of human sacrifice are purely sensationalism."

"And you have to admit it happens, like in Matamoros."

Marguerite said nothing.

"Assuming she is, would it make sense that Mother Love'd burn some victims and cut others?"

"It would depend on who she was making offerings to."

"So it wouldn't be inconsistent to light some victims and bleed others?"

"No. Now hush."

Frank did as instructed, vaguely distracted by Marguerite's supple movements.

"What are you doing?"

"This is called a *vevé*. Each spirit has its own design that it recognizes. We draw these to attract the spirit we're seeking."

"And which spirit are we seeking today?"

"Spirits," Marguerite corrected. "First Elegua. He's the master of the crossroads. He opens the gates, so to speak. And then Shango, as we did with Mr. Hernandez. He is the god to propitiate when a supplicant desires revenge or protection."

"But that's the Mother's god."

Marguerite's smile was patient.

"Do you think Jesus Christ belongs only to one person? We'll have to coax him and appease his fiery nature. We do this by offering him the things he loves."

"Roosters and crabs," Frank interjected.

Lifting a brow, Marguerite said, "You've been doing your homework. Therefore you must know that if we treat him well and respectfully, he will work with us."

Frank nodded to an altar in a corner of the room.

"That's for him?"

"Yes."

Marguerite finished her drawing. It was nothing Frank recognized.

"Do you have a god?"

"Yes."

"Which one?"

Marguerite smiled and all her harshness vanished.

"Are you always this talkative, Lieutenant, or just nervous?"

Standing over Frank, she daubed oil onto her face. Frank closed her eyes, aware how near Marguerite's breasts were. Her scent was rich and heavy and Frank hoped she couldn't read her mind.

"Just curious. I'm out of my realm here. Trying to understand something which makes no sense to me. So which is your god?"

"Ezili Freda," Marguerite said tenderly.

"Is that a good one?"

"They're all good. And they're all bad. They have human natures like we do. They can be angered, then they can be appeased. They can be funny or serious. They love a good time."

Marguerite pulled jars of herbs from a bookshelf. Mixing the

183

contents in a little clay bowl, she lit them, waving the smoke onto Frank.

"I'll be right back," she said, slipping out the door. When she returned, she was holding a large black rooster upside down by its legs. The animal didn't flap or struggle. She raised it toward Frank, stopping with it over her head when Frank asked, "What are you doing?"

"There are different remedies for different maladies," she explained. "Some spells can be counteracted and eliminated. Depending on the curse and the power of the person who has placed it. The stronger spells cannot be entirely removed. What we do with these is displace them. That's what I'm going to do to you. I'm going to draw off the negative energy and feed it to Shango. The gods are so much stronger than we are. What would cripple us, doesn't even faze them."

"What do you mean feed it?"

"Hush," Marguerite scolded again. "You'll see."

Again the thin high song. The mambo drew the uncomplaining bird over Frank's limbs and torso. Frank thought it was all pretty fucking weird, yet didn't stop it.

Marguerite held the cock over a bowl and before Frank could even think to protest she'd cleanly sliced its throat. She sang over the draining body, then returned to Frank. She poked a finger in the bird's neck. Frank watched the bloody finger come toward her, felt the sticky warm line Marguerite drew on her forehead. Dipping into the bird's neck again, she drew a line on Frank's cheek, still singing her calm, sweet song.

Tilting the stump to Frank, she ordered, "Touch your tongue to it."

"No way." Frank shook her head.

"You must."

"No."

Still Marguerite held the bird to her. Frank watched blood ooze around the neck bone. Marguerite moved the bird closer to Frank's lips.

"Go ahead," she commanded, gentle but insistent. "Don't be afraid."

Frank glanced from the headless bird to Marguerite. She stood before Frank, implacable and unyielding, yet oddly comforting. At a level she couldn't and wouldn't analyze, Frank trusted the mambo. She touched her tongue to the warm flesh. Marguerite continued her singing. Frank closed her eyes, the tang of rust in her mouth.

At the altar, the mambo mixed oils and herbs. She sang while she dressed the dead bird with the mixture. When she finished her song, she presented Frank with a small bundle. It looked like a silk onion decorated with ribbons and beads.

"Put this by your bed and leave it there."

"What is it?"

"It's a *paquette*, an offering to Shango. Leave it near you, where he can find it and watch over you. On your dashboard or by your bed."

"Why would Shango care about me? Isn't he busy enough looking out for people who actually believe in him?"

"*I* believe, Lieutenant. And for the time being that will have to do."

Her face clouded. She cocked her head, seemed about to say something, then stopped. Frank didn't think much about it when she said, "You have my number. Call if you need me."

"We're done?"

Marguerite nodded, opening the office door. As they walked out, Frank started to wipe the blood from her face.

"No! Leave it for at least an hour."

"Oh, sure. They'll love this over at Homicide."

Frank pulled her wallet from her pocket but Marguerite firmly pushed it away.

"*Lagniappe*," she said. "Where I come from that means a little something extra. This one's on the house, Lieutenant. I'm just glad you came."

Frank studied the rich brown eyes. They seemed to hold an ancient lineage of secrets, secrets Frank didn't want to know about.

185

"I don't get it. What's in it for you?"

Marguerite smiled. "Why are you a detective?"

"It's what I'm good at."

"What brought you to it?"

"I like catching bad guys."

"Are you one of the good guys?"

"I like to think so."

"Then it's true to say you at least believe in good and bad?"

"Yes," Frank allowed.

"You have the skills, the training, and the experience to catch bad people and protect innocent people, yes?"

"On a good day."

"I do the same thing you do, Lieutenant. Only you do it on a physical level. I do it on a metaphysical level. I have the skills and the knowledge to stop bad people and to protect innocent people." Marguerite jutted her head toward the window, asking, "Orange County's not in your jurisdiction, is it?"

"No."

"If you see a murder happening when you walk out this door will you just keep walking?"

"Big difference between this and a murder."

Marguerite frowned. "Not nearly as much as you'd like to think, Lieutenant. Good day."

31

"Hi. You're home early."

Gail was at her computer and Frank kissed her quickly, hoping she didn't stink of chicken blood.

"I had a drink with Johnnie and left. Figured the company was better here."

"Well, *that's* flattering."

"It is," Frank insisted, stripping her clothes off by the bathroom door. "You don't know how many times I've closed the Alibi with him."

"I don't *want* to know," Gail called as Frank stepped into the shower.

While the hot water sluiced away the day's strangeness, Frank debated telling Gail about her trip to Marguerite's. She decided against it, not wanting to spook the doc with stories about bad juju and blood sacrifices.

Toweling herself off, Frank was dismayed by what she saw in the mirror. Since she'd started dating Gail, she'd been eating more and working out less. She scowled at the belly forming over her blonde pubic hair. She jumped when Gail's image appeared behind her.

Gail grinned, "Do you like what you see?"

"Needs a little work," Frank admitted, wrapping the terrycloth around her waist. Gail trailed her fingers along Frank's spine, then over her toweled flank. The gesture was irksome and Frank tried to figure why she was wrapped so tight. Watching in the mirror, Gail asked, "Want to go to Kabuki's? Get an eel roll? A spider roll?"

"Why can't they give 'em better names?" Frank grinned. Belying her discomfort, she turned to hold Gail. She studied the doc's easy features, noting, "You must've taken your whole bottle of beautiful pills today. You know, you can't OD on those, but the people looking at you can. Be careful you don't make my heart stop one of these days."

Gail's response to Frank's compliments had evolved from self-deprecation to bemused silence. She smiled at her lover and Frank relaxed into their embrace.

She said into Gail's hair, "Let's go eat creepy-sounding food," but made no motion toward that end other than to glide her lips along Gail's neck. Gail tilted her head, encouraging the silky kisses. Like a candle left in the sun, Frank's tension liquefied. She felt her towel slip to the floor, unable to imagine how she could have ever found Gail's touch irritating.

When Frank staggered back from her, they were both bewildered, staring wide at each her. She heard Gail asking, "What's the matter?" but couldn't answer.

"Frank, what is it?"

Frank felt like a zombie. She could hear and feel and see but she couldn't respond. Gail stepped in front of her, looking scared. She touched Frank, and like the princess kissing the toad, she broke the spell.

"Jesus," Frank gasped. She groped for the sink and leaned over it like she was going to be sick. Gail hovered over her, asking "What's wrong? Baby, what is it?"

All Frank could do was shake her head, croaking, "Gimme a sec."

She remembered to breathe. In and out. That was enough for right now. In and out. She focused on the effort, aware of Gail's worry and the slick porcelain under her hands. Time was long for Frank, but after what was probably no more than a quarter minute, she swallowed hard and straightened. She brushed past Gail, saying, "I gotta get some clothes on."

Frank dressed quickly, ignoring Gail's silhouette in the doorway. When she tried slipping around her, Gail grabbed her arm, demanding, "Frank, what happened?"

She tried to find an answer in Gail's face, but it wasn't there. She put her hands on Gail's waist. She shook her head. "I don't know," was all she could say, and then she repeated it.

"Are you hurt?" Gail asked. "Is it your hand?"

"No," Frank insisted, folding the doc against her. "Jesus fucking Christ. I don't know what happened."

Her lips dumbly sought the comfort of Gail's neck, but Frank made a point to keep her eyes open, lest she slip back into that eerie place. The doc pulled away.

"You're starting to scare me."

"Shit," Frank choked with a half laugh-half sob, "I'm scaring myself. Come on," she added, tugging Gail to the couch, "I gotta sit."

She'd just as soon have a couple drinks and put the whole bizarre scene out of her mind, but Gail's silent expectation made Frank fumble for an explanation.

"It was like . . ." She couldn't go on because it was unlike anything Frank had ever felt before.

"It was like I left my body and walked into the bathroom and was watching us. It was so . . . *vivid*. I could see the towel and the loops it's made of. Then your arm shifted and in the shadow between us I could see the flatness where your breast used to be. It was so

189

normal. It was natural, like it had always been that way, like it was *supposed* to be that way. It felt like the whole thing had already happened—us, standing there, making out, me in a towel. It was like I'd scripted a movie and now I was watching it being filmed."

Frank gave her head a hard shake and swore.

"I been having these little déjà vus," she continued, "but this one. It was overpowering. I mean I wasn't even there. I was *gone*, Gail. I was *watching* us. From somewhere else. I wasn't me. I wasn't inside my own body."

Frank stood up and started pacing in a tight circle, Gail watching her. The doc's silence disappointed Frank. She wanted Gail to make it go away, to say something that would explain it all. Suddenly Frank demanded, "Am I losing my fucking mind or what?"

Gail's chuckle was small but comforting. She approached Frank and put her arms around her.

"While it's certainly a possibility I don't think it's the first conclusion we should jump to."

"Give me a better one."

"We-ll," Gail pointed out. "You've been working as hard as you always do. You swill coffee all day and never eat. You drink too much," she added gingerly. "And when was the last time you got a decent night's sleep? You're getting older, you know. You can't push yourself like you used to. At some point your body's going to rebel."

"So you *do* think I'm crazy."

"That's not crazy. It's just your body's way of saying maybe you'd better start taking care of yourself."

"So you think it's perfectly normal to have an out of body experience while you're cupcaking your girlfriend?"

Gail swooned against Frank, exclaiming, "Well, if cupcaking's what I think it is, I *always* have an out of body experience when you cupcake me."

"Very funny."

"It's true," Gail insisted. "I wouldn't worry about it if I were you. But I would consider taking better care of myself."

Gail tried to hold her, but Frank was too jumpy.

"Maybe you're right. Maybe I'm just getting old and need to get some sleep. I should go home, have a peanut butter sandwich and a glass of milk. Go to bed. I'm sure everything'll be fine in the morning," Frank lied, trying like hell to believe her own bullshit. Gail looked crestfallen and Frank had to step away.

"Baby," Gail started, "just stay. I'll make you something to eat. It's not a big deal."

"Making something to eat's not a big deal?"

"No. I mean whatever's going on with you. I'm sure it's nothing. Why don't—"

"Oh, you're sure it's nothing," Frank bridled. "Does this diagnosis come from your years of expertise in dealing with humanity or is this something you actually learned in med school?"

"What are you getting so upset about?"

"I'm not upset. I'm insane, remember?"

"Frank, I never said that. I just think you had a mild reaction to something. It happens all the time and you're making a mountain out of a molehill."

"Oh, really?" Frank said, nodding. "Is that what I'm doing?"

"Well, look at you."

Frank didn't want to look at herself. She wanted to get the hell out of there and go home. And fuck the peanut butter and milk—she was headed straight for the Scotch bottle. She gathered her work clothes, refilling the pockets with what she'd emptied onto the kitchen table.

Gail watched her, finally muttering, "You are being such an asshole."

"Then I guess you'll be happy when I'm gone," Frank answered, yanking at the door and slamming it shut behind her.

Frank was making love to Gail but Marguerite was in her head. Marguerite, naked and dancing, her huge breasts unbound, pushing into Frank's face. Frank's desire grew like rage. She felt starved for Gail and bit at her neck. The doc cried out, on one side or the other of the thin line between pain and passion. Frank didn't care which. She followed the exquisite hunger, steering Gail backwards toward her darkened bedroom. She chewed at Gail's neck, dragging her lover into the dark, like a lion dragging a gazelle into its lair.

Through the red haze of desire, Frank saw candles burning. Someone was beating a drum. Then she was dancing around a fire with a billion stars in her hair. She was naked and Marguerite was naked and the Mother was there, all of them dancing around the fire. Around and around they paraded, and Frank's hunger grew and swelled, roiling and crashing like waves pounding a sea. The Aegean sea at midnight. Fire on the shore. Women dancing under an ageless moon. Drums pounding in their heads like blood.

As happens in dreams, Frank was suddenly clothed, and she pulled the 9mm from under her jacket. Its grip was comforting. She trained the sight on the Mother. Fired. Again and again, but the Mother only laughed. She wouldn't go down. The bullets didn't even seem to hit her. Frank was a good shot and she was close. She couldn't have missed. How could she not be killing the Mother?

She trained the gun on herself, staring down the barrel.

"Go ahead," the Mother laughed. "Pull the trigger."

Marguerite kept dancing, a thousand secrets smiling from her eyes.

"You always have a choice," she shrugged.

Frank's finger was squeezing the trigger. She was afraid she was going to fire but she couldn't turn the gun around. She couldn't move it and her finger was getting tighter and tighter on the trigger.

She woke up screaming, *"Drop the gun! Drop the gun!"*

Frank rolled off the couch. She was up in an instant, looking for the Beretta, waiting to see the Mother holding it on her. There was nothing. Just the familiar reality of her den. Frank's head pounded and the overhead light hurt her eyes. But she didn't want to turn it off.

She stumbled to the bathroom, disgusted with the nightmare sweat sticking to her skin. She couldn't get into the shower fast enough. Not for the first time that night she wondered what the fuck was wrong with her.

She remembered storming out of Gail's, amazed at the pique she'd gotten into. She'd felt pretty stupid by the time she got home, but still angry. A couple stiff shots brought her down. She paced and drank, trying to figure out if she was just stressed like Gail said, or going postal, or something else. It was the something else that Frank had done a dark tango with all night. While not appealing, going nuts didn't seem nearly as frightening as Marguerite's postulation that the Mother was fucking with her head.

Frank stood in the shower, thinking that when you put all the weird events together, it made sense. As much as any of this could make sense. She'd had baby déjà vus before—she couldn't remember where or what about, but Frank had recognized the feeling when it happened at the Mother's. It had been a little odd and kind of disconcerting, but she'd forgotten about it. Then it happened again, twice, when the dog bit her. The déjà vu about the dog attack had been wildly clear. Frank hadn't been able to dismiss that so lightly, nor the freaky vision of the Mother standing in pools of blood. That had been slightly less real, but just as uncomfortable. Then it had happened again at the church and last night at Gail's. That last one was the granddaddy of the déjà vus, more powerful and absolutely real.

Realizing the visions were getting stronger, she shivered in the hot water. She turned it off, and put on her robe, even though she was still wet. Frank connected the dots, starting with the little déjà vu in the Mother's office, then the dog. No, she corrected, then she'd seen that thing in rags, right after the first déjà vu, right after she'd left the Mother's.

Frank had never seen this bum before, then all of a sudden the fucking thing's everywhere, even seeming to follow her. But that was impossible, right? As impossible as its being able to see out of those ruined eyes or let itself out of a locked interrogation box. (Frank had subsequently quizzed the entire station house—no one except Darcy had even admitted to seeing the relic).

There was the dream, too, with the relic and the soldier. That hadn't been as intense as the déjà vus, but it had been awfully real-istic. Familiar, was the word. Like Frank intimately knew that soldier in the carnage. Then the dog mauled her, a red dog, just like the Mother said. Coincidence? Possibly. As coincidental as anything else. But how coincidental was the timing of the events, and their growing frequency and intensity?

Frank wandered into the kitchen. She made coffee even though she'd rather have a drink. She rationalized that despite it being Saturday and despite that she wasn't on call, only drunks drank first thing in the morning. She might be going crazy, but she wasn't a drunk. Throwing away yesterday's coffee grounds, she saw Marguerite James's business card lying on top of the garbage like a little white surrender flag.

Frank took it out and put it on the counter. She ignored it until after she got the coffee brewing, then she smoothed the crumpled card against the tiles. It was barely five AM, but Frank grabbed the phone. If she didn't do it now she never would.

"It's Lieutenant Franco. Look, I'm sorry to wake you but I have to ask you something."

Marguerite had answered sleepily, but she sounded fully alert when she answered, "Yes?"

Frank sucked in a deep breath and told Marguerite everything. The déjà vus, the thing in rags, the dog, the dreams—everything.

"What the hell does it all mean?"

"I'm not sure," Marguerite came back. Frank thought Marguerite was hedging until she said, "For want of a better expla-nation, I'd liken it to a psychic awakening."

"What the fuck does that mean?" Frank asked in another abnor-mal burst of impatience.

"Lieutenant. It's five-fifteen in the morning. I don't care to be sworn at."

"I'm sorry," Frank gritted out. "This is a little new to me."

"Of course it is."

Marguerite sounded strong and reassuring.

"Basically, whether you believe it or not, Mother Love has awakened an innate psychic ability within you. At an instinctual level, you are aware of the threat she represents to you. Your psyche is trying to defend you, regardless of your lack of belief in her abilities and your ignorance of your own."

Bullshit, Frank wanted to say and hang up, but she'd made the call and she'd tough it out.

"What am I defending myself against?"

"Her intentions. That's the black pall I feel around you. Thoughts are energy, Lieutenant. Intentions are energy. Subtle yes, but effective in quantity and over time. And especially damaging when the source is able to focus her will and concentration as effectively as this woman apparently can."

"But why me?" Frank interrupted. "There are two other cops working this case. Why isn't she attacking them?"

Or maybe she is, Frank thought and they're not spilling. Impossible. She knew her cops too well. If this shit was going down on them, Noah would be the first in line to bitch about it and Frank was sure Lewis wouldn't be far behind.

"You there?"

"Yes. Bear with me."

Frank held on, wondering what the hell Marguerite was doing.

"I don't think this is about your work. Maybe inadvertently it is, but this . . . *malice* I feel around you, is much older than any case you're working on. It feels extremely old. It has an archaic form. I can't explain it more clearly than that. And I'm not sure it matters. What does matter is that you need help."

Marguerite abruptly switched gears.

"Are you a Christian, Lieutenant?"

"No. I'm not anything."

"Do you believe in any spiritual beings?"

"No."

"Yet you're calling me at five o'clock in the morning. Why is that?"

"I thought you could explain this."

"A Catholic priest could give you an explanation as well. Why didn't you call one of them?"

Frank almost shuddered, seeing Father Merrin stumbling in the ruins.

"Look, I'm sorry I bothered you. I didn't—"

"I'm not bothered, Lieutenant. What I'm asking is, why are you seeking an explanation from me when you know the answer I'll give you?"

Ah, now Frank saw it. Marguerite was good. She'd backed Frank into a corner and blocked the only exit. She should have been a cop.

"All right. You win. Can you help me?"

"I've won nothing, Lieutenant. This isn't about me. This is between you and that woman. I wanted to tell you this earlier, but I knew you'd laugh. I think you're finally ready to hear it."

Christ, now what? Switching the phone to her aching right hand, Frank sank her head into the palm of her left. The silence was so long Frank said, "You there?"

"Yes . . . I think it's so easy for me to see this because you are completely unaware and make no effort to hide it. I saw this when you walked into my house with Mr. Hernandez. It stunned me actually, but what could I have said? You wouldn't have believed me."

Another silence. This time Frank waited. She'd kill for a drink. Great, she thought, Johnnie and I should be going to AA meetings together.

"You have a tremendous power about you. I can see it as easily as I see this other woman's power. But where hers pulls in energy like a dark star, yours is *bright*. It pulses a wonderful light. And it seems very old, something you've carried for many, many lifetimes."

Frank rubbed at her eyes, not believing this conversation. Not believing she hadn't hung up yet.

"It's more like a shield, really. It envelops you and protects you for the work you do. You see, you've always been a warrior. For a very long time. Maybe always."

Marguerite's words jarred loose the image of the dream soldier, forever fighting.

"You're in a battle now," the mambo went on. "And it's not the first time. I can't see all your enemies, but I feel Mother Love so strongly upon you. And just as strongly, I can feel your courage and compassion. You will fight because you *have* to, not because you want to. You don't like to fight, but it's what you must do and you do it well. It appears to be your destiny."

Just like the soldier's, Frank thought. He didn't like it either, but it was what he had to do. He left the dead in the blowing sand and went on. Father Merrin, running after him, out of time. The dogs snarling in the desert. The red dog. *"Cry havoc and let slip the the dogs of war."*

"And Lieutenant?"

Marguerite brought Frank back.

"Make no mistake. This is a battle to the end."

Sure it was. Frank could see that with the soldier's eye. Her mind still tripped in puddles of confusion, but her *bones* knew. They understood what her brain couldn't. Darcy had said he accepted without understanding. Yeah, she could go that far. It all made sense in a way that couldn't be made sense of.

"A battle," Frank repeated.

"Yes."

And though she was sure of the answer, she had to ask.

"Who's winning?"

197

32

Lucian had the gift too. And it had been getting stronger. He hadn't told his mother that. Though he worshipped her with the awe of a child, like a child, he had come of age.

"You know, that decided it for me when Mama made me lay which you," he said to Lavinia. "Don't matter that we was already. She didn't know about that. That was what decided my mind for me. That she could go against her own children like that. It ain't right."

Lavinia snuggled into his ribs. Marcus was out collecting receipts and Mama Love was at the church. She had Lucian all to herself. Her silence helped Lucian justify his decision.

"She gonna bring us all down, she keep goin' on like this. I tried talkin' to her, but she just give me that bug-eye stare like she about to pop sense into my head. I love my mama, I do, but she won't listen to sense no more. Her head's got too big, n'mean? This seems harsh but it's the only way I can think of that you and me can be free and that this family can go on, n'mean?"

Lavinia's head rubbed assent against his chest. He felt himself getting hard again. Lavinia felt it too and her fingers encouraged his erection.

"Girl, what you doin'?" he asked.

"Takin' your mind off your troubles," she leered.

He slid down the sheets and took her into his big arms. He'd loved Lavinia from the first time he'd seen her. She knew after meeting Lucian she was dating the wrong brother, but by then it was too late. Marcus was already sweet on her. When she'd suggested breaking up Marcus had tattooed fist marks on her body. She and Lucian had tried to pretend the other didn't exist, but it had been impossible, living in the same house like they did. Finally they gave in.

Holding her hand against his heart, he said, "Not now, baby. We got to plan this out to the last detail. It all gots to go perfect or we fucked. And it's gotta go down soon."

Lucian rolled onto his back and Lavinia followed. Teasing him with her thigh, she asked, "Why's that? She ain't got nothing on us. Why it can't wait?"

"Cause that one-time's getting stronger. I can feel that, and I think Mama can too. And Mama's smart. She get her nose in this and I don't even want to think what could happen. Or if Marcus found out? Shit, girl."

Lucian shuddered under his brother's wife, "Uh-uh. It's gotta be soon. This weekend."

"Marcus don't know nothin'. He all about being a hater. He can't see nothing past his own anger."

"I know. He always been that way. And I'm countin' on that anger. We gonna turn it against him. And soon, baby girl. We can't wait no more."

"*I* can't wait no more," Lavinia corrected. Moving her hand down Lucian's broad belly she guided him into her waiting wetness.

33

The next morning Frank showed up at Gail's with lattes and croissants. It was a cheap bribe but it got her in the door.

"I'm sorry. You're right. I was an asshole."

Gail didn't say anything, but Frank thought it was a good sign that she plucked a croissant from the bag. She took a bite and flakes fell on the floor. Crumbs drove Frank nuts, but Gail never saw them. She seemed to be deliberately making a mess, but Frank refused the bait. Gail opened the lid off a coffee, and said, "You know, I'm still peeved. We hardly have any time together and then one of the few nights we do, you fly out of here on a broomstick."

Frank took the admonition with a small smile.

"I know. I fucked up. I'm sorry."

"And that's supposed to make it all okay?"

Instead of asking, *Now who's being the asshole?* Frank said, "It's over, Gail. I can't take it back. Do we stay mad or do we move on?"

Gail pouted. "I want to stay mad."

"If you were really mad," Frank wheedled, "you wouldn't be eating the food I brought."

"You're right." Gail sulked, dropping the croissant into the bag. Frank waited a beat.

"You know you want that."

Gail cast a longing eye over the greasy paper. Plucking the croissant back out, she declared, "Fight's over. I'm right. You were an asshole. I forgive you."

Frank smiled. Seeing as she was staying, she opened the other coffee.

"Look," she sighed. "I gotta tell you something. Might make my reaction last night a little more sensible."

"Well, in case we start fighting again, can I get a kiss first?"

Frank was happy to comply, after which they took breakfast out on the balcony.

"This is pretty bizarre, and it's probably going to sound as strange to you as it does to me, but here goes."

As she had a few hours ago, Frank admitted the events of the past few weeks. She added the last visit to Marguerite and their phone conversation. When she finished, Gail asked, "Why didn't you tell me all this earlier?"

"I didn't want to worry you. You were worried enough when I told you about the Mother the first time. I figured this would just worry you more. Besides, I didn't think it was anything worth mentioning."

"You didn't find any of this rather odd?"

"Not really. I mean it is in retrospect, and all put together, but at the time I just thought it was so much coincidence. Weird coincidence, but coincidence nonetheless."

Gail sat back with her feet on the railing while Frank considered the doc had cornered the market on great legs.

"Are you telling me you're *possessed*?"

"No," Frank laughed. "At least I don't think so. I mean, from

201

what I can gather, the Mother's just putting some bad vibes on me. It's like two phone lines getting crossed. Marguerite says—"

"And don't you think that's kind of odd that you *just happen* to hire a cop who *just happens* to have a wife that's a mambo priestess?"

"Ex wife. Again, in retrospect, yeah. That's one more thing that's got me thinking this isn't coincidence. That maybe there really is a pattern to this. A reason I can't understand or explain, but that it's happening nonetheless."

"Gee, you think?"

"Come on, Gay, you've got to admit it's pretty hard to swallow."

"Oh, I'm the first to admit it's bizarre. But what I find even more bizarre is that you didn't tell me about this until now. If somebody took a shot at you or stabbed you with a hunting knife, would you tell me? Am I a part of your life or not?"

"You're the best part," Frank replied without hesitation.

"Then why don't you talk to me? This all sounds pretty serious."

Frank saw Gail was hurt. She put herself in the doc's place, trying on how she'd feel if Gail was holding back on her.

"I'm sorry. You know, the main thing is, I probably didn't tell you because I didn't want to hear what you'd have to say about it. I didn't want to deal with it. I still don't, but it's looking like I don't have much choice."

Frank remembered Marguerite's dream words. She edged away from the memory, adding, "By not talking about all this I didn't have to admit how uncomfortable it makes me. I don't like dealing with stuff I can't touch or see. It's hard to fight something I don't even believe in."

Gail took Frank's hand.

"And the reason I still keep you around is because your candor, when it finally arrives, is completely disarming."

Frank acknowledged the comment with a mirthless smile. Swirling the dregs of her coffee, she admitted, "It's scary. I still don't know whether I'd rather believe this or that I'm flipping out. I was thinking I'd call Clay on Monday."

Frank had wanted to call the shrink last night, but he worked regular office hours. She continued, "He doesn't need to know about Glenda the Good Witch or the Wicked Witch of the West. I'll just outline what's been going on with me, see what he's got to say."

"It couldn't hurt. What did Glenda say about all this?"

Frank looked for derision in Gail's face, but found none. She drained her cup and sighed again.

"She told me to pray."

Frank had to go to the office. It was the center of her comfort zone and where she thought the best. She kissed Gail goodbye, making plans for an early dinner, then resigned herself to an hour in early afternoon traffic. Chin in hand, steering with her elbows, Frank reflected on Marguerite's advice.

She had told Frank she had to combat the Mother on a psychic level. When Frank had balked, Marguerite had spelled it out for her.

"Have you ever been with someone who knew what you were thinking even before you said it?"

Thinking of Noah, Frank had answered yes.

"How do you suppose that happens?"

"Shared history. Experience. Coincidence."

Coming to dislike that word, Frank had amended, "We just happen to think the same way."

"Fine. Can you include the possibility that you may have a connection deeper than that which appears on the surface? Would you be willing to consider a metaphysical explanation for why you have the same thought patterns?"

"Sure," Frank had caved. "What the hell. Why not?"

"I know I'm asking you to stretch, but remember, you called me."

Rub it in, Frank had thought.

"If you can have this unspoken bond with one person, what is there to say you couldn't have it with another?"

"Nothing, I guess."

"Exactly. And if this person is aware of that metaphysical connection, and using it, don't you think you'd be apt to feel it? Somehow?"

"I guess."

"Maybe you can understand it easier as instinct. Don't all cops have some sort of instinct?"

"Good ones. But again, that comes from experience. It's developed over time."

"When you were a rookie you never followed your instinct? You played it by the book always or did nothing?"

Frank remembered a couple good calls she'd made early on, but she also remembered some real boners.

"Look. Just tell me what I need to do. I don't have a lot of options right now, so I'm willing to follow your lead."

"Are you sure?"

"I've gone this far," Frank said, recalling the taste of blood in her mouth.

"I want you to get on your knees, Lieutenant, and pray."

"Pray?"

"Yes. It doesn't matter to whom. It can be Mickey Mouse or Joe Dimaggio. Just pray."

"Been a long time since I've done that."

"Yes, I know. Even if you don't believe it, or mean it, I want you to pray for help in defeating this woman. Because believe me, you can't beat her alone. I will do what I can but at some point that's not enough."

"I have to believe," Frank had finished for her.

"Exactly."

"What if I can't?"

"I wouldn't say."

"Couldn't or wouldn't?"

"You said you'd follow my lead, Lieutenant. Will you or won't you?"

Then it was Marguerite's turn to hang in the space between words.

"Guess I don't have a choice," Frank had conceded.

"That's ridiculous. You always have a choice. Either you will or you won't. This is as far as I can go with you, Lieutenant. The rest is up to you."

You always have a choice, Frank had silently repeated. That's what Marguerite had said in the dream last night when she was thinking of pulling the trigger on herself.

"Fine," Frank had relented. "I'll pray."

34

Frank cleared papers and folders off her desk pad. The pad was a monthly calendar where Frank usually scribbled phone numbers and names. She looked at today's date. There it was. In red pen.

Bembe 1730—Slauson

She stared a long time at the careful print. She remembered the Mother inviting her, but didn't remember writing down where or when. Maybe she *was* losing it. Which is easier to accept, she wondered, insanity or the idea that some crazy old broad was fucking with her head? Couched that way, the latter option looked more attractive.

At least Frank could do something about that. It was almost two o'clock. The way traffic was, she should give herself at least forty-five minutes to get to Slauson. That left her plenty of time to think about why she should go.

Danny Duncan's murder book was on Lewis's desk. Frank studied it, thought about calling Noah. What would she say? I want to bust the Mother today—what have you got on her? She'd just lectured Lewis the other day that homicide was a waiting game. Thing was, Frank didn't have much time to wait. How many more déjà vus would she have? Frank had been *gone* last night; she was somewhere out of herself and didn't care to repeat the experience. Was she just supposed to let them get stronger and longer until she didn't come out of it one day?

And what other weird shit was going to happen? What followed the crazed dog attack and The Thing in rags? Frank didn't even want to consider it. She *had* to beat the Mother, even if it meant playing on her own court, by her own rules. She always had a choice, Marguerite had said. She could choose to engage the Mother or not. Lying back and taking whatever life handed her wasn't Frank's style. Fighting was. She was good at it. Marguerite had said that too.

Frank shook her head. A week ago she didn't know Marguerite James's name. Now she was making life or death decisions based on the mambo's advice. She thought about calling Clay at home. She glanced at the clock. Two-twenty. Her eyes moved to Lewis's phone. She picked up the receiver, then replaced it.

No, her gut said. As crazy as this all sounded, she had to see it through. Go to the *bembe*, if for no other reason than to show the Mother she was still around and still watching. Sooner or later everyone got sloppy. Sooner or later everyone slipped. Frank would be waiting when the Mother did.

Maybe, Frank thought, she'd forgotten she'd invited her. Frank hoped she'd show up and startle the Mother. It'd be nice to have the shoe on the other foot for a change. But Frank doubted the Mother forgot very much.

Frank stretched and paced. She'd been doing her damnedest to ignore the pit of dread in her belly, now she gave it an ear. It was the same knot she'd felt the night Danny Duncan was killed. Something was happening. Something Frank couldn't put a finger on. There was a sense of largeness, like a great storm cloud gathering just beyond the horizon. And there was no shelter.

Frank paced. She checked the clock often.

She didn't have to go. No one would be the wiser if she tucked tail and went home. Even as she had the thought, she dismissed it. She'd know. And Frank was certain that the Mother would know.

The clock read 3:10. Frank had an idea and jogged out of the office. It was quiet as she went through the lobby out front. She walked up the block and entered a small store just yards from the station. Frank hadn't been inside in years, but the *botanica* hadn't changed at all. The hand-lettered windows were still crammed with dusty, sun-bleached curios. Incense, powders, herbs, and magical oils mingled in the musty air. Two older Latino women sat on stools next to a cluttered counter. They stopped talking when she walked in. Frank raised a hand.

"*Hola,*" she smiled. "*Habla ingles?*"

She added in pitiful Spanish that she had a question.

The women looked at each other. Neither would take her bait.

"Okay," Frank tried again. "*Tiene libro de bembe?*"

The woman who shook her head pointed at an assortment of books scattered among the prayer candles and plaster statuettes. She slid off her stool and picked out a couple. She spoke in Spanish and handed them to Frank.

"*Que es bembe?*" Frank tried. The woman shrugged.

"You read those," she answered in fair English. "They tell you."

One of the books was wrapped in plastic and the other was torn and dog-geared. Frank agreed and the woman rang her up on an old fashioned cash register. Frank pointed at a cluster of charms and trinkets under the glass.

"How much is the heart?"

The woman pulled out a stamped tin heart, painted red with blue and yellow edging.

"Two dollars," she grunted.

Frank nodded and paid, not caring that 50¢ was written in wax pencil on the back. She pocketed the heart and picked up the books. Back in her office she read that a *bembe* was a large party for new *santería* priests. It involved specific drumming and offerings of food, liquor, and trinkets. Its purpose was to entice the *orishas* down to earth to "mount" the initiates. Mounting was possession by the gods.

"Great," Frank said under her breath, "*The Exorcist* redux."

The *bembe* started with ceremonial chanting and drumming, and then established priests or priestesses presented the initiates to the *orishas*. The drumming increased and eventually the initiate was mounted by his or her *orisha*. While possessed, they exhibited all the characteristics of the god riding them. The *orishas* loved to experience sensation but could only do so in human form, therefore there was a tendency toward extreme behavior whenever a human was mounted. Trained, non-mounted participants made sure the possessed weren't used to the point of endangerment.

Frank thumbed through the used book. With minor variations it corroborated what she'd already read. Frank thought a *bembe* sounded a lot like the Latin version of a holy roller baptism, with everybody rolling around and hollering that they'd been touched by Jesus. Tossing the books into a drawer, she figured the evening would at least be entertaining.

She made a phone call and Gail answered on the second ring.

"Hey. Something's come up. I'm going to be late."

"What is it?"

"I'll tell you later."

"Did you get called out?"

"No. Go ahead and eat without me."

"Fra-ank," Gail warned, "you're being evasive. What's going on?"

"I can't talk right now. Gotta go."

"Okay. Be safe."

Frank was surprised by a hunger to tell Gail she loved her. Answering, "Roger that," she checked the impulse.

35

Clouds moved in from the west. Frank fiddled with the radio dial until it hit a weather report. A front moving in, cooler and partly cloudy through tomorrow. A fat drop hit Frank's windshield, then another. The forecast said nothing about rain.

By the time she turned onto Slauson, the drops were falling faster and harder. Thick clouds padded the sky, but the view in her rearview mirror was bright and blue. Lightning danced under the clouds and Frank ceded, "All right. Very impressive. You can quit with the special effects. Just help me do my job, okay? You do yours and I'll do mine. Give me something to hang this little old lady with and we'll make this fucked up world of yours a better place. Deal?"

Frank felt stupid talking to an empty car, but when Frank had asked Gail how to pray, Gail had said just talk. Say whatever came to mind. What came to Frank's mind was that this was ridiculous. Her bones impelled her to Mother Love's while her head insisted she had no business at the bembe.

The old slaughterhouse grew against the skyline. Rain streaked down its bricks, darkening them the color of dried blood. Frank parked on the Slauson side, bolting for the door through the pelting rain. She didn't bother knocking and the handle turned in her good hand. She stepped into what looked like a reception area. A young woman came from behind a counter.

"You must be Lieutenant Franco," she smiled.

"I am," Frank said, shaking water off. She heard muffled drumming. It was similar to her dream drumming, and she thought she was going to have another déjà vu. The absolute worst time or place for that to happen. Frank willed herself to stay focused.

Opening a door, the woman told Frank, "Mother Love said you might come. I'll take you to her."

Alice in Wonderland, Frank thought, following the girl through a maze of brick walls. She missed Lewis behind her this time, and with a tiny hitch of panic she regretted not telling anyone where she was going. Frank steadied herself. They were getting closer to the drumming. It was slower and not as loud, but Frank was sure it was the same beat she'd heard in her dream. Her mouth went dry and she promised herself as many beers as she wanted when this was over.

The drumming grew louder and louder. The girl stopped in front of a red door, her hand resting on an old brass handle. She smiled again, calling over the tempo, "Here we are."

Frank realized she didn't like the girl's smile. It was too bright. Too false. An alarm tripped in Frank's gut. Thunderous drumming overwhelmed it as the girl pushed the door open. Frank had no choice but to follow. Marguerite spoke clearly in her head, *you always have a choice*.

Irrationally, Frank snapped back, *not this time*.

The room was lit like a scene from hell. Shadows spawned from torches and candles clambered over the walls. Against them, a half-dozen men sat blindfolded, naked to the waist. They pounded on the drums, their skin glistening in the coppery light.

Frank sensed rather than saw the twins standing on either side of the door. Near the center of the room, the Mother waited to meet Frank's eyes. Frank wouldn't look there, suddenly very afraid of what she would see.

The drummers increased their tempo. Frank's heartbeat kept time. Behind her, the twins blocked the door. Hot sweat rolled down her ribs. The incessant rhythm made it hard to think, but one thing was obvious. There was no bembe. Frank was the one they'd been waiting for.

Cold fury rippled through her. Frank raged that she had so profoundly fallen for the set-up. Like a punk-ass civilian, straight off the plane from Podunk, Iowa.

But that was all part of the plan, wasn't it?

Before she could stop it, another memory swamped her. The certainty that she was meant to be here staggered her. She knew the rhythm the drummers were beating out. Her bones cherished it. The twisting shadows and blinded men, the Mother's foreboding patience and the twins behind her, Azazel and Belial, each detail perfectly fitted Frank's memory. In a different world, this moment had already happened and been preserved. Frank was only revisiting it. It was inevitable that she face the Mother. Always fighting, always the soldier. Forever and ever, amen. Father Merrin confronting his monstrous desert gods. Tripping in the desiccated ruins. Dogs snarling and snapping.

She felt herself falling. Instinct made her reach for her weapon. The twins lunged for either arm. Her bad hand closed awkwardly on the grip. She lifted the 9mm, but the wasted milliseconds cost her. The twins pinned her, one of them taking the Beretta.

Lifting Frank with minimal effort, they carried her to the Mother. Frank still hadn't looked at her. Now she concentrated on a line dangling from the ceiling. It looked like a rope, one of those thick ones they used on ships. There was another behind it, looped through a pulley. Only Frank realized they were chains.

Jesus Christ.

The chains that had kept Danny Duncan immobilized. Terror reared like a stricken horse, but again Frank reined it in.

Get mad, she heard her father say. She dredged up the slap of his palms on her face. *Get mad and stay mad.*

Frank slammed her eyes into the Mother's, too angry to even be pleased that for an instant the Mother's hubris wavered.

Words, even if they had been necessary, would have been useless against the crescendo of the drums. The adversaries glared, neither cognizant of defeat. With a crisp nod from their mother, the twins hustled Frank to the waiting chains. One pinioned her while the other knelt to secure her ankles. Frank thought to kick him in the face, break his nose, and try to manhandle the other brother. Even if she did break free she'd still have to deal with the Mother and her six drummers drumming. Her odds were slim to nil and Frank couldn't accept the possibility of failing in front of the Mother.

The twin jerked the metal tight around her ankle bones. Frank tried to think that the pain was probably a pleasure compared to what was coming. She held the same thought while he chained her wrists, wincing where he touched her fresh scars. The other brother hauled the ankle chain through the pulley. She couldn't hear it, but the vibrations rattled through her ankles. He stopped pulling just as the metal dug into her skin. Then he worked the hand chain until Frank's arms were horizontal behind her back. Muscles and tendons pulled. Frank reflexively stretched onto her toes, trying for some slack but it wasn't enough. She'd only held the position for seconds and already it was excruciating

Get mad! Frank screamed into the pain.

The Mother whirled and bent to one of the drummers. She said something in his ear and his timing changed. The other drummers, all old men, responded intimately. Frank wondered how many times they'd played this pin-the-tail-on-the-donkey game. One of the twins went out the red door. The other watched Frank with his arms folded over his massive chest.

You fucking stupid magilla, Frank glowered at him. *Like I could*

actually do anything. You got me trussed up like that fucking gimp in Pulp Fiction. *I'ma get medieval on yo' ass.*

How long would they keep her like this? The Mother was swigging from a bottle and spraying the contents over her drummers. When she was done with them she sprayed the twin, then chugged and turned to Frank. Frank closed her eyes as the mist blasted her face. She recognized the smell of rum and licked her lips before shaking the rest off her face.

The Mother walked back to her elaborate altar. She held a gourd up to each corner of the room and sprinkled something from it. Then she took a sip and held it to the lips of each drummer.

The twin returned with the girl. They were both carrying boxes. The Mother paused to hold the gourd up for them. Frank watched them sip. Then the twin guarding her took a drink. When the Mother approached Frank, her eyes screamed, *Don't even fucking try it!*

The Mother smiled.

"Proud to the end," she purred in a deep voice. "It's pride that makes the angels fall."

She dipped three fingers into the mix and smeared them against Frank's lips. Frank snapped, biting only air. The Mother started, recoiling her clawed fingers. Anger flashed from the ravening eyes and Frank grinned. The Mother moved away, continuing her ablutions.

Frank tried to stretch even higher on her toes. But she couldn't relieve the pull of the chain.

God, it fucking hurt. How long was this fucking dog and pony show gonna take? Longer the better, she thought with a genuine stab of fear, afraid to think what would happen when it was over.

How did she get into this? And now that she was here, what the fuck was she going to do about it?

"Pray," she heard Marguerite say. To Mickey Mouse or Joe Dimaggio, just pray. *Fine,* Frank conceded. She'd pray to Noah. They had that link. The Vulcan mind meld, Johnnie had said. If anyone could get her out of here it would be Noah. She called him in her head, repeating his name in time to the thundering drums.

Hey, No. Listen up buddy. Hear me calling you? Help me, buddy. Help me. I'm at the Mother's place on Slauson. It's Frank, No. You gotta help me. Noah. Help me. The Mother's place. Slauson. Come on, buddy. I need you bad. Listen to me, No. Stop what you're doing and listen. Yeah, buddy, it's me, Frank. Come on, get your ass over here. I need you, No.

Returning the gourd to the altar, the Mother started sprinkling designs onto the floor like Marguerite had done. The Mother straightened, breaking into a chant. Frank was momentarily distracted from her pain, amazed at the deep bellow issuing from the Mother, rising over the cacophony of the drums. Frank tried to recognize the language. It was like none she'd ever heard.

Come on, No. The Mother's place on Slauson. It's Frank. Come get me, No. HQ for Marie Laveau. Come on, No, come on. It's Frank.

The Mother spoke to the lead drummer and he changed the tempo again. The drums thrummed faster and tighter. Reaching into one of the boxes, the Mother pulled out a pigeon. She held the bird over her head, braying like she was Mephistopheles. Ripping the bird's head off, she walked around the room sprinkling blood on everyone. The drummers sang responses to her chant. She did the same thing with another pigeon, then repeated the procedure with a rooster. The bodies were dumped into a black kettle in front of the altar.

Noah! The Mother's place! Slauson! Get your fucking ass over here, buddy. ASAP! Pronto, No. We're killing birds over here!

The girl who led Frank into the room brought in a lamb covered with a red cloth. Frank understood that the sacrifices were getting larger. Kneeling before the altar, the Mother sang, "Obi aro obi aye obi ofo."

Frank answered, *Obi Wan Kenobi, where are you? Scooby Doo, motherfucker, we got some work to do. Come on, Noah. Mother Love's place. Please don't let me be next on the menu, No.*

She pictured the wet brick building. The street address. She watched the Mother dress the lamb with the sticky stuff in the gourd. The animal didn't protest at all and Frank wondered if they'd drugged it. Christ, she wished they'd have drugged her. Her arms were finally getting numb but her back was wrenching into spasms. She twisted into them as best she could.

The drummers chanted, "Firolo, firolo," and Frank sang, *Figaro, Figaro*, against the daggers down her back and sides. *Jesus fucking sweet Jesus the pain. Noah, buddy. Noah, help me for Christ's sake. Look, No. It's me. Frank. The Mother's got me. At Slauson. Come on, bud. Come on. Come through for me, No.*

The Mother walked toward Frank, intent and business-like. She jammed something into Frank's mouth and Frank spat it out. It tasted of coconut and pepper. The Mother picked up the wad and rubbed it into the lamb's forehead. The twin who'd brought the birds in tied the lamb's legs together. He flipped it onto a bed of banana leaves by the altar and nodded at his brother. The twin glowered at Frank. She lunged at him as best she could. He started and she grinned, shouting, "Made you jump, stupid motherfucker."

The brothers stretched the lamb lengthwise and the drummers wailed on their heads between their legs. The Mother bawled one of her ditties and her six blind mice offered the answering refrain. They did that three times, then she neatly severed the lamb's throat. Its blood spouted into a brightly painted tureen.

Jesus, Noah, hurry. Please. I'm begging you. Whoever the fuck is out there. Mickey Mouse, Jesus, Buddha. Whoever the fuck, whatever, if anybody's listening, now is the time to do something. Look! I'm begging. I'm not proud here. Look. No pride. Please. I'm asking nice. Pretty please.

The first twin cut the lamb's head off. The Mother poured salt into the neck, swabbing the wound with a clear, sticky goo. Chanting, her drummers answering, the Mother carried the head to Frank. She lifted it, letting warm blood rain onto Frank's face.

"Washed in the blood of the lamb," Frank murmured.

The Mother laughed deeply, like a man. She nodded at the twins and they walked behind Frank. They dropped her arms to her ass.

She couldn't feel them, but the blood rushing into the surrounding area felt like her veins were infused with acid. She flinched at the pain, cursing these bastards for even getting that much from her.

The tempo of the drumming was furious, like Hell's own cattle herd stampeding. The Mother put the lamb's head into the pot with the birds. She carefully cleaned her knife. It was long and grooved, a wicked looking instrument. Frank turned away from it. She just hoped it was sharp.

Oh fucking sweet Jesus, I am so fucked. Oh goddamn. Come on, No, quit dicking around. I need you man, oh please, I need you. I'm running out of time here, No. Running out of time, Boy-o.

Frank could relate to Father Merrin scrabbling through the dusky ruins, with Pazzuzu's face leering over him as his final confrontation played out to its irrevocable conclusion. But the priest had gone down swinging. In the end, he had his pride. Was that why he fell? Did he choke on his own arrogance?

The Mother came toward Frank. She held the knife with both hands, as if offering atonement. The blade winked in the burnt light. Bile rose in Frank's throat. The Mother stood before her, the boys behind. She passed the knife to the twin who'd been assisting her.

"Lucian has been touched by Ogun," she said reverently. "He's allowed to handle the sacrificial instruments."

"Glad we cleared that up," Frank spat, "I like to know who's gonna slit my fucking throat."

The Mother's words were audible above the din of the drums, but Frank's were swallowed alive. She stared into the terrible blackness of the Mother's eyes. All things repelled by daylight glinted from those twin hells. In them, jinn and lilim cavorted by smokeless fires, the desert night stirring restlessly beyond them. Hobbled inside the pale, Azazel's goat bleated for mercy. Jackals paced restlessly with the hyenas, awaiting the blooded sacrifice. The moon turned away, but the stars looked on with indifference.

Soundlessly, the Mother spun the old tale, luring Frank with promises as old as the sands upon which they were made. This wasn't the first time the dark covenant had winked at Frank or cocked a crooked finger at her.

Frank closed her eyes against the desolate visions. She listened to the Mother's laugh, echoing as if from a black and reeking well.

Laugh, you cankerous old bitch. Go ahead. We'll see who's standing at the end. Odds were excellent it would be the Mother but Frank refused to believe that. Couldn't believe that. Even as the Mother gave Lucian the nod.

Grabbing Frank's shirt, he ran the knife along it. He pulled the cloth apart and bared her chest. Deftly running the blade along her arms he stripped the rest of the shirt free.

Frank didn't like that one little bit, but it was buying her time.

For what? she questioned bitterly. *For the psychic hotline to kick in? Fuck you, Marguerite, fuck you, Noah. Fuck you all very much. Fuck you Mickey Mouse. Fuck you god, if you're even there. Yeah, I'm choking on my pride, too.*

Lucian yanked her jeans down with her underwear, slitting them loose from the chain. For the first time in her life, Frank wished she wore a bra. One more thing to cut away. One more minute to buy.

Frank no longer hoped a miraculous intervention would save her. She just wanted to live a few minutes longer. Life had suddenly become intensely sweet and she wasn't ready to give it up. She wanted to cry, but refused to feed the Mother's triumph.

The Mother returned to her altar, took up the chanting in that unnervingly male voice. Frank was almost senseless with gratitude for the extra moments. The Mother brought a bowl to Frank, rubbing her up and down with an orange oil. Frank avoided those Stygian eyes. She didn't want them to be the last thing she saw.

She thought about Gail and the tin heart still in her pocket. She was pissed she wasn't going to be able to give it to her, more pissed she hadn't said, "I love you" on the phone. Frank cursed her cowardice and her anger refueled her.

It ain't over 'til the fat lady sings and I ain't going down easy. All I got left's pride.

Marguerite had said she was a warrior. Always fighting. Always.

The Mother lifted her hand and Frank's feet were swept from under her. She tried breaking the fall with her shoulder but had no leverage to turn. She arched her neck, but her skull hit the floor.

Frank blinked at colored lights arcing across a gray background. The twins pulled steadily on her ankle chain and her face scraped across the concrete. She felt the warmth and wetness of blood, but she wasn't feeling much pain. The numbness was good news. The bad news was that the dullness signaled some degree of concussion; her body had closed down the ancillary pain receptors to combat this latest crisis. She was drowsy and nauseous.

Just sleep, she told herself. *Don't give them the satisfaction of any pain.* Frank gagged. Her body's desperate plea for oxygen suddenly sharpened her thoughts. She coughed, gulping in air. If she puked upside down she'd probably suffocate herself.

Not an option, she managed to think. *They can slit my fucking throat but I will not choke on my own puke. Pride, yeah. Puke, no. Fuck you, motherfuckers. Ain't goin' down easy. Okay, No. I'm giving you one last chance. Running out of time here. Come on. Come and get me, No. Mickey Mouse. Somebody. Slauson, buddy, La Casa de Love.*

With a last heave, Frank's head dangled over the floor, her ankles supporting all one hundred and sixty three pounds. A moan slipped between her clenched teeth. She couldn't stop it and didn't care.

The blood backed up into her brain and squeezed behind her eyes. Black dots hovered like malevolent cherubs. She wondered how long before she passed out?

Motherfuckers, motherfuckers, she droned lazily. *Get mad. Stay mad. Running out of mad. Noah. Hear me, buddy?*

Frank saw the reverse order of her world through the fog of concussion and rushing blood. The brothers were beside her and the Mother was behind her. She was singing in a high wail like she had just before she slaughtered the lamb. Frank thought if she went as quickly as that it wouldn't be so bad.

Helluva picture to hang over the coffee pot. Lieutenant L.A. Franco, sold into white slavery. Come on, No, I'm naked. You know you always wanted to see me naked. Now's your chance. Better hurry .

The pain was dulling again and grayness crept at the edge of her vision. She was fading and knew it.

"Gotta stay mad," she mumbled indifferently. "Stay mad."

She was aware enough to see the brothers pivot. Heard their deep voices above the drums. The drumming faltered, the beat breaking down skin by skin. Frank heard another voice. It was familiar but she was too woozy to place it. The Mother was yelling but the drummers jabbering and the boys shouting jumbled all their words up.

Must be the audience participation part of the show, Frank thought dimly. She mustered enough strength for a weak twist against the chains, still curious about what fresh hell waited her.

The pain ratcheted through her confusion, and just before the dimness made its final, rushing assault, Frank had a fraction of a second to think, *What the fuck is he doing here?*

36

She repeated the question to him from her hospital bed.

Darcy's smile was sheepish.

"Fubar's going to be asking you the same thing."

"He on his way?"

Darcy nodded. "With an entourage of big hats."

"At least I bought some time," Frank said, indicating the curtained wall. "He's probably still busy fucking up the scene."

Frank was exhausted, but nonetheless grateful for her fatigue and dull pain.

"Give me the lowdown before he gets here."

"It's pretty wild," he said, pulling the only chair up to her bed.

"You don't know the half of it," she said. "Or maybe you do."

He nodded.

"Turns out, this whole thing was a setup, and not just on you. Lucian—one of the twins—he and his brother's wife set this scam up on the Mother. Like begets like. According to him, she was starting to believe her own legends, acting like she was invincible. He saw after she killed her own nephew how far she'd go and how far she'd already gone. He didn't want to go down with her.

"The *bembe* was his idea. He was sure you'd come and she went along with it. The plan was to have you in imminent danger, then have the cops bust in at the last minute. No way the Mother could get off for jacking a cop. He didn't want you to die, but it was a chance he was willing to take."

"Yeah, I saw."

"The point was to set the Mother up. The son—Lucian—he was going to cop to everything so that the old lady would get sent away forever. But the plan slipped. When we came in, the other brother, Marcus, he fired shots and we took him out. Lavinia and the Mother went and hid behind you. The Mother had a knife on you and that pretty much stopped us. She called Lucian over to her and he went. He stood behind her and next thing we know he's got a gun on her. He said, 'I'm sorry, Mama,' and just like that he pulled the trigger. He dropped the gun and just stood there. He said one way or another somebody was going to die and that by killing her he ended the killing."

Through the haze of her concussion and meds, Frank stated, "That's beautiful. 'I'm sorry, Mama'. Sorry my ass. I bet he meant to smoke her."

"Probably, huh?"

"I wouldn't want the Mother alive after I'd ratted her out. If he'd already seen how far she'd go, what would keep her from frying her own son alive? There's no way he'd get out of that except by killing her. Then his army of lawyers get him off on self-defense and the kid's running an empire."

Frank studied the ceiling.

"Lavinia. She the skinny girl in the black dress?"

"Marcus's wife. She and Lucian cooked this up together."

Frank nodded, "She was going in and out. She's the one who

222

called you." Frank had to close her eyes.

"But why did she call *you*?"

"This is where it really gets strange. Maybe you should rest a spell. The captain'll be here any minute."

Frank recognized the stall and said, "If I need to cover your ass, I better know about it."

Darcy huffed, "Who's covering whose ass?"

"Spill it."

"You're not going to believe it," he argued.

Frank's smile was weak, but she replied, "Try me. You might be surprised."

Darcy glanced toward the door.

"I was home working on a paper."

That had been another revelation about Darcy. For all his resemblance to a Hell's Angel, her cop had a PhD in criminal psychology and was published regularly in law enforcement journals. She watched him fidget, noting he'd cut his hair.

"I was trying to concentrate on it but I kept getting this picture of you in my head. It felt like you were in trouble. It seemed like Noah was with you, but that you were the one in trouble."

The blanket over Frank suddenly seemed thin. Darcy paused.

"Go on," she said grimly.

"I tried calling both of you but didn't get an answer. I left a page for you and when you didn't respond I got worried. Really worried. The feeling kept intensifying, that something was seriously wrong. And I kept getting these flashes of a brick building. Bobby and I'd driven past the Mother's place and I thought that was what it was. It looked like the same place."

Frank watched Darcy stare at his hands. Lifting his head, his blue eyes met hers.

"I was getting scared. I just couldn't shake that you were in trouble. So I got on the bike and drove over. I swear, the sense of . . . *urgency* got stronger the closer I got. I was scared. For you.

"And wet," he tried to laugh, but it didn't come off. "I drove right into a thunderstorm. I didn't want to go in there, Frank, but I felt like I had to. I thought about calling backup but what was I going to tell them? I tried the door and it was open. I heard those drums, and I tell you, I about fainted I was so fucking scared. I followed them straight to you."

"So Lavinia didn't call you."

"No. She called the station. Two cars rolled a couple minutes behind me."

The implication of that made Frank queasy. When he'd been confronted with a particularly bizarre outcome of timing, Joe Girardi had frequently muttered, "Seconds and inches."

Sometimes that was all that separated the living from the dying.

In a hush, Frank said, "I was calling Noah. Marguerite told me to pray and I didn't know how so I was calling Noah."

Darcy nodded as if that cleared up any ambiguity.

Frank didn't want to think anymore. She just wanted to close her eyes for a while. "Do me a favor," she said. "Another one. Call this number."

She waited for him to get his pen.

"It's Doc Lawless' number. Tell her I'm okay, but tell her where I am. Now let me get some sleep before Fubar gets here."

Darcy's chair scraped back and as he pushed the curtain aside, Frank said, "Hey."

He turned.

"How do I thank you for something like this?"

He shrugged and disappeared.

Gail arrived just as the hats were leaving. The men stared at her breathless entry. They seemed to collectively decide they didn't want to know any more and almost pushed each other out the door.

Perching on the edge of the bed, Gail demanded, "What the hell happened to you. You look *terrible*."

"I'm fine," Frank assured, offering what she could of a smile. Her face was swollen and scraped and she wondered what she'd feel like when the drugs wore off. Reveling in the luxury of touching Gail's cheek, she added, "Just a little banged up. Nothing that doesn't happen to a good quarterback a couple times a season."

Gail pointed out, "You're not a quarterback, Frank. What happened? That damned Darcy won't tell me a thing."

"That damned Darcy saved my ass tonight."

Frank gave Gail the short version of the story. How she'd gone over on a hunch, how the whole thing had been a scam, how she'd tried praying, and how Darcy had stepped in at the last minute.

Gail blanched and kept repeating, "Oh my God."

"Yeah. Somebody's God. Pretty freaky, huh?"

Gail started to cry.

"Hey," Frank soothed, touching a tear with her thumb. "Hey."

"I don't know whether to hit you or kiss you. You *knew* what you were getting into and you didn't tell me!"

"Jesus, Gail, I *didn't* know. I knew I had to go, and I didn't know why. I knew I didn't want to go, but I had no fucking idea all this was going to go down. I wouldn't have gone in, at least not alone, if I had. Give me *some* credit. I just thought it was a church thing. Like a party."

"Then why didn't you tell me where you were going?"

"It just seemed silly. I didn't want to break dinner because I had to go to a party. I don't know. I didn't have a good reason for going, but I felt like I had to. I can't explain it."

Frank shrugged and the movement made her flinch.

"What sort of a relationship can we ever have if you can't tell me the truth, Frank?"

"The truth is I didn't know what I was doing. I didn't plan on going there when I left you. I just remembered I'd been invited, and it seemed dumb to go, but I was . . . drawn. I *had* to go."

"Well then why couldn't you have just said that?"

Gail's voice was rising and Frank was too tired for another fight.

"I don't know. I honestly can't tell you. I'm sorry I didn't. And I can't argue with you right now. I was wrong. You're right. It's over.

The whole fucking thing is over and I just want to move on. Can we do that?"

She was still pissed, but Frank could at least see Gail considering her request. Before she could answer, Frank said, "Hey. I got something for you. Darcy said he brought my wallet and stuff. Do you see it?"

Frowning, Gail pulled a plastic hospital bag from under the bed.

"How can I impress upon you the need to communicate with me?"

"How can I impress upon you that I'm trying? I'm not used to communicating with myself, nonetheless another human being, Gay. I'm not good at it. I'll be the first to admit that. But I'm trying."

Finding the tin heart in her pants pocket, she told Gail, "Close your eyes and put out your hand."

Gail sighed, but did as instructed. Frank put the heart in her palm.

"Okay."

The doc opened her eyes and Frank said, "You're holding my heart in the palm of your hand."

Gail studied it a long time before answering, "I'll be very careful with it."

Cupping Gail's fingers around the stamped heart, Frank was at last able to say, "I love you."

Epilogue

On his way home from school, a boy stops by a pile of blankets. They are dirty and smell like his baby sister when her diaper needs changing. He sucks thoughtfully on his Tootsie-Pop, calculating how long before he gets to the chocolate center. He takes the candy out, studies it, then looks back at the blankets.

They are heaped in the middle like they're covering something. Maybe there's a backpack underneath. Or a radio. The boy looks around for the blanket's owner. The alley is empty. Only blind cars pass on his left. He nudges the blankets with the toe of his sneaker. Nothing happens. Again he looks around. He kicks the pile, scattering the mounded blankets.

The smell of old pee lifts into the air. And a nasty smell, like from that cat his uncle hung in the basement. The boy waves his hand in front of his nose and swears. He doesn't notice the hot breeze that snakes around his ankles. Or that the pigeons on the wire above have suddenly cried out and taken flight.

Publications from
BELLA BOOKS, INC.
The best in contemporary lesbian fiction

P.O. Box 10543, Tallahassee, FL 32302
Phone: 800-729-4992
www.bellabooks.com

ONE DEGREE OF SEPARATION by Karin Kallmaker. 232 pp.
Can an Iowa City librarian find love and passion when a California
girl surfs into the close-knit Dyke Capital of the Midwest?
ISBN 1-931513-30-9 $12.95

CRY HAVOC: A Detective Franco Mystery by Baxter Clare. 240 pp.
A dead hustler with a headless rooster in his lap sends Lt. L.A.
Franco headfirst against Mother Love.   ISBN 1-931513931-7 $12.95

DISTANT THUNDER by Peggy J. Herring. 294 pp. Bankrobbing
drifter Cordy awakens strange new feelings in Leo in this romantic
tale set in the old West.   ISBN 1-931513-28-7 $12.95

COP OUT by Claire McNab. 216 pp. 4th Detective Inspector
Carol Ashton Mystery.   ISBN 1-931513-29-5 $12.95

BLOOD LINK by Claire McNab. 159 pp. 15th Detective
Inspector Carol Ashton Mystery. Is Carol unwittingly playing
into a deadly plan?   ISBN 1-931513-27-9 $12.95

TALK OF THE TOWN by Saxon Bennett. 239 pp.
With enough beer, barbecue and B.S., anything
is possible!   ISBN 1-931513-18-X $12.95

MAYBE NEXT TIME by Karin Kallmaker. 256 pp. Sabrina
Starling has it all: fame, money, women—and pain. Nothing
hurts like the one that got away.   ISBN 1-931513-26-0 $12.95

WHEN GOOD GIRLS GO BAD: A Motor City Thriller by
Therese Szymanski. 230 pp. Brett, Randi, and Allie join forces
to stop a serial killer.   ISBN 1-931513-11-2   12.95

A DAY TOO LONG: A Helen Black Mystery by Pat Welch. 328 pp. This time Helen's fate is in her own hands.
ISBN 1-931513-22-8 $12.95

THE RED LINE OF YARMALD by Diana Rivers. 256 pp. The Hadra's only hope lies in a magical red line . . . Climactic sequel to *Clouds of War*.   ISBN 1-931513-23-6 $12.95

OUTSIDE THE FLOCK by Jackie Calhoun. 224 pp. Jo embraces her new love and life.   ISBN 1-931513-13-9 $12.95

LEGACY OF LOVE by Marianne K. Martin. 224 pp. Read the whole Sage Bristo story.   ISBN 1-931513-15-5 $12.95

STREET RULES: A Detective Franco Mystery by Baxter Clare. 304 pp. Gritty, fast-paced mystery with compelling Detective L.A. Franco   ISBN 1-931513-14-7 $12.95

RECOGNITION FACTOR: 4th Denise Cleever Thriller by Claire McNab. 176 pp. Denise Cleever tracks a notorious terrorist to America.   ISBN 1-931513-24-4 $12.95

NORA AND LIZ by Nancy Garden. 296 pp. Lesbian romance by the author of *Annie on My Mind*.   ISBN 1931513-20-1 $12.95

MIDAS TOUCH by Frankie J. Jones. 208 pp. Sandra had everything but love.   ISBN 1-931513-21-X $12.95

BEYOND ALL REASON by Peggy J. Herring. 240 pp. A romance hotter than Texas.   ISBN 1-9513-25-2 $12.95

ACCIDENTAL MURDER: 14th Detective Inspector Carol Ashton Mystery by Claire McNab. 208 pp.Carol Ashton tracks an elusive killer.   ISBN 1-931513-16-3 $12.95

SEEDS OF FIRE:Tunnel of Light Trilogy, Book 2 by Karin Kallmaker writing as Laura Adams. 274 pp. Intriguing sequel to *Sleight of Hand*.   ISBN 1-931513-19-8 $12.95

DRIFTING AT THE BOTTOM OF THE WORLD by Auden Bailey. 288 pp. Beautifully written first novel set in Antarctica.   ISBN 1-931513-17-1 $12.95

CLOUDS OF WAR by Diana Rivers. 288 pp. Women unite to defend Zelindar!   ISBN 1-931513-12-0 $12.95

DEATHS OF JOCASTA: 2nd Micky Knight Mystery by J.M. Redmann. 408 pp. Sexy and intriguing Lambda Literary Award-nominated mystery.   ISBN 1-931513-10-4 $12.95

LOVE IN THE BALANCE by Marianne K. Martin. 256 pp.
The classic lesbian love story, back in print! ISBN 1-931513-08-2 $12.95

THE COMFORT OF STRANGERS by Peggy J. Herring. 272 pp.
Lela's work was her passion . . . until now. ISBN 1-931513-09-0 $12.95

CHICKEN by Paula Martinac. 208 pp. Lynn finds that the
only thing harder than being in a lesbian relationship is ending
one.   ISBN 1-931513-07-4 $11.95

TAMARACK CREEK by Jackie Calhoun. 208 pp. An intriguing
story of love and danger.   ISBN 1-931513-06-6 $11.95

DEATH BY THE RIVERSIDE: 1st Micky Knight Mystery by
J.M. Redmann. 320 pp. Finally back in print, the book that
launched the Lambda Literary Award-winning Micky Knight
mystery series.   ISBN 1-931513-05-8 $11.95

EIGHTH DAY: A Cassidy James Mystery by Kate Calloway.
272 pp. In the eighth installment of the Cassidy James
mystery series, Cassidy goes undercover at a camp for troubled
teens.   ISBN 1-931513-04-X $11.95

MIRRORS by Marianne K. Martin. 208 pp. Jean Carson and Shayna
Bradley fight for a future together.   ISBN 1-931513-02-3 $11.95

THE ULTIMATE EXIT STRATEGY: A Virginia Kelly
Mystery by Nikki Baker. 240 pp. The long-awaited return of
the wickedly observant Virginia Kelly.   ISBN 1-931513-03-1 $11.95

FOREVER AND THE NIGHT by Laura DeHart Young. 224 pp.
Desire and passion ignite the frozen Arctic in this exciting
sequel to the classic romantic adventure *Love on the Line*.
                                               ISBN 0-931513-00-7 $11.95

WINGED ISIS by Jean Stewart. 240 pp. The long-awaited
sequel to *Warriors of Isis* and the fourth in the exciting Isis
series.   ISBN 1-931513-01-5 $11.95

ROOM FOR LOVE by Frankie J. Jones. 192 pp. Jo and Beth
must overcome the past in order to have a future together.
                                               ISBN 0-9677753-9-6 $11.95

THE QUESTION OF SABOTAGE by Bonnie J. Morris.
144 pp. A charming, sexy tale of romance, intrigue, and
coming of age.   ISBN 0-9677753-8-8 $11.95

SLEIGHT OF HAND by Karin Kallmaker writing as
Laura Adams. 256 pp. A journey of passion, heartbreak
and triumph that reunites two women for a final chance at
their destiny.   ISBN 0-9677753-7-X $11.95

MOVING TARGETS: A Helen Black Mystery by Pat Welch.
240 pp. Helen must decide if getting to the bottom of a mystery
is worth hitting bottom.   ISBN 0-9677753-6-1 $11.95

CALM BEFORE THE STORM by Peggy J. Herring. 208 pp.
Colonel Robicheaux retires from the military and comes out of
the closet.   ISBN 0-9677753-1-0 $12.95

OFF SEASON by Jackie Calhoun. 208 pp. Pam threatens Jenny
and Rita's fledgling relationship.   ISBN 0-9677753-0-2 $11.95

WHEN EVIL CHANGES FACE: A Motor City Thriller by
Therese Szymanski. 240 pp. Brett Higgins is back in another
heart-pounding thriller.   ISBN 0-9677753-3-7 $11.95

BOLD COAST LOVE by Diana Tremain Braund. 208 pp.
Jackie Claymont fights for her reputation and the right to love
the woman she chooses.   ISBN 0-9677753-2-9 $11.95

THE WILD ONE by Lyn Denison. 176 pp. Rachel never
expected that Quinn's wild yearnings would change her life
forever.   ISBN 0-9677753-4-5 $12.95

SWEET FIRE by Saxon Bennett. 224 pp. Welcome to
Heroy—the town with more lesbians per capita than any
other place on the planet!   ISBN 0-9677753-5-3 $11.95

Visit

Bella Books

at

BellaBooks.com

or call our toll-free number

1-800-729-4992